The Bond That Heals Us

CHRISTINE D'ABO

Ellora's Cave
Romantica Publishing

An Ellora's Cave Romantica Publication

www.ellorascave.com

The Bond That Heals Us

ISBN 9781419961120
ALL RIGHTS RESERVED.
The Bond That Heals Us Copyright © 2008 Christine d'Abo
Edited by Briana St. James.
Photography and cover art by Les Byerley.

This book printed in the U.S.A. by Jasmine-Jade Enterprises, LLC.

Electronic book publication May 2008
Trade paperback publication September 2010

With the exception of quotes used in reviews, this book may not be reproduced or used in whole or in part by any means existing without written permission from the publisher, Ellora's Cave Publishing, Inc.® 1056 Home Avenue, Akron OH 44310-3502.

Warning: The unauthorized reproduction or distribution of this copyrighted work is illegal. Criminal copyright infringement, including infringement without monetary gain, is investigated by the FBI and is punishable by up to 5 years in federal prison and a fine of $250,000.
(http://www.fbi.gov/ipr/)

This book is a work of fiction and any resemblance to persons, living or dead, or places, events or locales is purely coincidental.

The characters are productions of the author's imagination and used fictitiously.

THE BOND THAT HEALS US

∞

Chapter One

༒

Sara Fergus raced through the door to the meeting room and practically threw herself into the only empty seat at the conference table. The chair shifted, making a scraping noise as it absorbed her moving body.

"Sorry I'm late. One of the engineers had a severe laceration on his leg after a conduit exploded and sent metal flying. I had to rush him into surgery. Bloody mess everywhere." She muttered the last under her breath.

She blew a strand of hair away from her face before she finally looked up at the people who were now all staring at her. Her best friend and chief of security, Haylie, was sitting at the end of the table next to her husband Kamran, grinning like a fool. He stared at her, trying to maintain an air of diplomatic professionalism, but Sara couldn't miss the twinkle in his eyes or the slight smirk on his face. Sara didn't need to look around at the rest of the participants to know what their expressions would be.

Dumb, stupid space cadet!

"Sorry, I didn't mean to cause a disturbance," she said and felt a blush heat her face.

"Not at all. We all appreciate how busy you are," Kamran said, unable to contain his smile anymore. "You are just in time to hear about our supply situation."

Thank god her two friends were here to smooth things over. Sara had been an unorganized mess most of her life. Haylie had been around for most of it and knew how to keep her in line. Now that her friend had formed a mental bond with her husband, Sara suddenly found herself with another powerful friend—and someone who could help keep her out of trouble. Not that she *intended* to get into trouble, but it always seemed to follow her.

Kamran looked down at Haylie and Sara watched as his smile changed. She knew they were probably sharing some silent thought, a comment or private joke communicated through their bond. Despite the close friendship the three of them shared, she couldn't help but feel uncomfortable around them sometimes. She didn't like that she'd lost some of the intimacy she'd shared with her best friend for years. Hated that she couldn't claim to know Haylie's mind as well as her husband did.

Petty jealously, she supposed.

Sara gave her head a shake and tried to focus her attention on the portly man in the brown suit who was now talking. A data pad was pushed in front of her and automatically began to flick from report to report, detailing the state of the colony as the man talked. She had to fight back a sudden wave of exhaustion and stifle a yawn when he began droning on about regulations. She really didn't have time for this crap.

"Administrator Kamran, after taking a closer look at our supply reserves and comparing that against how much profit we can earn from sales of silicate ore from our mines, we will be running dangerously close to the wire for the next six months." The man leaned his fleshy arms across the table and pressed his belly firmly against the edge. "We will need to increase production if we are to maintain the colony."

"Why is this just coming to light now?" Kamran asked, his hands folded together in front of him. "We should have had warning long before now."

"Sir, we don't have the luxury of trying to figure out how this happened. We need to get matters resolved quickly before this colony is at risk. We need triple shifts."

Was this guy for real?

"I don't recommend that at all," Sara cut in. She made sure all eyes were on her before continuing. "I've already had five miners report to the med bay in the past week from exhaustion-related injuries. They barely seem to know where they are or what they are doing. I've had to take three of them off active duty and send them on mandatory rest leave. They're being pushed to their limits already."

The man in brown snorted. "They're simply taking advantage of your bleeding heart, Doctor. I very much doubt things are as dire as you are leading us to believe. And the triple shifts will let us—"

Somewhere in her head she registered the sudden sharp intake of breath as Haylie's, but she was far too pissed off to acknowledge it. Sara was on her feet, leaning across the Briel who sat beside her, so she could glare at the odious man.

"What is your name?" she ground out.

"I don't see what that—"

"What...is...your...*name*?"

"Grant," he squeaked.

"Well *Grant*, you may take issue with many things about me, but don't you ever, *ever* call into question the validity of any of my diagnoses. The health and wellbeing of my patients are the most important thing to me and under no circumstance will I have my ethics as a doctor disputed by a small-minded *bureaucrat*. Do I make myself clear, *little* man?"

By the end of her speech, Sara's voice was dangerously close to a yell and her body was shaking. For his part, sitting wide mouthed and sputtering, Grant could only nod. Sara flopped back into her chair, folded her hands across her lap and shot her gaze to a blank spot on the wall. Her heart was pounding and it took all her concentration to relax.

"Thank you for your recommendations, *both* your recommendations, on the situation at the mines." Kamran's calm, steady voice filled the uncomfortable silence in the room. "If the situation is as dire as we are led to believe, I'll appoint a representative from the colony to start a recruiting campaign to entice some additional personnel to relocate to Eurus. That should help both the production and the physical conditions of the miners."

"Thank you," she said, casting a glance at Grant.

"We need to look into getting a better forecasting system in place to prevent this sort of thing from happening again," Haylie said, sitting back in her chair, her arms across her stomach.

"Of course," Grant nodded, looking strangely pleased.

Kamran nodded. "Good. I'd also like to arrange a tour of the mines. I've put off checking the conditions—"

"I don't recommend that currently, Administrator," Grant cut in. "Conditions aren't ideal at the moment. We had one of the secondary caves collapse and need to get it cleaned up."

"Can't have a mess in the mines," Sara muttered, a bit louder than she'd intended.

Sara felt her face heat for the second time since her arrival at the meeting. She quickly flicked her gaze to Kamran, who only winked at her. Haylie rolled her eyes but winced suddenly afterward. Her husband's hand immediately went to hers and gave it a squeeze.

Something's wrong.

"Were there any other items on the agenda?" Kamran's voice, while still even, had taken on a concerned note.

The murmur in the room faded out when Kamran gave his head a sharp nod. "Excellent. We'll meet again next week. Thank you for coming."

Grant practically bowled Sara over trying to escape the room, but she really didn't give a shit about his little snit right now. Haylie was sick. Sara strode across the room as fast as her short legs would carry her until she was at her friend's side.

"What the hell's the matter with you and why haven't you called me sooner?"

"Sara, there's nothing—"

"She's been sick for over a week now," Kamran said, his hand wrapped around her shoulder. "She's barely eating and what she does eat, she can't keep down. And she's moody, worse than normal."

Haylie hit her husband hard across the chest. He completely ignored her.

"Any weight loss or weight gain?" she asked Kamran, blocking out Haylie's annoyed protests.

"Yes, some weight loss. And she's been sleeping more than normal."

Haylie sighed. "I miss one little meeting—"

"She missed a meeting?" Sara couldn't hide her surprise. That was something she would have done, but never Haylie.

"That was yesterday. I had a hard time getting her out of bed again today."

Kamran ran his hand through Haylie's long brown hair and frowned. Sara knew they were communicating through their mental bond when Haylie sighed and nodded.

"Go ahead. But I swear nothing's wrong with me. It's probably just the flu."

Sara immediately set to work checking her over. The last time Haylie had exhibited strange symptoms, Sara had ignored them. It turned out to be the effects of an alien pheromone manipulation, something that had created a temporary mating bond between Haylie and Kamran. Sara had been thrilled when the Briel council had found a way to make their bond permanent a little over a year ago. She'd never seen her friend this happy.

This time she wasn't about to ignore any strange goings on when it came to Haylie. The quick check of her vitals revealed lower than normal blood pressure and heart rate. It wasn't until she pulled out her portable bio scanner that Sara clued in to the problem. The excitement that zipped through her brought an instant grin to her face.

"What?" Haylie and Kamran asked at the same time.

"You, my dearest and oldest friend, are going to be perfectly fine."

"See," Haylie said and whacked Kamran across the chest again. "It's just the flu."

"Then what's wrong with her, Sara? She's not acting herself. And please don't tell me it's the flu."

Not wanting to worry either of them, Sara stood up, taking Haylie's hand with her. She reached for Kamran's and laced the two of them together. "I have to say that this is my favorite part of being a doctor. I have the utmost pleasure to be able to tell you that you should expect an addition to your family in about twelve months."

Kamran was on his feet, eyes wide. "A baby?"

"Twelve months!" Haylie was on her feet just as fast. "What happened to nine?"

Sara couldn't help but laugh. "Well, the normal gestation period for a Briel baby is fifteen months. I figure it's somewhere in the middle and took a guess. I'll be able to give you a more accurate reading once I can get you back to the med bay."

"A baby," Kamran repeated with a grin fixed firmly on his face. He suddenly picked up Haylie in his arms and gave her a hug. Haylie giggled and, after a brief protest, relaxed against him.

"I'll leave you two alone. But I want you to check in later on today so we can start some blood work to make sure everything's in order. And until I do so, consider yourself off duty, Chief."

She couldn't be sure either of them heard her at that moment. They were so lost in each other that Sara took the opportunity to slip away.

Light from outside streamed in through the windows that lined the outside wall of the colony's main building. Since the Ecada attack last year, they'd expanded the colony to include a second building. Sara slowed as she approached one of the windows so she could stare at the half-finished structure. Men and women in EV suits were outside welding metal frames that would soon be fitted with reinforced plastic panels. Another six months, maybe a year and they'd be finished. The Eurus colony would see another explosion of colonists arrive to seek out adventure on the frontier. That, combined with the gradual influx of explorers from neighboring star systems, pirates and wanderers, and the colony would be at its capacity sooner than anyone anticipated.

Sara ran her fingers along her neck, trying to rub out the stiff muscles. With any luck, there would be a few more doctors with the new group and she'd get a rest.

Shaking off her exhaustion, Sara made her way back toward her office, knowing there was a pile of work waiting for her. As she walked, she smiled at the people she passed, trying to mentally review each of their names and, for the most part, *actually* remembering them. She had no problem recalling the symptoms of most human diseases and more than a few alien ones as well, but give her someone's name and she was lost. Not for the first time, she envied Haylie's photographic memory.

The doors hissed closed behind her as she walked into the unusually quiet med bay. Several of the Briel doctors had taken the day off to prepare for some sort of ceremony, which for the life of her, Sara couldn't remember. It was important— that much she knew. What it meant was she needed to pull a double shift until Jaylin returned.

She'd been more than a little suspicious of the new Briel doctor when he'd arrived shortly after Ray's death. The elder council vouched for him and his abilities until she was satisfied he wouldn't launch an attack against them. But it didn't stop her from having Haylie and Taber run a background check anyway. She wasn't taking any more chances when it came to who she worked with.

"Hey, Doc. I thought you had a meeting?" Rachael asked, throwing a nutrition bar at her.

Sara smiled at her head nurse as she ripped into the packaging and pulled off a piece of the moist bar.

"I did. Showed up late, got out early. Anything exciting going on here?"

"Nope. Quiet enough that you can steal a nap in the isolation room," Rachael said and winked.

The temptation was certainly there. Instead, Sara sighed and made her way toward her office. "No, I have a pile of reports I need to get through. Earth Medical sent me another nasty communication yesterday, and if I don't get these done, they've vowed to replace me."

"Well, we don't want them tossing our favorite Earth doctor out an airlock."

Sara grinned at Rachael. "I better get at it then. Yell if anything exciting happens."

Her office was blessedly cool and quiet. Before sliding behind her desk to tackle the data pads stacked there, she made her way over to the food dispenser as she chewed on the mostly bland bar.

"Large glass of water."

Instantly, her request appeared in the small slot in front of her. She would never get tired of that particular piece of Briel technology. Instead of drinking, Sara poured the water over the large Briel plant Kamran had given her as a birthday present a few months ago. He swore she couldn't kill it, and so far she hadn't let him down.

But anything could happen.

With nothing left to help her procrastinate, Sara began to work away at the reports. As she read, her eyelids became heavy and she had to adjust her body in her seat several times to keep from nodding off. When she realized she'd read the same paragraph on the data pad three times, she pushed it aside.

"Just a quick nap."

Leaning back as far as her chair would allow, Sara tucked her feet under her butt, crossed her arms across her chest and let her mind wander. She couldn't help but think of Haylie and Kamran and how happy they were. Someday, she wanted that for herself. All she needed was to find a man who could look past her particular idiosyncrasies and love her.

Not normally much of a dreamer, Sara felt oddly aware of her surroundings as she slipped into sleep.

She was on a beach back on Earth, one she hadn't been to since she was a kid. The tide was up as the waves crashed on the sandy beach, pulling and pushing seashells with it as it moved. Sara wandered close and enjoyed the feeling of the water on her feet. It had always relaxed both her body and mind.

She heard a person, a man, come up behind her and wrap his arms around her body. Leaning back, she soaked in his warmth and his scent as it mixed with the salt air. She kept her eyes closed, scared to wake up and lose the comfort of her dream lover. She'd been so lonely over the past year, it felt wonderful to have someone just for her. To have that same type of closeness Haylie shared with Kamran.

"I'm so tired," she whispered.

Her dream lover placed a slow, sensuous kiss on her neck. Sara tilted her head to the side to give him better access. As he nipped and licked the sensitive skin, he moved his hands to reach up and cup her breasts.

"I'll look after you." He spoke the words against her damp neck.

"But you're not real."

"I'm here with you now. That's all that matters."

She sighed as his fingers brushed over her nipples lightly before he gently rolled the swollen tips, stoking her desire. His breath came out in hot pants and she could feel his hard cock pressing against the small of her back.

"I could so fuck you right now," he whispered.

Sara's body instantly reacted to his words as she arched her back hard against him. Her pussy was soaked, ready for him to push inside her, take her as his own.

"Please, I need you." The words rushed out of her.

"Only if you look at me. I want to see your face."

Her heart began to pound. She knew if she did what he asked, the spell would be broken, everything would fade away.

"Sara, look at me."

His voice was demanding, needy and very tempting.

"Sara?"

"Yes."

Slowly, she spun in her dream lover's arms, but she kept her eyes closed. His chest felt hard against her sensitive breasts. Her heartbeat was loud in her ears as she felt him lean forward and place a kiss on the tip of her nose.

"That's cheating."

"Hey, it's my dream."

"Open your eyes. I want you to see me."

She opened her mouth to argue, but nothing came out. Why didn't she just open her eyes? It *was* only a dream.

As she was about to give him what he wanted, a loud siren blared, instinctively forcing her to open her eyes. Instead of her dream lover, the only thing Sara saw was her office. It took her a few seconds to realize the siren was real. Sara was on her feet and in front of the computer console before she'd even given it thought.

"Eurus control, this is Dr. Fergus in med bay. What's the emergency?"

The face of a young Briel soldier immediately filled the screen. She'd sized him up instantly as one of Taber's new recruits. A nervous one from the look of him.

"Doctor, we have a shuttle of unknown origin on an emergency descent to the colony. They contacted us long enough to say they have casualties before their com gave out."

"Which bay will they be near?" When he didn't answer her right away, Sara couldn't hold back her annoyance. "Damn it, which bay!"

"East bay. A security detail will meet you there."

Not waiting to sign off, Sara bolted from her office into the main med bay. Rachael already had two emergency med kits ready to go and held one out to Sara.

"What's the scoop?"

"Shuttle about to crash land near the east bay. We'll have to hurry."

The two women set out at a jog toward the transport tube that would take them to the lower level. They didn't speak and the crowds parted to let them pass through unimpeded. They were slowed briefly as they made their way through the bazaar until Rachael yelled for people to clear the way. That gave them enough of an opening to hop into the tube.

"Shuttle level," Sara barked at the computer.

Her body hummed from the adrenaline and unfulfilled desire, sending her into hyper-mode. Her heart pounded harder than it should have and her palms were sweating as she gripped the coated cord of the med kit's strap. She knew she would crash hard after the emergency was done and probably have a killer headache to show for it. For now, she needed to focus and get through this.

When they came out of the tube, Taber and a small group of security personnel were waiting for them. Sara and Rachael fell into step with the group and they made their way to the east bay.

"Do we know what we're dealing with?" Sara asked Taber as they reached the outer blast door.

Taber's normally composed face currently had a deep frown fixed on it. That told her more than his words would ever say.

"I don't want either of you to come in until we have cleared the area," he said, shooting a sideways glance at her. "Haylie won't forgive me if you get hurt."

"Yes, she must be chomping at the bit wanting to come down here." She couldn't help but smile. "I bet Kamran has his hands full right now."

"I haven't heard her use such…*interesting* human expressions before."

They looked at each other and she saw Taber's lips threaten to twitch into a smile.

"So I'm assuming they told you?"

Taber nodded. "I'd wondered about her behavior changes. I'm very pleased for them."

"Commander," Taber's communicator cut in. "The ship is on final approach. It looks like the captain has enough control left to land in the bay. But they are coming in hard."

"Damn good pilot," Taber muttered. "Stand back everyone," Taber said and physically took Sara by the arm and moved her several paces away from the door firmly behind him.

"Excuse me!"

"Your friend's wrath is far greater than yours," he said over his shoulder.

"Yes, but I can make your next physical a living hell."

For a second, Sara actually thought she heard Taber chuckle.

All her rebuttals and smart remarks were pushed aside when she heard the rumble and creaking metal of the outer blast doors being raised. Unable to see, she relied on her ears to give her an idea as to what was going on. The wind began to howl as it whipped into the open shuttle bay. Very faint in the distance, like a high-pitched buzz coming in above the wind, Sara could make out the howl of a damaged stardrive.

"Rachael, get ready for plasma burns and radiation poisoning."

"On it."

The group grew silent, waiting for the inevitable crash that was due to come any second. The screeching of the stardrive grew louder and louder until it was punctuated with a deafening bang and screeching of metal on metal. She couldn't help but jump at the noise and she felt Taber reach out to give her arm a quick squeeze.

"Wait here until I give you the all clear," he said again.

"Not moving." *So not moving.*

Taber motioned for the security personnel to follow and cautiously approached the inner blast door.

"Computer, status of the east shuttle bay?" His calm voice filled the corridor.

The system paused before the too-pleasant-sounding voice finally answered. "External doors secured. Atmosphere purged of contaminants."

"Computer, release security lock on inner east bay door. Authorize Taber zero-delta-five."

"Access granted."

The stench of burning wire mixed with the heavy sulfur from the planet's surface turned Sara's stomach. Rachael began to cough and had to cover her face with a bio mask. Sara inched her way closer to the open door, trying to see what they were in for. She gasped at the sight in front of her. The damaged ship, larger than a short-range shuttle but not as large as a passenger ship, was resting half on its side with the nose jammed hard against a bulkhead. The metal had peeled back, exposing conduits and cables as gases vented into the bay. How it hadn't exploded she wasn't sure.

Taber and the security force were quickly putting out the few flames that had erupted with a suppression gas. It took a few seconds, but everything was eventually extinguished.

"Looks like a cruiser," Sara said over her shoulder. "Maybe five to ten for a crew. We should call for two more medics."

Rachael was looking a little pale. Sara knew she was timid of unknown alien visitors since the Ecada attack. But she thought Rachael had gotten over it through a few months of talking with a psychologist from Earth. Rachael swallowed hard, her eyes glued to the ship, panic clear on her face.

"I'll get them," Rachael offered a bit too quickly and took off down the corridor without a backward glance.

"Nice," Sara muttered, turning back to wait for Taber's signal. She'd have to see about getting Rachael a bit more help.

In the shuttle bay, she watched Taber and the security guards edge cautiously toward the shuttle door, their weapons drawn and pointed at the cockpit, which was showing no sign of life.

"Occupants of the shuttle. You've crash landed on Eurus colony." Taber's commanding voice echoed loud and clear. "Open your door so we may offer assistance."

Sara rolled her eyes. "You're supposed to say *please*, Taber. And don't point your weapons at them," she muttered to herself.

When a loud hiss of atmosphere vented from the shuttle door, every security guard in the bay raised their weapons a fraction higher, fixing them on the spot. Sara gasped when the most unusually handsome man she'd ever laid eyes gripped the now open entrance and leaned out of the ship to stare directly at Taber. His shoulder-length brown hair fell forward, partially covering his face.

"I have wounded in here. I need a doctor," he snapped.

Before she had time to blink, he retreated inside the shuttle. Kicking her body into overdrive, Sara was through the door and halfway across the shuttle bay before Taber could turn around.

"Sara!"

"Come with me if you want, but I'm not stopping. You heard him—they need help."

Somehow she managed to skirt past Taber and throw her med kit up into the open door. The entrance, which would normally be only a foot from the ground, was a full five feet in the air. For not the first time in her life, Sara cursed her five feet five inches and tried to pull herself in.

"Let me help," a voice said from above.

Sara looked up and into the most amazing golden eyes she'd ever seen. His irises were reptilian shaped and Sara found herself unable to look away.

"You're the doctor, I assume?" His voice was deep with an unusual accent. His English was surprisingly good for a race she'd never seen before. And he sounded more than a little amused, despite the circumstances he was currently in.

She had the distinct impression he was laughing at her. She *hated* it when people laughed at her.

"Are you going to help me up or not?"

"Sara, let me," Taber said from behind.

She found herself being pushed and pulled up—directly into the waiting arms of her unusual alien. The air in her lungs whooshed out, leaving her shaking and very much aware of the large, firm, male chest she was currently pressed against. He wasn't as tall as Taber or any of the other Briel on the planet, but he was more than big enough for Sara. A full head taller, she was forced to tilt her head back to look into his golden eyes.

"Under better circumstance, I'd take great pleasure in our current position." He practically purred as he spoke and then he winked. "But I have people in need of help."

"Dr. Fergus, step back please."

The edge in Taber's voice was enough to shake her out of her momentary haze. Thankfully, the alien let her move to the side and turned his attention to Taber.

"Name's Davin. I'm the captain of this bucket. Some of my crew were wounded in the crash. I just managed to get the cabin door unjammed to get out. My copilot was knocked unconscious when we took damage entering the atmosphere."

"Your ship isn't registered for this sector." Taber took a step closer. "My crew will have to inspect it for contraband."

"*After* your doctor looks at my men. When she's done, go ahead. You won't find anything." Davin crossed his arms and leveled a stare at Taber.

Taber stiffened slightly. "Because there is nothing to find or because it's well hidden?"

Sara had to clear her throat twice before either of them would look at her. "Hi. I'm going to help the dying people. Once you are done with your pissing match, I could use a hand."

Shaking her head, she moved toward the front of the ship to where she hoped the wounded crew member was. Her exit wouldn't be half as dramatic if she had to turn around and come back. She'd just shoved the cabin door release when she felt Davin come up behind her.

"My copilot, Rafe, took a nasty crack to the head when we entered the planet's atmosphere. I tried to stop the bleeding, but had my hands full trying to keep the ship together as she came down."

When the door opened, Sara could smell the blood in the air. Ignoring Davin behind her, she crossed the small space to where a man sat slumped forward in his seat across a control console. Sara pulled him back to reveal half the man's face covered in burns and blood.

"Med kit," she said to Davin over her shoulder.

"Hang on—"

"Now!"

In the next second, she felt the weight of the strap in her hand. She pulled it around and tore into it until she found her scanner. Grimacing at what it told her, she looked up at Davin.

"I need to get him to med bay now or he's dead. He has massive cerebral hemorrhaging and I need to get him into surgery right away to relieve the pressure. Are there any others? Anyone else hurt?"

Davin frowned and clenched his fists. "Three with the engines. They were keeping us going, but I'm not sure if they're hurt or not."

"Rachael should be back by now. I'll send her and the other medics to the engine room."

She draped the wounded man's arm around hers and tried to pull him to his feet. Davin stepped beside her and helped get his copilot up. He started muttering something under his breath, like he was arguing with himself. When she tried to pull the injured man away, Davin resisted with a sigh. She didn't have time to fight with him and was about to call for her med team.

Before she could yell for help and a stretcher, Davin said something that sounded like a curse, placed his hand in the middle of the injured man's chest and closed his eyes. Sara watched as he seemed to focus his attention on the other man. For a moment she wanted to hit him, wake him up from his trance. But then she felt a tingle of energy coming from the wounded man, as if Davin was sending a jolt through his body. She was about to ask what was going on when the injured man sucked in a deep breath and began to moan. Davin opened his eyes and looked at her quickly, as if he'd been caught doing something wrong.

"What did you do?" she asked, completely awestruck.

"Nothing. Bought us a little time. Let's get him to your med bay, Doctor."

"Sara!" Rachael popped her head in from the shuttle bay floor. "I have a stretcher here if you need it."

"Call med bay. Have them prep the operating room."

"You got it."

Davin helped hand his co-pilot down to the security guards and medics waiting below. "Take care of Rafe. I need him back in one piece."

Sara turned to look at him, trying to size up the captain. "Are you hurt?"

"No, I'm lucky that way." And he winked at her.

"You fucking bastard!" a voice behind them barked.

Both Sara and Davin spun around to face an extremely pissed-off, burly man barreling down on them. Before she had time to react, Sara was shoved aside as the man took a swing at Davin.

"You're trying to fucking kill us!" The man was blindly swinging at Davin, connecting several times with his jaw.

"Calm down, Silas." Davin managed to say, spitting out a mouthful of blood. He took a swing of his own and landed a punch on the side of Silas' head. "We made it in one piece."

"Fuck you!"

When Silas swung this time, Davin blocked him and managed to land a kick that knocked the large man back into Sara. The last thing she remembered was being thrown back against the bulkhead and hearing a loud crack as darkness overtook her.

Chapter Two
∞

When Sara finally regained consciousness, she felt as if her brain was on fire. She tried to push her body into a sitting position, but her head pounded harder at the change of elevation. She fell back against the pillow and tried to brace herself against the pain.

"Shit," she muttered.

"Nice to see you up and running again." Haylie's concerned voice floated over to her.

Sara turned her head so she could see her friend sitting in the visitor's chair. The look on Haylie's face told her she'd given everyone a scare.

"How long?" She rubbed her temples, looking for relief.

"Long enough for Taber to throw your assaulter in the brig and tear his ship apart looking for anything illegal so he could keep him there. Just over four hours."

"Shit!" Sara sat up again, ignoring the wave of nausea that slammed into her. "What about the copilot? He needed surgery."

"I know this might come as a shock to you, but there *are* other doctors on this colony." Haylie was on her feet and moving to Sara's side. "He was in and out in under an hour. He'll be fine."

Sara's mind began to whiz through the events leading up to her crack on the head. "Wait a minute, Taber threw Davin in the brig?"

"Well, he went a bit ape-shit crazy when you got knocked out. Apparently, he just about took his engineer's head off."

"Davin or Taber?"

"The captain."

A shiver of desire rolled down Sara's back. Davin had been upset that she'd been hurt. She didn't know why, but the idea was very appealing.

"Now I know that look, Doctor Fergus," Haylie said and chuckled. "Your mysterious captain must be cute."

"Oh please. He gave me a concussion. And he was a bit of a pompous ass."

"Definitely cute. I'd go down and check him out myself, but I'm not currently on active duty." Haylie paused, bit her lip and looked over her shoulder briefly. "Look, think you're up to giving me the go ahead to return to work? I'm going a bit crazy."

"It's only been a day. Not even."

"Sara, please."

It was Sara's turn to chuckle. "You're asking your doctor, who has a concussion and is unfit to dispense a bandage at the moment, to give you medical clearance. I haven't even run a full exam on you yet to satisfy myself that you *are* fit for duty."

"I'm sure the baby is fine." Haylie rolled her eyes and sighed. "You're going to be as bad as Kamran, aren't you?"

"Probably worse. It's not like we have any previous cases of human-Briel mating to draw on. For now, I want you as far away from the action as I can get you."

"That's what I told her," a familiar voice said.

Both women turned to look at Kamran as he entered the room. Taber was trailing close behind him, wearing a scowl. Sara knew he was annoyed with her.

"How are you feeling?" Kamran asked as he gave Sara's hand a squeeze.

Sara shrugged, the motion sending a dull ache down her neck and along her left arm. "Nothing a little shot of pain meds won't cure." She looked up at Taber and offered him a small smile. "Sorry to have caused trouble."

"For once, you were not the cause, simply caught in the crossfire," Taber said in his normally even voice.

She really wanted to be offended at his comment, but she caught the slight smirk on his face in time. When had Taber developed a sense of humor?

"How is Davin? I hope you didn't rough him up too much."

Kamran straightened. "We were on our way to talk to him. I wanted to stop by and make sure you were okay first. He's been asking about you."

Sara's heart began to pound. Before anyone could protest, she slid off the gurney and walked over to the med dispenser.

"Should you be up?" Haylie was beside her instantly. "I doubt even you would let your patients up this fast."

"No, I'd probably tie them down. But I'm a lousy patient. All I need is a little shot of this." She pressed an injection into her arm. The drug instantly took the edge off her pounding head, making it easier to breathe. "Now I'm going to check my patient in the brig and make sure that my charming, but overly protective, security escort didn't cause him any harm."

Not waiting for anyone to answer, Sara turned and marched out of the room. She'd made it half way down the hall before Taber fell into step beside her.

"You...are a stubborn woman," he said simply.

"You've known me for over a year and you're just coming to that conclusion now?"

She swore she heard Taber sigh.

"Kamran will be joining us shortly. It seems his mate is under the impression that she can save the planet in her current condition."

"The only way we're going to keep Haylie off a case is to give her something else to do. She needs a mystery to unravel. Preferably one that will keep her in front of the computer."

"I'll mention that to Kamran."

They walked the rest of the way to the brig in silence. Since the Ecada attack last year, the colony had rarely needed use of the lower-level cells. Haylie and Taber had converted one of the side storage rooms close to her office as an intermediate brig. Sara couldn't remember the last time it had been used.

The doors to the brig whooshed open and she immediately saw Davin standing, arms crossed over his chest, in the middle of the cell. She swore when his reptilian gaze landed on her, relief washed across his face. She felt a blush heat her cheeks when he licked his lips and offered her a lopsided smirk.

"There's the little blaster. Nice to see you back in the land of the conscious, Doctor."

Sara straightened her back and walked purposefully over to stand in front of his cell. Neither one of them said anything at first. Sara really looked at him this time. Davin's brown hair was long, kissing the top of his shoulders and falling over his golden eyes. His broad shoulders were tucked into a black leather vest that held an assortment of survival gear. He wore no shirt underneath and she saw an intricate pattern of tattoos covering both his biceps and forearms. Interestingly, he wore a pair of black leather gloves that covered his hands and wrists.

When Davin chuckled, Sara's gaze snapped back to his. He cocked an eyebrow, issuing either a silent challenge or seeking her approval.

"I see you survived your brawl," Sara asked, clearing her throat. "Where is your friend?"

"Silas? You'll have to ask your Briel attack *ravak*. I haven't seen him since they hauled my ass in here."

The door behind her whooshed open and Sara looked over her shoulder to see Kamran walk in. Taber was by his side, whispering to him, most likely filling Kamran in on the pertinent details of their unexpected guest. When she looked back at Davin, she quickly noted the change in his demeanor.

His arms were now clasped behind his back and his face had lost some of its humor.

"It's okay," she whispered. "Kamran is one of the fairest people I know."

Davin didn't respond, his jaw tensing instead. Sara stepped to the side, allowing Kamran room to stand in front of the cell.

"Hello, Captain...I'm sorry, I didn't catch your last name," Kamran said with a smile.

"Davin Jagt." The two words came out clipped.

If Kamran noticed the hostility, he completely ignored it. "If you could be so kind as to tell us what damaged your ship. Both the head of human and Briel security are wondering if they should be planning a defense against an alien invasion force bound on getting you back. Or getting back at you."

The two men locked gazes and Sara fought the urge to squirm with the sudden intensity in the room. Kamran had a way of getting information from others that didn't require he do any more than raise an eyebrow. Davin wasn't immune to Kamran's gaze, which gave her a strange sense of comfort.

"Your colony is fine. We'd dropped off a shipment of supplies to Radon Three and got caught in the gravitational eddies of the asteroid belt."

Taber made some sort of noise Sara could only assume was a sigh as he left the room.

Davin chuckled, softening the harsh lines of his face. "I take it that because your *ravak* left, you believe me?"

"Of course. We simply needed to confirm what our own engineers suspected. You do realize Radon Three is under martial law and is off limits to outsiders?" Kamran asked, his eyebrow raised.

"Of course. It's the reason we were smuggling supplies to the rebels. Even the bad guys need to eat."

Kamran smiled. "If one would consider them *bad* instead of merely fighting for what they believe."

That seemed to catch Davin off guard. "You know of the conflict then?"

"Of course. Computer, release the security locks for cell two."

The door popped open and Kamran took a step back. Davin hesitated for only a moment before stepping out, right beside Sara. Again, she couldn't help but let her gaze travel over his body, drinking in every luscious inch. A distinctly male scent washed over her and she enjoyed the spicy musk.

"Please forgive our rude treatment when you first arrived." Kamran held out his hand. "Welcome to Eurus colony."

Davin eyed Kamran's outstretched arm. "Your reputation precedes you, Ambassador. They say you always get what you want and do it with a smile."

Kamran didn't move, though the very smile Davin mentioned played on his lips. Finally, Davin reached out and gripped his hand. From her position, Sara was better able to see the tattoos on his arm. Blues and blacks twined together like a snake crawling down his arm. Kamran noticed too.

"You're a Raqulian."

Sara gave her head a shake. "I can't keep up with all of the planets in this sector. Where is that one?"

"Farthest away from Briel, if I'm not mistaken. You certainly have a tremendous understanding of your distant neighbors." Davin said and dropped Kamran's hand.

"It's my job to know. While you and your crew are here, please enjoy the recreation facilities of the colony. I'm sure Sara won't mind showing you around."

"I should really get back to med bay. I'm sure there are–"

"I believe you told my wife you weren't fit to issue her a medical clearance. I assume that means you need your rest."

Kamran winked at her. "I'm sure the colony will survive without you for a day. Besides, you should enjoy the festivities tonight."

Sara couldn't believe it. She opened her mouth to protest, but nothing came out. Not that Davin had any such problem.

"Festivities?" Davin grinned. "It seems we chose an opportune day to crash."

"We would be happy to have you attend. And Sara wouldn't mind giving you a tour. That is, if she is feeling up to it?"

"Of course, I'm fine." Like she would admit to feeling like shit in front of them.

"I would love a guided tour. Thank you for your hospitality, Ambassador."

"It's administrator now. In any case, you are most welcome. Now, if you'll excuse me, my wife is about to do something foolish."

With a small bow, Kamran turned and walked out of the room.

Davin looked at Sara and frowned. "Bonded?"

"Oh yeah."

"I pity his wife," Davin muttered.

"Don't. She gives as good as she gets." Sara snorted. "Haylie would kick his ass if he gave her a reason."

Davin turned and faced her. Relief seemed to settle over him. Whether it was relief from being free of his cell or from being released from Kamran's presence, she wasn't sure.

Sara felt the air rush from her lungs when he took half a step closer to her, closing the already small distance between them.

"So, Doctor. I see you are feeling better." His voice was smooth and seductive, with a hint of mischief in it.

"I'm conscious, if that's what you mean," she said and began to walk away.

Unfortunately, she turned too quickly and a wave of dizziness washed over her. Before she knew what was happening, Davin had his arm around her waist, holding her up. Sara suddenly found it difficult to breathe and it had nothing to do with her injury. Being this close to him, having his body pressed against hers, made her insides quiver. When she looked up into his golden, reptilian eyes, she couldn't help but suck in a deep breath. They seemed to see straight through her, see what she was thinking.

"Easy now, Doc. I much prefer to have you awake. I don't think your security boyfriend would much appreciate you ending up unconscious."

Sara couldn't help but chuckle. "Me and Taber? He just hates it when someone steps on his toes. There's nothing between us."

"Really?"

The way Davin said the word made Sara shiver. He ran his thumb over the arm he held in his hand, letting his gaze travel over her face to stop on her breasts. She felt the blush return with a vengeance and withdrew her arm from his grip.

"Not that it's any concern of yours," she muttered. Straightening, she tucked a loose strand of hair behind her ear. "I suppose you'd like to see the station?"

Davin licked his lips and smiled his slow, half smile. "I wouldn't miss it. Lead on, Doc."

Not wanting to be caught under his devouring look for too long, Sara crossed her arms across her chest and walked out of the room, Davin half a step behind her. As Sara led him through the corridors, she could feel her skin tingle from his nearness. Her body would lead her down a dangerous path with him if she wasn't careful.

When he leaned his head down so it was near her ear, she shivered.

"So is this a silent tour? I should try to guess what it is I'm seeing?"

Sara cringed. "Sorry. I guess that crack on my head didn't knock any manners into me."

Davin reached up and brushed a strand of her hair that'd escaped her ponytail. "Consider yourself forgiven."

He draped his arm around her shoulder and Sara felt his body heat penetrate her. It should be a criminal offense to have that much sex appeal and use it on a woman in public. She tried to ignore the strange looks people gave her as they passed by. Not wanting to give him the satisfaction of letting him know he'd gotten to her, Sara acted like she didn't have a care in the world.

"We're coming up to the bazaar. It looks better now than it did a year ago. The Ecada tore this place apart when they attacked us." Her thoughts threatened to drift back to the day of the attack, so she gave her head a soft shake and quickly regretted the motion when it made her head throb. The pain brought her back to the present. "Tore it apart."

She looked up to see him frown and nod.

"I heard about the attack from some of the traders out on the rim. I'm surprised you're here to tell the tale."

"If it wasn't for Haylie and Kamran, we wouldn't be. And Sean too, though he wouldn't admit to his part in helping."

She felt her heart ache at the thought of Sean and the shell of a man he'd turned into since the Ecada were defeated. She'd tried to work with him over the past few months, but nothing seemed to help. He hated himself for the part, however outside of his control, he'd played.

"And where were you during the attack? On the front lines, saving lives, I imagine."

For a moment she thought he was being flippant. It wasn't until she looked into his eyes that she realized he was serious. Sara stopped walking and turned to face him. The crowd and noise around her seemed to fade away until there was only Davin.

"It was horrible," she whispered. The pain and fear she'd felt came rushing back in a heartbeat. "They kept bringing the bodies to us to patch up, but we couldn't keep up. I couldn't even look at their faces, knowing I would heal them just so they'd be thrown back into the fight. And Ecada broke through the front lines and almost wiped out me and my team."

Sara swayed, her head suddenly feeling dizzy. Davin's arms were around her as she leaned hard against him. The strength and warmth from his body seemed to seep into her, giving her a slight boost but not enough to help her overcome the overwhelming pull of her emotions.

"I think you hit your head a bit harder than you realized. I need to get you back to med bay," he said with more concern than a stranger really should.

"My quarters are closer. I have a med kit there."

She tried to walk away, but Davin scooped her up in his arms. Sara would have fought him under normal conditions, but it was easier to give in. If anyone thought it odd that their chief of medical was being carried away by an alien they'd never seen before, no one said anything.

Davin managed to get her close to her quarters with little direction on her part. When she was only a short distance away, she tried to get him to put her down so she could walk under her own power.

"And lose my chance to touch your sweet ass, I don't think so," he said in a voice loud enough to turn the head of a passing engineer.

"Do you try to embarrass people?" she said, her face flaming.

"People? No. Apparently just you. This yours?"

"Thank god. I'd hate to have to share this honor."

Still, he didn't set her down. Instead, Sara was forced to lean over and press her hand against the ID scanner to unlock her door.

The air inside was cool as the door whooshed shut behind them. Davin walked across her small living room and set her gently on her couch. Instead of moving away, he sat down beside her and began to remove his gloves.

"Nice place. Roomy."

Suddenly feeling nervous being this close to him, all alone, Sara began to chatter away. "You should have seen the room we had when we first arrived. They had us sharing quarters in a place half this size. Thank god I was sharing with Haylie or I would have gone — what the hell are you doing?"

Davin had tossed his gloves aside on the coffee table and reached up to place his hand in the middle of her chest.

"I'm making your head better. Now sit still."

"I don't think so, buddy. I've just met you, you're the reason I have a bump on my head in the first place and now you want to feel me up!"

"Feel you up?"

The confused look on his face was almost cute. Sara sighed and rolled her eyes.

"Touching my breasts. You know, these things."

She motioned her hands in front of her breasts as if to cup them. Davin's gaze followed her action and she watched as he licked his lips.

"Perhaps we'll save that for another time. Right now, I simply want to heal your wound."

Dropping her hands in her lap, Sara shook her head. "And how to do you propose to do that?"

"What do you know about my people?" He said the words quietly, his normal teasing tone surprisingly gone.

"Nothing." She shrugged, sneaking a glance at his arms. "Who did Kamran say your people are?"

"Raqulians."

Unable to stop herself anymore, Sara reached up and traced her finger down along his arm. She could almost feel the lines of the tattoo and the intricate patters woven on his skin.

"Do all your people have these?" she spoke quietly, enjoying the feeling of touching him.

Davin didn't move. His eyes were fixed on her face while she stared at where her finger connected with his skin.

"We do, but they are different depending on which cast you are born into. And which cast you pledge yourself to."

She continued to trace the tattoo all the way down his forearm to the top of his hands. When she started to retrace her path, he caught her wrist, lifting it an inch.

"Touch is a very powerful thing for my people. It has the power to heal, the power to kill. Or the power to arouse."

Sara's gaze shot to his and she could see it. See the desire dancing in his golden eyes, the tightness of his jaw as he swallowed hard. Her heart began to pound and she found herself being drawn into his arousal. Her nipples hardened and she couldn't get enough air into her lungs.

"I've only just met you," she said, her voice shaking.

"I brought you here to heal your head. Not claim you as my mate."

She shivered at the thought of being in his bed, under him as he slammed his cock hard into her. That is, if he had a cock. Sara looked down between his legs and could see the outline of a large bulge straining in his pants. Davin took her hand that he was holding and pressed it to his cock.

"I trust we are compatible," he drawled, a sexy half smile on his face.

Whether it was from the concussion or her own ignored desires, Sara wrapped her hand around his shaft and squeezed. She sucked in a breath, amazed at his girth. "I thought you weren't going to...do this?"

"Can you blame me? A beautiful temptress is sitting practically on top of me, devouring me with her eyes." He chuckled. "But you are correct."

Gently, he lifted her wrist again, this time placing it back in her lap. Sara flexed her fingers and bit down on her bottom lip. "So how do you want to heal me?"

"Do you trust me?" He asked the words with all seriousness, even though his eyes were twinkling.

"No," she snorted. "I just met you."

"Fair enough. I'm going to place my hand on your chest, like I did with my co-pilot. You'll feel a tingle, but that should be all."

Sara couldn't help but frown. "And that will fix a concussion?"

Davin shrugged. "Ready?"

"No."

Sara jumped up on unsteady legs and made her way over to the med kit she had stuffed in the corner. It took her a minute, but she found the medical scanner hiding under the compresses and sedatives. Standing up, she quickly scanned herself to confirm she still had the concussion.

"Don't believe me?" he asked chuckling.

"I just want a baseline comparison. In case anything else changes. Can never be too careful around you aliens."

"Did you ever stop to consider that the humans in the sector are the aliens? This is *my* home."

She frowned as she made her way back to the couch. "I never looked at it that way."

Davin sat up on the couch when Sara rejoined him. She placed the medical scanner on the table in front of her, took a deep breath and tried to relax. Her whole body seemed to tingle from his closeness and her heart was racing. Once he was done with her, she needed him to get the hell out.

"Ready," she said in a voice far calmer than she felt.

When she looked up into his eyes, she felt the instant attraction again. Her nipples tightened as he raised his hand and gently pressed it to the middle of her chest, in between her breasts. He didn't look away from her, instead keeping his gaze locked to hers.

The tingling began in her chest. It felt as if a warm compress now lay against her naked skin and was sending out waves of heat. Instead of the warmth going into her body, it seemed to travel along the surface of her skin, over her breasts to the tips of her nipples, teasing each one. She wanted to look down to see if he'd moved his hand but she knew he hadn't.

His eyes were dancing with amusement, teasing her, as if he really were caressing her, only from the inside. When Sara went to frown, she found she couldn't move her lips. After a final tweak of pleasure, she felt the warmth finally move from her breasts to deeper inside her chest. The warmth seemed to envelop her lungs, muscles, even her ribs as Davin probed deeper. Slowly, he moved from her chest to her neck and into her head.

For a moment, Sara swore he was trying to kill her. The room seemed to go dark and her head began to spin. She had to lean forward fully onto his hand for support. The world was tilting out of control and she could barely hold on for the ride.

"Shh, you're okay," Davin's voice drifted to her ears, sounding as if he were far away. "It's been a while since I've done this."

Her entire head was tingling now. Every hair alive with energy, every muscle being massaged from the inside out. And suddenly she felt it—felt the area of her brain where there was damage. Davin's other hand was now on her head, rubbing slow circles around the injury. The headache she'd had since waking up in med bay an hour ago was suddenly gone.

It took Sara several blinks for her vision to clear. Once it did, she realized Davin's face was only inches away from hers. The hand on her head was massaging her hair, drifting down to the back of her neck to caress her tense muscles.

"How did you do that?" she whispered.

"I told you. It's a gift some of my people have. Very common."

Sara wasn't sure if she had leaned forward or if Davin had tugged her head closer. Either way their lips were close to brushing together.

"Did you fix me?" As she spoke, her eyes searched his, looking for something, anything that should be scaring her off.

"You didn't need fixing, *shara*."

His hand on her chest didn't shift position, but she felt his fingers flex against her uniform.

"I haven't seen a more beautiful woman in the entire sector. And I've seen quite a few."

"I bet you have."

Davin chuckled. "Jealous, *shara*? I forgot about that with human women. It's been a long time since I met one."

When she started to pull away, Davin increased his grip.

"Let me go," she said the words more with annoyance than fear. She wasn't used to being out of control, and with Davin she felt her grip definitely slipping.

"We haven't talked about my payment. I'm not in the habit of performing services and not getting paid."

The way his eyes dipped down to her lips, Sara knew exactly what he wanted when it came to *payment*.

"You're a bastard, Davin."

But her heart was beating loud and hard. He only smiled and moved his hand from the middle of her chest to cover her heart.

"Then why are you so excited. I have to assume you're excited. You don't look like the type to scare easily."

"I have a fast heart rate."

His grin widened. "One…little…kiss. Hardly a harsh price to fix your head."

As he brought his lips on hers, Sara's eyes slipped closed. He didn't kiss her hard, or was demanding with his advances. Davin took his time, exploring her, tasting her at an infuriatingly slow pace. His mouth was warm and tasted of exotic spices, so different Sara wanted to eat him whole. She slid her tongue into his mouth to caress his and she felt his body stiffen before he let out a groan.

His hand slid down to cup her breast through her uniform, taking time to tease her already painfully erect nipple. Sara moaned and pushed her breast hard against him. Her hands began to explore his body as well. She ran her hands up his forearms to his biceps, following the raised marks of his tattoos. Davin groaned again into her mouth, pinching her nipple and deepening their kiss.

Desperate for air, Sara pulled back, tipping her head and exposing her neck to him. Davin quickly took what she offered and licked up the length of her neck to stop at her earlobe.

"I want nothing more than to fuck you right now." His words were hot against her ear.

Sara's breath hitched and she tightened her grip on his arms. "Davin..."

They stayed that way, clutching each other, panting for several minutes. Finally he pulled back and ran his hand through his hair.

"I should go." He stood quickly and took two steps away before turning back to face her. "I didn't intend that."

"It's okay, I—"

"No, it's not."

Davin took another step before turning around and coming back. He grabbed Sara by the head and she forgot to breathe when he ravaged her mouth with another forceful kiss. This time, when he pulled away, he seemed to be searching her eyes. Sara couldn't help but think he was looking for something, some sign of approval or rejection.

"I'm glad your head is better," he said, releasing her head.

Without another word, he left her alone.

Chapter Three

Davin paced the main living quarters of his ship, fighting the urge to hit something.

"Fucking humans," he muttered. "A bane on the galaxy."

His body was still humming from the kiss he'd shared with Sara hours earlier. Since leaving her, he'd holed up in his ship and had decided he wasn't coming out until it was repaired. It would be the only way he'd be able to maintain his sanity. Silas had calmed down enough for Davin to talk some sense into him and get him out of the brig as well. It also helped that Rafe was out of surgery and recovering nicely. Davin had been friends with Rafe a long time and had never wanted him to get hurt. Especially since the whole fucking mess was Davin's fault.

You'd think I'd learn to stop helping people.

When he turned around, he slammed his fist into the center console, his knuckle landing squarely on a rivet. Blood began to trickle down his hand to drip several drops onto the floor. He couldn't help but watch the drops pool on the floor, splattering into patters. His life was complicated—he couldn't do that to anyone, let alone someone like Sara.

"Warning, approaching intruder," the metallic voice of the computer screeched at him.

"Identify," he said and closed his eyes, placing his hand over his injured fist. It took only a second to repair the damage, but he wasn't pleased about having to use his healing gift for a third time in one day. Hard to stay under anyone's notice when you're flaunting your talents.

"Administrator Kamran," the computer responded.

"Fuck," he muttered.

The familiar tingle was quickly gone and Davin went in search of his gloves. It wasn't until he had them safely in place and he'd taken several deep breaths that he opened the shuttle's main door and let his cocky smirk slide on his face.

"What a surprise to see you here, Administrator. I trust none of my crew is causing you any problems."

The tall Briel walked up the temporary stairs the Eurus security guards had placed there for easy entry into the ship. Once again, Davin felt the Briel's piercing gaze assessing him. Measuring him not just as a captain but as a man. He somehow doubted he'd measure up in the eyes of a man like Kamran.

"Not at all. In fact, other than your copilot in med bay, we've barely seen any of you."

Davin offered him a seat, taking the one closest to the cockpit. "We've been busy trying to get this bucket back together. Don't want to trespass on your hospitality for too long."

Kamran stared at him long enough that Davin almost felt the urge to squirm. Almost. But when Kamran smiled, he started to get nervous.

"You made quite the impression with Sara. She said you fixed her head."

"She told you that?"

"No, but she told my wife. What she knows, I know."

He'd forgotten about the Briel bonding and how close their mates were. Davin didn't think he could ever be like that with any woman. But if any woman were to tempt him, it would be Sara.

"I fixed her head. It was nothing."

"It's been a long time since I've spent any time with a Raqulian. There aren't as many of you around helping travelers these days."

Davin didn't like where this line of conversation was going. "We're around. Why did you come here, Administrator? I'd like to get back to fixing my ship."

"Please, call me Kamran. There is no rush for you or your crew to leave. Your ship has taken a lot of damage and your crew looks tired. We are having a celebration, starting tonight. It's to be an annual event honoring those who died in the attack on the colony last year. You're more than welcome to attend."

Davin looked hard at Kamran, wishing he could get inside the other man's head to discover his intentions. He didn't trust him—not that Davin trusted many people. Realistically, he couldn't say no and his crew needed the rest. They'd been on the run for months and were all near the point of breaking.

"We appreciate the offer. Thank you," he said and nodded his head.

"I'll arrange for quarters for you and your crew. No sense in staying in a ship when you have an entire station at your disposal. There will be an engineering team assigned to assist you with your repairs in the morning."

Kamran stood and offered his hand. This time, Davin took it without hesitation. "I'll let them know."

"Apparently, Sara is working and, as my wife informs me, doesn't plan on attending the festivities."

Davin crossed his arms across his chest. *So this is why Kamran came.* "Oh?"

"She's had a tough time adjusting to things over the past year. She could stand to get out and have some fun."

"She mentioned she was on the frontlines. It must have been difficult for her."

Kamran nodded. "She's very brave. And the last person I'd want to get in the way of when she has an agenda. But that attack shook her hard. She'd been trying to ignore rather than accept what happened back then."

Davin could tell. He had felt the pull of her emotional scars when he'd healed her head, knew how deep her pain ran. For a moment, he'd been tempted to do something about them. But only for a moment. "Well, I will have to make sure she enjoys herself."

"I'm very pleased to hear that. Have a good time yourself, Captain." With a half smile of his own, Kamran turned and left the shuttle.

Davin was still standing there dumbfounded when Silas came up from the engine room.

"It's pretty much fucked back there." He slapped his sweat- and dust-covered bandana against his thigh. "It's going to take a week or more to get everything back online. And that would be with an entire team of engineers."

"Ask and I shall provide." Davin turned and smiled.

"What the fuck are you talking about?"

"We will have a full engineering team at our disposal until the ship is fixed. Starting tomorrow."

Silas's moth dropped open. "Who did you bribe to get that?"

"Not a soul. The administrator offered."

"Well, I'll be. Probably wants us out of his precious colony."

Davin shrugged. "Not so sure of that. He offered us rooms and use of the station while we're here. No rush on the leaving part."

"Holy shit. And what do you have to do in return?"

"Take the lovely doctor on a date."

Silas laughed. "Make sure to tell her you're sorry for cracking her skull."

"I believe it was your body that knocked her into the wall. Besides, she knows already. I said my apologies this afternoon." He winked at Silas.

"And she still wants you? Ha!"

"Just remember the things I do—it's all for you and the crew. Every hardship," Davin said, pressing his hand to his chest and batting his eyes.

"The only hard thing on you will be your cock!"

"Make sure everyone enjoys the festivities tonight. I don't want to see even one of your sorry asses here. You all deserve it after the month we've had."

"Aye, sir."

On his walk back to his quarters, Davin's mind drifted back to Sara. The feel of her soft lips, the sound of her moans in his ear made his body buzz, sent his blood rushing through his ears. His cock grew stiff and hard and he knew there was only one way to ease his pain.

No, showing the doctor a good time wouldn't be a hardship at all.

* * * * *

Davin nodded to the group of people he passed in the hall on his way to the med bay. He'd spent the last few hours working with Silas getting the shuttle cleaned up. There was more damage than either of them had realized at first, including most of the stardrive. It would take them longer than Silas had estimated, even with the help of Kamran's engineers working around the clock. He'd dismissed his crew with strict orders to get drunk at the festivities tonight. If they were going to be stuck here, they might as well enjoy it.

Now all he was interested in was finding a certain doctor and enjoying the night himself.

When he walked into med bay, he quickly located Sara. She was talking to a man, a miner from the look of his filthy clothing, who was looking more than a little angry. Not willing to risk Sara getting attacked, Davin sauntered close and was about to interrupt when she heard her speak.

"You're killing yourself, Sean. If you don't stop taking unnecessary risks like this, you'll be dead in a year."

The concern Davin heard in her voice told him this was more than a doctor talking to a casual patient.

Sean stood tall, about Davin's height. He couldn't see the other man's face but could tell by the lean cut of his build he'd spent a while working in the mines.

"Am I cleared to return to work?" Sean's voice was hard, jaded.

"No!" She threw her hands in the air. "And I'm not approving your return until you have at least forty-eight hours' rest. You were sucking in dust from the surface for at least five minutes. That's enough to kill a person."

"I'm still here, aren't I?"

"Forty-eight hours. And I want to see you back in here for another physical."

Sean didn't respond, turning instead so Davin could see his face. His blond hair was cut short and his blue eyes seemed to pierce through to the back of Davin's head. He could feel the pull of emotions, a wounded soul coming from the other man. The feelings beat against Davin's inner barrier, demanding that he let his gift come out, begging it to help him. Sean took a step forward and put his body in such a position he could easily defend Sara if the need arose.

And despite the fact he was here to show Sara a good time, Davin would have been more than happy to fight this man if he got in his way. Not that he'd be winning any favor with Sara if he punched a friend.

At least he hoped Sean was *only* a friend.

"Hello, Davin." Sara pushed past Sean and smiled at him, though lacking some enthusiasm. "What brings you here?"

"I wanted to check up on you. Make sure you were feeling better," he said and looked directly at Sean. "I didn't realize you were with a patient."

"Oh, Davin, this is Sean Donaldson. Sean, Davin's ship is the one that crashed landed in the east bay this morning."

Despite Davin being in the best shape of his life, one look at Sean and he realized he'd put up one hell of a fight if it ever came to that. For whatever reason, the fire that flashed in Sean's eyes died to be replaced with a dead cold.

"Learn to fly," he muttered and pushed past Sara and Davin.

Sara sighed and squeezed Davin's hand. "Sorry. He's had a death wish ever since the Ecada left. It's been all I can do to keep him going. Psychologist I'm not."

"I've seen men like him before. It's hard to bring them back from whatever demon is eating at them."

He pushed back the memories of his father's work with the refugees on Cryus Planes. The haunted look in the soldiers' eyes when they returned from the battlefield had given him nightmares as a child. Worse was being forced to climb inside their heads, trying to heal their pain. Davin gave his head a shake. No, he'd never do that again.

"You okay?" Sara asked, sliding her hand up along the bare skin of his arm.

The snake of desire began to uncoil inside him at her touch. He tried to push back the overwhelming need to strip her bare and slam his cock inside her over and over. That was the warrior in him wanting to come out and play. His chosen profession after he'd abandoned the calling of his cast.

Davin smiled at her and watched as she bit down on her bottom lip, making it red from the impact.

"I am in need of a party. And I've been told there is one *javen* of one going on tonight."

Sara frowned. "So why are you here? I'm working."

"To be honest, if I want my ship fixed, I must take you out and show you a good time."

"What?"

"By orders of the administrator of this Eurus colony."

Sara's face grew red and she began to sputter.

"I'm going to kill Kamran. No! Haylie. He wouldn't even think of it if she hadn't been nattering in his ear. I'm going to — put me down!"

Davin threw Sara over his shoulder and carried her out of the med bay. She slammed her fists into his back and kicked at his chest. He only laughed and spanked her ass. Instead of the shocked cry of outrage he'd expected, Sara gasped and squirmed against him.

"You like that, do you? I'll have to keep that in mind." And he gave her another slap.

"Where the hell are you taking me?"

"To my quarters. You can't expect me to take you out dressed like that?"

"I'm not *going* anywhere. Get it through your thick alien skull! Take me back."

"You're lucky the administrator found me a room near med bay. I don't think you'd want too many people seeing you like this."

"Bastard."

He laughed. "This is becoming a habit, me carrying you to a bedroom. It's only going to end badly for you sooner or later."

Sara muttered, "I'll kick your ass, buddy."

Not wishing to tempt fate or test his restraint, he set Sara down and pushed her inside when he opened the door to his quarters. Davin crossed his arms and grinned.

"Inside on the bed is an outfit for you. I won't let you out until you put it on."

She ground her teeth and clenched her fists. "I need to get back to work. I'm on duty."

"No, I believe they found you a replacement."

"I'll call security. Have them throw you back in the brig."

"Your friend Haylie has given me her approval. Even gave me your clothing size."

Sara covered her face with both hands and groaned. "I'm going to kill her."

Gently, Davin took her wrists and pulled her hands away from her face. She looked suddenly very tired and very scared. He remembered what Kamran had said about her, and knew what that level of fear could do to a person. It had her running and he knew the type of damage that would do to her. The only way she could get over this was to face it head on.

He'd been tempted to try to help but had pulled away before he got too close. Now a small part of him wished he had despite his reservations. Right now she didn't need tenderness. His fiery doctor needed to have an insane amount of fun. Davin took a step closer, using his height to seduce her. It seemed to work, as her breathing grew shallow and her gaze flicked from his lips to his chest and arms.

"Your friends have all agreed you need a night with a scoundrel. You need to forget the rules and enjoy yourself."

"And are you a scoundrel?" Her voice quivered slightly as she spoke.

"You're about to find out." He leaned in and licked her bottom lip. She tasted soft and sweet, more tempting than he wanted to admit. "Consider yourself kidnapped. Put on the outfit in there and be back at this door in ten minutes."

"And what if I take longer. Or don't come out at all?"

Davin smiled, reached around and cupped her ass with his hand, squeezing hard. "I'll come in after you. Either way, you'll have a good time."

He shoved her gently backward into the room and let the door close between them. Now he had to wait. He hated waiting. Crossing his arms across his chest, Davin pressed his back against the wall and closed his eyes.

The rumble of residual turmoil left over from his brief encounter with Sean was making his head ache. It had been a long time since he'd experienced contact with that kind of psychological hurt. He'd made a point of staying far away from damaged people, not knowing how strong his mental barrier really was. The buzzing left in his ears was driving him insane. Breathing deep, he tried to push it away, even though he knew it wouldn't work. There was only one thing he could do—heal it.

Mentally, he corralled the turbulent emotions, getting them balled up in a small part of his mind. He didn't let his guard down completely, scared he wouldn't be able to regain his control once he was done. Davin concentrated on the pain, the guilt and used his long-rusty skills to smooth the emotions down. There was a sudden surge when Sean's torment threatened to overtake him, trying to fuse with his emotions. With effort, he pushed them back. Over and over he stroked them, shrinking them until there was nothing left.

Davin exhaled a long, shaky breath. His body trembled as his hands tried to grip the smooth wall behind him. When he opened his eyes, his body felt lighter. The dull glow of the corridor lights was brighter than it had been a moment ago. He'd done it.

The whoosh of the door beside him caught his attention. When Sara stepped out, he forgot to breathe. The green silk of her dress clung to every curve of her body, drawing his gaze to her breasts and swell of her hips. The neckline was low, revealing the tops of her creamy, white breasts, making his mouth water. She'd pulled her blonde hair out of the binding she'd worn a few minutes ago and the long strands fell seductively over her shoulder and down her back. The bottom of the dress came to just below her knees but had a long split up the side to tease him with glances of her thigh.

"It's not going to be much of a night out if we stand in the corridor staring at each other." Her amused tone shook him from his infatuation.

Davin pushed away from the wall and offered her his arm. "I believe there is food at the bazaar. Hungry?"

When she slipped her arm into the crook of his, Davin felt his skin tingle. The top of her head came up to his jaw and her body fit nicely against his. His cock sprang to life and he had to think of every disgusting thing in the sector to try to calm his raging desire. They walked the nearly empty corridors in silence until they were finally in the hall that led to the bazaar.

"Where did you get this dress? I didn't think they had anything like it here," she asked, breaking the silence between them.

"Your friend. She said it was going to be your birthday present."

Sara sighed. "I should have known."

"I love it." He bumped her body as they walked.

"You would." She bumped back.

She looked up at him and he couldn't help but wink at her. Her lips twitched into a small grin. His heart rate picked up speed and he found himself lost in her blue eyes.

The entrance to the bazaar was in front of them and there was already a crowd of people swarming the various booths. Laughter rolled above the chattering and the buzz of good emotions pricked at Davin's mind. When a trio of miners walked past them and whistled at Sara, she stiffened. The only thing that kept Davin from turning around and smashing them in the face was how Sara clung a bit harder to his arm.

"Do you want to go back?" he asked softly.

Sara's jaw tightened for a moment and her back stiffened. Then, just as suddenly, her whole body relaxed. She spun around to face him, grabbed both his hands and grinned.

"There was a time not that long ago I would have joined those three guys just to see what kind of trouble I'd get myself into. Since the attack…let's go have some fun."

The rebel in him grinned back. "I'm sure I can get you into more than enough trouble for your liking."

The next several hours were all a blur to him. He laughed, ate and drank more than he had in months as they walked through the crowds of the bazaar. Davin's head was spinning, not from the alcohol but rather from Sara's constant touch. She had a fascination with his arms and the tattoos that covered them. At one point, when someone had bumped into him and gotten some sort of food on his biceps, Sara was there.

"Let me clean that up for you," she said in a low, seductive voice. Leaning in, she ran her tongue up his arm, licking up every last spot of the sticky substance. "Yummy."

Before he had a chance to grab her for a kiss, Sara pulled away laughing and made her way through the crowd to one of the colony's bars. The music pounded into his chest when Davin finally caught up to her in the middle of the floor. People of all races were dancing, drinking and laughing, their bodies being pressed together before pulling apart.

Sara closed her eyes and began to sway to the rhythmic sounds. She was more relaxed than she'd been since he met her and Davin found the change in her intoxicating. She was wild and free, an attitude he'd chased for himself his entire life. He spun her around and pressed her body against his.

Keeping her eyes closed, Sara swayed against him, her hands reaching up to trace a pattern over his chest and down to his hips. They were bumped and she fell forward, pressing her breasts hard against him. He could feel her erect nipples through the thin fabric of her dress. His cock somehow grew harder and Davin couldn't hold back anymore. He grabbed Sara by the hips and ground against her.

Her eyes flew open as she gasped. He ground again, this time in beat with the music, so anyone watching would think they were simply dancing. But not Sara. He could tell by her eyes that she knew exactly what he was doing.

Marking her for his own.

Her hands found the edge of his black shirt and slipped beneath. She raked her nails along his stomach just above the waistband of his pants. Teasing, she ran her thumbs over his stomach muscles, each tingle going straight to his cock.

"You're killing me," he groaned.

Sara looked around, and seeing something, began to pull at him. "Come with me."

It took them a while to push their way through the crowd. Anonymous hands would reach out and touch him, caressing his back and ass as he passed people. Sara wasn't immune to their touch either as both men and women reached out for her. With every touch, she squeezed his hand tighter, scare to get lost in the crowd. Finally, they emerged from the crowd close to the bar. Sara waved to a man and led Davin through a side door and into a short hallway. The loud music still reached them though it was now muted by the door. Davin pushed her against the wall and licked a trail from her shoulder to her neck. She tasted like sweat and desire.

"Where are we?" he muttered against her, sucking her earlobe into his mouth.

"Service corridor. I had a patient here last month."

"Someone could walk in and see us."

He didn't let her answer, ravaging her mouth with a possessive kiss. Sara's hands were on his face and in his hair, pulling him as close as he could get. Unlike the kiss they'd shared before, this one was frantic, needy and more erotic than any other he'd ever had.

Her tongue explored his mouth, dueling with his, wisps of caresses sending chills through her body. He could taste the mixture of drinks and food they'd sampled and something that was uniquely Sara. His blood simmered close to a boil—making him needy.

Davin breathed in deep and shifted his attention from her mouth back to her neck. The overwhelming desire to bite her, mark her as his hit him hard. Somehow he ignored it and licked the skin instead. Sara moaned and ran her leg up the length of his thigh. He grabbed her under her knee and held her body open to him, her dress parting at the slit to give him access. Leaning in, he pressed his erection against her hot pussy.

"I want to fuck you right now." He nipped at her shoulder.

"Oh shit," she whispered, her body trembling.

"You want me to fuck here right here, wild one? Take you right now?"

He pressed even harder against her, this time reaching down with his hand and cupping her breast. Her nipple was hard and he took great pleasure in rolling it between his thumb and finger.

"Might...not be compatible." Sara sighed before biting down on her lip.

Enjoying the invitation, he slid his gloved hand from her knee, along the inside of her thigh to her pussy. Quickly pushing past her panties, he found her wet opening and pushed a finger inside. Sara gasped and her gaze locked on his.

"Feels compatible to me."

"Davin!"

He continued to push in, feeling her cream ease the motion of his gloved finger. When he pulled back to circle her swollen clit, her entire body tensed.

"You like that, do you?" When she didn't respond, he pulled his hand away. "Do you?"

"Yes, please don't stop."

Chuckling, he brought his glove to his face and used his teeth to pull it off. Dropping it to the floor, he returned his hand to her hot pussy.

"That's better," he said and dipped his finger into her cream. As his finger played deep inside her, he let his thumb stroke her clit.

"Shit, you're killing me," she whispered, arching her body against his hand.

"Good thing I know a doctor."

Repeatedly he thrust his finger into her until her juices covered his hand. When he thought she could take it, he added a second finger. Sara's body shuddered and she leaned forward resting her head on his shoulder.

"This is what I want to be doing with my cock right now. Over and over again." He punctuated each word with the thrust of his hand.

Sara managed a whimper before he kissed her again. Her hands clung tightly to him, bunching his shirt in her fists. All rational thought fled from his mind. With his free hand, Davin tugged her neckline down, exposing her breast. He lowered his head and caught her nipple in his mouth, sucking hard. He felt her pussy clamp around his fingers and her cream flood his hand. She was so close to the edge now.

The dull music suddenly became a loud blare when the door that separated the hall from the bar opened. Davin leaned forward and shielded Sara's half-naked body from the intruder.

"Get the fuck out," he spat out at the pair of drunk men who now stood gawking at them.

"Holy shit!"

"That's fucking hot."

"Get...out...now," Davin turned his face to glare at them.

"No problem, buddy. Relax." The one on the left said. "Let's go."

"Man, I want to watch."

"He looks like he'll rip your head off, come on."

And as suddenly as they'd arrived, the pair was gone. One look at Sara told him the moment was gone as well.

"You okay?" he asked, brushing a strand of her hair away.

She was panting and her eyes were wide. Carefully, she looked around him at the door.

"Do you think they saw me?"

The Bond that Heals Us

"Not your face, if that's what you mean."

"I..." She looked back at him and grinned shyly.

"Everyone's a bit crazy tonight. I doubt they'd remember it was you even if they did see." When she didn't answer, Davin placed a kiss on her forehead. "Let me get you home."

"No!" She grabbed at his arms, preventing him from pulling away. "We're not done."

Davin's heart pounded and the blood went straight to his cock. "Oh I'm far from done with you. But I'll be forced to kill the next man who stares at you that way. I'd rather not get arrested before I make you come."

Chapter Four

ಸಾ

Sara didn't remember getting back to her quarters, only the constant caresses and kisses from Davin. When the two guys had interrupted them, she'd felt a strange mix of embarrassment and excitement. It had only served to intensify her needs and she'd be damned if she wasn't going to satisfy them.

The whoosh of the closing door was silent permission for them to let loose. Davin grabbed her by the waist and lifted her up, allowing Sara to wrap her legs around his hips. Her dress rode high up on her thighs, keeping her precious inches away from his cock. *Fuck, I want him so bad.* She felt him tug at the buttons on the side of her dress, sending more than a few flying through the air.

"Are you sure you want this?" His words came out harsh against her ear.

She reached down between them and squeezed his shaft through is pants. "In me. Now."

"Wild one."

She *did* feel wild. Crazy. Not caring about the consequences of her actions. She wanted Davin now, despite knowing nothing about him or his people. She needed his warmth and his touch so she could forget. He dropped her on the bed, quickly following. Sara closed her eyes and held on for dear life.

Again, he started at her neck, nipping and licking her skin as he slowly pulled her dress from her breasts. The air was cool, making her already sensitive nipples pulse with pleasure. Davin still wore one glove and the contrast of the heat of his skin to the cool glove sent shivers through her. When he brought it up to caress her face, Sara grabbed his wrist and tugged it off.

"I want to feel you." To help ease the loss of his garment, she sucked his finger into her mouth, teasing the tip with her tongue.

"Not before I get my taste."

Davin rose up on his knees, straddling her thighs with his. With a quick jerk he pulled off the tight-fitting black shirt that accentuated more than it hid and threw it somewhere over his shoulder. With Davin now bare from the waist up, Sara was able to really looked at her alien lover for the first time.

A long, deep scar stitched its way along his side, stopping just above the bottom of his ribcage. The tattoos that covered his arms continued over his shoulders to stop above his pecs. Kneeling in front of her looking dangerous, his golden eyes hooded and hungry, Sara suddenly felt she was about to be consumed.

"You were wounded?"

"I was a warrior for my people. A soldier."

The idea excited her more than it should have. Knowing that he could protect her, that he wasn't afraid to save the people he cared about, thrilled her.

"Pull your dress down. I want to see you naked."

Sara felt the blush heat her face as she looked up at him. Despite his carefree attitude, she knew this was a man who was used to getting exactly what he wanted. She half rose up on her arms, bringing her face close to his groin. She let her gaze dip there while she slowly shrugged her arms out of the loose dress. She held the material for a moment before leaning back and slowly peeling it away.

"*Joural,* you're beautiful."

Sara watched as he stood up, leaned forward and gripped the soft material to pull it down. Davin didn't rush, and the slow pace at which he was baring her body to him made her writhe on the bed. Finally, she was naked except for the slip of panties she wore. Davin dropped to his knees on the floor and pulled her to the edge of the bed. Before she could think, he had her legs spread wide, her body completely open to him.

He pressed his mouth to her pussy and blew hot air against her. The heat sent shivers up and down her spine, forcing her to half sit to see him. He looked up and grinned

"Yes, I want you to watch me. I'm going to lick you until you scream my name."

Oh fuck! "How did you know—?"

"I've worked with humans for years. Men...talk."

She could barely control her breathing, her voice was useless. All she could do was sit and watch. Davin pushed her panties aside, exposing her pussy to him. She watched as he reached up and twirled his finger through the hair that covered her mound.

"I bet you taste as good as you smell." He leaned his face an inch closer to her clit. "Should I find out?"

When he didn't move, Sara nodded her head. Davin smiled and brushed his nose against her clit. She bit her lip but didn't move, keeping her eyes fixed to the spot where he touched her.

"More?" he asked, his hot breath teasing her.

She managed another nod and was rewarded when his tongue dipped out to flick across her hot, swollen nub. The contact was electrifying, making her forget to breathe. Again, he stuck his tongue out, this time flattening it and licking full contact along her. Sara moaned, her hands flexing against the bed.

He sucked her swollen, hard clit into his mouth and Sara cried out. The constant pressure brought her to the brink of orgasm. But he wasn't going to free her from his sensual torture that quickly. Her eyes drifted closed as she tried to fight back the overpowering sight of what he was doing to her.

"Now, now, now, that's not being a good girl."

The sudden loss of his body heat wasn't as surprising as finding herself being flipped over onto her stomach so her body lay across his lap.

"What the hell—ouch!"

The smack echoed in the room, mingling with her shocked cry. Davin rubbed his hand over the wounded cheek of her ass as the heat and sting soaked into her.

"You didn't listen," he said with a chuckle.

Sara wanted to protest but found herself enjoying being at his mercy. "I'll behave."

Another smack, this time on the other cheek, sent the warm tingle to her pussy. She squirmed on his lap, both to taunt and to escape him.

"I think you like it." He ran a finger down the crack of her ass and on to the wet opening of her cunt. "I think you like it very much."

Sara was almost in tears from the gentleness of his touch. "Please, I need to come."

Davin smacked her ass again but this time far lighter than before. "Not yet."

He helped turn her over so the small of her back was resting directly on top of his cock. She could feel how hard it pressed against her. She had the sudden urge to taste him. To feel what an alien cock was like. But she couldn't do anything with Davin controlling her. He bent his head to kiss her while he used both hands on her breasts. The mix of pain and pleasure of him tweaking her nipples almost made her orgasm right there.

"I want to watch you come." His words were as hot as his breath. "I want you to scream over and over."

His hand was once again sliding down her body to circle her clit. Sara's gaze was locked on his, hypnotized by his golden eyes.

"You're so wet and tight. When I fuck you, you'll come so hard."

"Davin?"

"Hum?"

"Lick me."

"Promise me you'll watch."

"Promise."

This time when he settled his face between her legs, Sara watched. The sight of what he was doing mixed with the sensations was earth shattering. He didn't hold back. His fingers found her pussy and he pushed two inside. With his eyes half closed, he sucked and licked at her clit as he caressed her G-spot.

Sara couldn't take any more. Her legs went numb and her arms and chest began to tingle. She sucked in a deep breath long enough to let out a scream as her orgasm slammed into her. Her body tensed and she grabbed his head pulling his mouth hard against her.

Davin didn't stop, didn't slow down. His fingers continued their assault long past the end of her orgasm. His tongue lapped at her cream, licking every drop until she fell, completely spent, back on the bed.

She couldn't see. Couldn't open her eyes, didn't have the strength to even try. She felt him crawl on the bed beside her and pull her along the length of his side. For the next several minutes Davin whispered a language she didn't understand in her ear, licking and nibbling as he spoke. When she finally opened her eyes, she felt him chuckle.

"Welcome back."

"That was…you're…"

"I'm glad I met your expectations."

Sara could feel the pressure of his erection pressing against her. She shifted her hips to rub against him. "But we're not done."

"I wanted to give you some time to recover."

She turned her head so she could rub her nose with his. With his mouth a close temptation, Sara sucked on his bottom lip, running her tongue over the sensitive skin before releasing it.

"I want you," she said and licked the seam of his mouth once more.

He smiled, reached down and flicked her nipple with this forefinger.

"How do you want me?"

Ideas whizzed through her mind. But one more than any other stood out. Something she'd been unable to get out of her mind since she'd first laid eyes on him.

"Please," she whispered against his mouth. "Let me taste you."

A low rumble in his chest and the smile on his face let her know he approved of the idea. Sara rolled away from him and onto the floor as Davin stood in front of her. He began to free the opening of his pants when she put her hands on his.

"Let me."

The fastening of his pants was difficult to undo because her hands were shaking. After a few minutes of struggling, Sara finally pulled them free, letting them fall to a heap on the floor. Now completely naked and faced with his large, swollen cock, Sara was suddenly nervous. He was bigger and thicker than any man she'd been with. His slightly golden skin darkened around his shaft, and Sara wanted to run her fingers over him.

His scent was stronger now than it had been before. Leaning in, she pressed her closed lips to the base of his shaft and slowly rubbed her way up. Davin groaned but made no move to touch her, direct her actions. Wanting to tease him as badly as he'd teased her, Sara gently touched the tip of her tongue along the vein that ran down the length of his cock.

"Yummy," she said and grinned.

Again she ran her tongue up his shaft, this time stopping at the head and circling the tip. Leaning forward, she took the head into her mouth and sucked gently, adjusting to him. She ran her hands up the inside of his thighs, stopping at his balls. They were soft and felt heavy. When she raked her nails over the sensitive skin, Davin grabbed her head.

"Too much of that and this will be over quickly."

Pulling back, she winked at him. "What if I do this?"

She sucked one of his balls into her mouth and licked it with her tongue. Davin's grip tightened.

"*Friken*!"

Releasing his testicle with a pop, Sara returned to his cock. Wanting to take as much of him into her mouth as she could, she rose up high on her knees. As she milked him with her mouth, she pumped his shaft with her hand until she found the perfect rhythm.

Davin's legs began to shake and his hands flexed in her hair, encouraging her on. She could taste his pre-cum, salty and spicy at the same time. Not able to get enough of him, Sara licked and swallowed until everything around her faded away and all she could focus on was devouring his cock. When he suddenly pulled her back, she groaned, wanting more.

"Not like this. I want to be inside you when I spill my seed," he spoke the words in between pants.

Once more Sara found herself on her back, only this time she was quickly covered by Davin's long, hard body. Spreading her legs wide, Sara moaned and clutched at his shoulders when he positioned the tip of his cock at the opening of her pussy. Slowly, inch by inch, he pushed inside her. Sara felt her muscles stretch to accommodate his girth.

"You're so sweet, wild one. I've never...felt a woman...like you before."

When he was all the way inside her, Davin stopped, letting her adjust. She felt his body shaking from the control, something she didn't want him to use right now. Bucking her hips, Sara leaned up and licked one of his nipples, raking her fingers through the black hair that covered his chest.

"Fuck me hard, Davin."

He looked down at her, his expression one of wanting and concern. "Once I start, I can't stop."

She bucked her hips again and ran her hands down his arms. "Now."

A wicked grin crossed his face for a second before his eyes rolled into the back of his head as he began to thrust into her. Sara let her hands and mouth explore his chest and throat. With each thrust, he ground against her clit and she felt the beginning of another orgasm growing.

The tempo of their thrusts grew faster and faster. Sara switched from a casual explorer to holding on for her life. Gripping her legs around his lower back, she didn't even attempt to meet his pounding hips. The buildup of her orgasm was sudden.

"God, shit! I'm coming!"

She cried out before biting down on his shoulder. Davin growled and returned the bite on her shoulder. The pain mingled with the orgasm and another wave rolled over her. Davin's thrusts were frantic, driving her deep into the mattress until he lifted his head and cried out. An enormous shudder racked his body as he collapsed on her.

They stayed that way for several minutes, only the sounds of their breathing and heartbeats echoing in the room. Davin rolled to the side, pulling Sara as he went so she lay half draped over his body. Every nerve in her seemed to hum with satisfied pleasure.

"Wow," she managed after swallowing hard.

He dipped his head and licked her neck where he'd bitten her. "Sorry. When you bit me I couldn't stop myself. It's a part of our…it doesn't matter. I'm sorry."

He placed the gentlest kiss on her lips as he laced his fingers through her hair. Sara's mind began to wander and she had to struggle to keep from falling asleep.

"Don't fight it. You deserve a rest." His words were soft against her temple.

"No, I wanna talk."

"You do too much talking. Sleep."

"Biting?"

"Sleep."

Yawning, she flipped onto her other side, pressing her bottom against his belly and let the sexually induced exhaustion take her over.

* * * * *

Davin lay wide awake while Sara snored lightly as she slept. His heart hadn't stopped pounding since he'd spilled his seed inside the feisty doctor. When she'd bit him, every instinct in him yelled out that this was a woman who was worthy to be his mate. He'd spent so many years running from the ways of his people. To find such a basic need, basic drive bundled up in this little human both scared and confused him.

She'd never stay with him.

Rolling away carefully, he stood and walked away to the shower. The steam from the water filled the room within a matter of minutes. Davin stepped into the shower, the hot water hit his skin, instantly relaxing his tired muscles. He'd lived most of his adult life aboard spaceships and couldn't afford the luxury of a shower whenever he'd been planet side.

Small rivers of water trickled down his hair and skin, easing the tension of his muscles. A small bar of soap was tucked into the corner of the stall, which he grabbed and quickly lathered up. Rubbing the suds over his body and into his hair felt wonderful. For the first time in months, he felt like he could breathe.

Somehow over the hiss of the shower, he heard the quiet click of the door open. Davin looked up to see Sara standing there naked, biting her bottom lip. She smiled, shrugged and stepped into the shower with him.

"Let me wash your back," she said taking the bar of soap from his hand.

"Not a lot of room in here." He smiled and turned around.

When her hands touched his skin, Davin sighed. Her fingers began to rub small circles into his tired muscles, working the tension out of them. Sara began to move down his spine to his buttocks, where she continued to massage with gentle strokes.

"When I woke up, I thought you'd left." She placed a kiss in the middle of his spine. "Then I heard the shower."

"A shower is almost as big a temptation as you are," he said over his shoulder.

When she reached around to rub soap on his chest, Davin had to fight himself to stand still.

"I guess you don't get many of these on your ship, do you?"

"None."

"I guess I better make this as memorable as possible then."

Sara slid her hands down his chest to his cock, rubbing soap over his balls as she cupped them. His shaft instantly hardened as she began to stroke him. Davin grabbed the wall with his hands and tried to hold on.

"I can't believe how big you are," she said, adding some more lather to her hands.

"I'm sure you say that to all your lovers."

He hissed when she pulled her hands back, stroking his hips and thighs.

"There hasn't been a man in a long time. Not since coming to Eurus."

"Then I'm honored to have been your first choice."

"You should be."

He felt her laugh as her hands continued to explore his body. Her fingers found the scar on his side. It didn't hurt as much as it had a few years ago, but the skin was still sensitive. A constant reminder never to do stupid things again—like help people.

"Don't ask." The words were out of him just as he felt her draw in a deep breath.

"I was going to say this is sexy."

"No, you weren't. You were going to ask. They all do."

She lightly smacked his ass and the water made a loud sucking sound. "Play nice."

"I don't play *nice*."

Davin turned around in the small shower and pressed Sara hard against the wall. He could feel her tight nipples pressing against his chest as she breathed hard. His erection was trapped against her stomach and he ground it against her.

"I don't think you would be attracted to me if I was a *nice* man."

"There's nothing wrong with nice. Kamran is nice."

"Married."

"Taber is nice."

"Distant. You want bad, don't you, Doctor?" He thrust his cock against her stomach. "You need bad to chase away the evil you see every day."

Sara's gasp quickly turned into a moan when he pushed the head of his cock between her legs. Her damp hair clung to her neck, making her large blue eyes look even bigger. More innocent than the woman he knew she was. But it made him want her all the more.

"I'm going to show you. Show you how much you like bad." Davin pushed inside her with a single thrust. "I want to hear you scream."

Unlike earlier, he had absolute control over his body. This was about testing himself, testing her. He needed to know that nothing would ever work between them beyond a quick fuck on a layover.

Sara clutched his shoulders, her eyes shut tight. The soft mewling sounds she made were like a string to his cock. He grew even harder, pulled her closer, wanting to fill even the tiniest space that kept them apart.

"Davin, please."

He knew what she wanted and dipped his head to her breast, flicking her nipple with his tongue. Her fingers curled in his hair and a shiver passed through him when she tugged him closer. Each thrust of his cock brought him one step away from control and closer to chaos.

"Sara," he murmured her name against her slick skin.

"Make me come. I want to come so badly."

Lifting her leg, he thrust even deeper into her body, letting him grind against her swollen clit. She cried out, her body tense, but still didn't tumble into bliss. It wasn't until he slipped his hand between them to stroke her that she shattered around him with a scream.

Her cunt tightened around his shaft, choking him with pleasure. He felt his balls tighten as he began to pound into her uncontrollably. With every jut of his seed inside her, Davin knew he was in trouble.

Finally, they slipped in a heap to the floor. The water from the shower spilled over them, soothing his once more tired muscles.

"Water," she muttered against his shoulder.

Davin reached over and turned it off. Looking back at her, he couldn't help but chuckle.

"You look like a drowned *lenact*."

She opened her mouth to say something but stopped and gave her head a shake. "A what?"

"I believe you call it a rat."

"Well, you look like a…" She rolled her eyes. "Wet Greek god doesn't seem to have the sort of sting I'm looking for."

"Unless a Greek god is a horrible beast. Then perhaps it would be a perfect description. Seeing as I have no idea what you are referencing, I'll take it as a compliment. "

That comment brought the smile back to her face. "Shit, I've probably used up my water allowance for the week."

"Two weeks."

"Maybe a month. Kamran will have to cut me off."

"You can always use the steam shower on my ship."

Sara smiled, caressing his arm with her hands. "I didn't think you'd be around that long."

A sudden awkwardness passed between them. Sara shivered and pushed her hair away from her face. "I better get dressed. I don't even know what time it is."

Davin ground his teeth together but stood up and helped Sara to her feet. When they got out of the shower, she found them two towels to dry off. He managed to avoid looking directly at her while they got dressed.

"I need to get back to my ship," he said when she finally came out of the back room.

Inwardly, he cursed when she winced before fixing a too bright smile on her face.

"Hey, no worries. I need to get back to med bay anyway. I'm sure they're going nuts not knowing where I'm at anyway."

"Sara—"

"Look, I don't want you going all possessive alien on me. We didn't have any promises beyond enjoying ourselves. We had some of the best sex I can remember in forever. I had a great night's sleep and now it's time to go."

She tried to move past him toward the door, but Davin caught her arm. Beyond that he didn't know what to do. How in *Joural's* name had he let himself get so caught up with a woman? A woman he'd just met. He let his gaze travel over her body once more, memorizing every detail. When she didn't pull her arm away, he reached up and tried to tug her shirt over the exposed part of her shoulder.

"I left a mark." He said the words with a mixture of possessiveness and regret.

"You wouldn't be the first."

When she pulled away this time, he let her go.

Chapter Five

Sara sat behind her desk and stared at the wall. She wasn't even going to pretend to work—no point really. Everyone seemed to know about her wild night with Davin. The guys who had walked into the hall on them must have recognized her after all. Shit, it had been three days ago and Rachael still was teasing her about him. Thank god he'd avoided her since then.

"Stupid idiot."

She had no idea if she was cursing him or herself. Despite her playful image, she didn't sleep around. Sure, she liked to have fun and, admittedly, was a terrible flirt. But when it came to sex there'd been very few conquests. It wasn't worth the inevitable heartache that came the next day.

Pushing away from the desk, Sara stood, grabbed her lab coat and turned the collar up. The bruise on her neck was mostly healed now, but she didn't want to bring any undo attention to it. Haylie's freak-out session the day after she'd slept with Davin had been hard enough. It was only after she'd assured her it came as part of the best sex of her life that Haylie had backed down and promised not to arrest him.

Having someone notice and say something at the weekly department meeting would be just painful. Slipping out of her office and past the few people in med bay, pausing only to adjust a sling of one of the miners, she made her way into the corridor.

Where she ran straight into Davin.

He was leaning against the wall opposite med bay, wearing a heavy scowl.

"Your face will stick that way if you don't stop," she said and walked past him.

His body heat was a comfort when he fell into step beside her, though she'd be damned if she let him know that.

"Might be an improvement," he muttered.

She couldn't help but chuckle. "How's your ship, Captain? Repairs well underway, I assume."

"Progressing."

Sara let the silence carry on between them for half a corridor length before she stopped and turned on him.

"So what can I do for you? Or did you just feel like stalking me? Because if that's the case, I do believe Haylie or Taber would be happy to show you to the brig again."

"I've been asked by your charming administrator to accompany you to a meeting."

From the look on his face, he was less than happy about it.

"Why the hell would he want you to come? It's nothing but updates."

Davin shrugged, his eyes skimming over her body, lingering at the spot where he'd bitten her.

"I'll have to show up to find out."

"So why come here?"

Sara tried not to react to the nearness of his body, the erotic scent that rolled off him, teasing her when he stepped close.

"I didn't know where the meeting was."

"You could have asked someone." She swallowed hard but kept her eyes locked on his.

"I didn't want to ask someone. I wanted to follow you."

"So we're back to you being a stalker." As much as she'd never admit it to him, she was glad to see him again. Sara rolled her eyes. "Come on or we'll be late."

They continued their journey to the meeting room and Sara did her best to ignore the sensations in her body. The corridor had very few people, partially because this section of the station was primarily for administration, but mostly because this was the wing where the explosion that had almost killed Kamran had taken place. If given a choice, most of the Briel didn't come this way. And the humans on the station were just as superstitious.

Despite the fact they'd lost a large portion of the Briel Elder Council, Kamran had insisted they rebuild and reuse this room as a meeting area. Sara had always admired him for his strength. God, she didn't think she'd have been able to do it if it had been *her* life that had almost ended here. But he'd been the first one to walk in this wing after the reconstruction, Haylie by his side.

"So what do you normally do in these meetings?" Davin asked, looking around the hall. "Doesn't seem like there would be many relevant updates for you."

"I make sure the rest of the bureaucrats don't do stupid things. Like set up triple shifts for the miners."

"They'll have a revolt if they try something that stupid."

She looked over at him. "And what do you know of miners and shift schedules?"

"I run supplies to rebel forces. People who are fighting against that type of thing. They can only be pushed so far and then they break. Or kill people."

"That's what I tried to tell them. But there's this guy, Grant something-or-other, who thought it was a *brilliant* idea."

Sara had to shake her head. Yesterday the man in question had the gall to come into her office and try to convince her to change her stance on the miners. He was relentless in his persistence, which made no sense. Haylie had told her the reserves of ore weren't as low as Grant had first led them to believe. Sara couldn't belive that one man could be that much of an ass, but Grant had tested that theory with his unreasonable request. Thankfully, Rachael was there to step in before Sara punched him.

"I pity the man who would try to go against you."

Looking up at him, Sara could see he was laughing at her. The golden twinkle in his eyes brightened his face, making him look less severe than he had a few minutes earlier. He was wearing a shirt that had short sleeves, covering a portion of his tattoos. His gloves were still in place and this time he had on a wide utility belt. Hooked on the side was a phase pistol. Davin looked as sexy and dangerous as ever. But there was something else. Something she hadn't noticed right away.

"You look tired," she said, averting her gaze. "I hope you've been resting well."

"Any idea what the topic of this meeting will be?" He didn't look at her and gave no indication he'd heard her question. "I've been trying to guess why your administrator would want me there."

Sara's chest tightened, but she did her best to ignore it. If he didn't want to talk to her, then she wasn't going to push him. "Not sure. It's not our normal meeting time. Something important must have come up for Kamran to call this on such short notice."

"I guess I'll find out soon enough."

They turned the corner to see Taber standing outside the door, arms crossed over his chest.

"There is a man in need of a good fuck," Davin whispered to her.

Sara let out a surprised laugh that she tried to cover up with her hand.

"Doctor Fergus, Captain Jagt." Taber nodded to both of them as they approached. "They are expecting you inside."

Taber kept his gaze locked on Davin as they entered the meeting room. Taber had a hard time trusting people he didn't know and Davin seemed to take great pleasure in pushing every button Taber had. Almost like he didn't want Taber to trust him at all.

But Sara did. There was something about him, the way he was around her that made her have absolute confidence in him. She couldn't have slept with him otherwise. Though with his sexy body, she would have been tempted to regardless.

"Good, I'm glad you were both able to make it." Kamran stood up.

Haylie was tapping away on a data pad, frowning furiously as she made notes. She didn't notice them and Sara smiled. When Haylie had a puzzle to figure out, nothing short of the world exploding could distract her. Not even Kamran.

"Not to sound ungrateful, but why am I here?" Davin was first to speak once Taber triggered the door closed.

Kamran waited for Taber to sit before looking around the room at the five of them.

"We have a problem."

Those four words sent shivers down Sara's spine. The last time they'd *had a problem*, the entire colony had almost been overrun with aliens intent on killing them all.

"It's not the Ecada?" She had to know, even though the words were painful to say.

Haylie looked up and gave her a weak smile. "No, hon, nothing that immediate, thankfully."

"Captain Jagt." Kamran turned and leveled Davin with a look that made Sara want to squirm. "What is the purpose of your trip to Eurus?"

Davin frowned. "I had no intention of coming here at all. We sustained damage and crashed. What the fuck is going on?"

"See, I told you they were trying to take advantage of the situation," Haylie said, returning her attention back to the data pad.

"Forgive me. Haylie intercepted a communication from someone in the underground market here. Your name was mentioned."

Davin sat back in his chair, crossing his ankle over his knee. "You think someone is going to get in touch with me? Smuggling opportunity?"

"Possibly. But I think this would be one smuggling job you'd want to pass on."

Haylie handed Kamran the data pad. He quickly read over the contents. With a snort, Kamran slid it across the table to Davin. He sighed before picking it up to read. Slowly, his foot dropped to the floor and he began to lean forward.

"Is this legitimate? They don't honestly expect someone to be stupid enough to do this?"

This time, Taber spoke. "We've checked both our Briel and human sources. It seems they are that foolish."

"What?" Sara asked, knocking on the table for attention. "What the hell is going on?"

Haylie and Kamran looked at each other for a moment before Haylie straightened up. "They are looking to trade for stocolran gel."

Sara was on her feet, her mouth open in silent outrage, staring at her friend.

"I wouldn't touch that deal no matter how much they offered," Davin said quietly.

"I didn't think so. But I'm happy to hear it from you all the same," Kamran said and sat back in his seat. "But the fact remains that someone on this planet is trying to get their hands on a bio weapon."

In all her years as a doctor, the fear someone would use a bio weapon on her planet wasn't one she'd had to face. In some ways, it was more terrifying than facing an entire army of Ecada.

"They'll try others if they don't get what they want from me," she heard Davin say.

"What do you suggest?" This time it was Taber talking.

"Sara, hon, are you okay?" Haylie began to stand.

"Please sit. I'm sorry." She took her own chair again, rubbing her hand along the back of her neck. "What are we going to do about this?"

Kamran leaned forward, resting his forearms on the table. "I was hoping *we* could hire you instead, Captain. I don't like the idea of having a bunch of saboteurs on my colony."

"A setup?" Davin grinned. "This might be amusing."

"We'll let them come to you, make the offer and then we can catch them in the act. Once they are in possession with the gel, then we can safely arrest them," Haylie's own grin was just as mischievous.

"*We* won't be doing anything." Kamran frowned at Haylie.

"I'm perfectly capable—"

"Taber and the captain will head this up. Sara, I wanted you here in case things get out of hand and we can't catch them. I want worse-case-disaster scenarios worked up in case, goddess forbid, they find what they are looking for from another source and release the gel on the station."

"Of course. I'll get on it as soon as I get back to med bay."

"How did you find out about this?" Davin slid the data pad over to Taber. "If I'm going to stick my neck out, I want to make sure the source is trustworthy."

"We have a man in the mines who intercepted the message. I trust him," Kamran said and laced his hand with Haylie's.

Sara knew there were very few people Kamran trusted that well. Most of them were in this room. "Sean?"

Davin shivered beside her. "The man from med bay the other night?"

"He saved our lives. Despite what he's been going through the past year, the fact he brought this to our attention lets me know how serious it is." Kamran stood. "For now, I'll keep you apprised of information as soon as I get it. I want to keep this in as tight a circle as possible. The last thing this colony needs is another panic. Especially with it being so close to the anniversary of the attack."

Sara stayed seated while the others left the room. She smiled at Haylie when she passed by. "I expect to see you later."

"Yes, Doc."

Finally she was alone. She dropped her head to the table and sighed. One of the things she was aware of when she agreed to be a colonist was the potential for danger. Sara just didn't think it would be happening with such frequency.

"There you are," Davin said from the doorway behind her.

"I'd like to be alone if that's okay."

"I don't think so."

The next thing she knew, she felt his hands on her back, massaging her muscles. When he reached her neck, Sara sighed and felt her body relax.

"You should consider a career change," she muttered.

"I don't think Silas is big on neck rubs. Not from me, at least."

"I'm sure there are women in every space port who'd be more than happy to pay for your services."

"Strangely, it's not as much fun when it's expected."

Sara almost drifted off when she felt Davin tug the collar of her shirt back, exposing her neck. He bent down and placed a kiss on the bite. A shiver of awareness raced through her, making her nipples hard and her pussy damp.

"I can't get you out of my mind." His words were hot against her. Davin licked her neck. "Your smell is everywhere."

Hissing out her held breath, Sara turned her face so she could rub against him.

"I've been dreaming about you," she said and brushed her lips against his.

"Do I fuck you in them?"

Sara shivered.

"Do I?" He nipped at her neck.

"Yes."

The admission was thrilling and terrifying. For the past two nights she'd been determined to get him out of her mind. But every time she closed her eyes, all she could see was Davin's naked body. She'd rubbed her clit sore at the thought of him fucking her again. As much as she'd been annoyed with him, she wanted him more than before.

"Come with me." Davin tugged at her shoulders to stand up.

"Where?"

"My ship."

"Why?"

"It's closer than your room."

Before she really thought about it, Sara was on her feet and following Davin out the door. His grip was tight, almost painful around her hand as he led her down the corridors, through the crowds of the bazaar to the lift. As soon as the door closed, Davin threw her against the wall and began to kiss her neck. She ran her hands through his hair and down his back. She didn't want to think about anything else except him. When he ground his hard cock against her, there was no doubt as to what he wanted to show her in his ship.

Davin grabbed her breast and rolled her clothing-clad nipple between his thumb and forefinger.

"You're fucking ready for me already, aren't you?"

"God, Davin, I want you so much."

The computer quietly announced their arrival on the lower deck. Davin pulled away from her just as the door was opening. Sara prayed her face didn't go too red as Davin led her past the group of engineers who were waiting to get into the lift. She heard their chuckles as the doors closed behind them.

"Shit, everyone on the station is going to know about us."

"Good. That way I won't have to kill every man who tries to touch you," Davin snapped.

She had to admit, his possessiveness turned her on. There was something special about being his. She had the impression he didn't let himself get out of control like this, not normally. The fact she drove him to it was a heady sensation.

The hangar bay was nearly deserted when they entered. The ship looked better than it had when they'd crashed, but she could tell it still needed a lot of work. Davin turned when they reached the stairs that had been placed for entrance to the ship, picked her up and threw her over his shoulder.

"What are you doing?" She gave him several hard smacks on his back and ass.

"Kidnapping the colony's beautiful doctor. I plan on stealing you away so no one will ever find you."

Sara couldn't help but giggle. "But how are you going to escape? Your ship is broken."

"I'm working on that part. It was an impulse decision."

The air in the ship was cool and had the same exotic spice smell that clung to Davin. He turned to press the door close button, letting Sara see Silas approach from behind.

"I'd offer to help you, Doctor, but I'm not sure if you'd take it."

"Out, Silas. You can finish up later." Davin opened the door again.

The engineer stopped by Sara and gave her a kiss on the cheek. "I never did properly thank you for fixing up Rafe. Or apologize for hurting you."

"Thank you and you're forgiven." She tried to smile, but all the blood was rushing to her face, making it feel strange.

"Get out, human," Davin ground out.

"Don't let this Raqulian prick mistreat you, Doctor."

"Out!"

Silas' chuckle echoed in the hanger until Davin closed the door, blocking out the noise.

"Are you going to put me down now?"

Instead of answering, he continued to carry her down the hall. She couldn't see much of the ship, except that it was small and cramped. Containers of goods, medical supplies and engineering parts were tucked here and there on the floor, forcing Davin to walk around them.

When they finally reached a door near the back of the corridor, Sara was sure her head would explode from all of the blood. Davin opened the lock, stepped inside and swung her from over his shoulder into his arms. The sudden head rush made everything spin, forcing her to rest her head on his shoulder.

"Welcome to my humble home."

She looked around the small quarters and for the first time felt like she was seeing the true part of Davin. Most of the room was filled by a large bed. Light-colored furs covered it, and she couldn't help but imagine Davin's naked body lying under them. There were candles placed around the room and she swore there was a hint of spice in the room.

Davin walked over to the bed and set her down in the middle of it. Sara couldn't help but run her fingers over the soft furs, bending down to rub her face against them. Davin growled, her gaze going to his.

"I've dreamed of seeing you in my bed."

"It's beautiful. I've never felt anything like this before."

Discarding his belt and pulling his shirt off, he slid beside her. "On our planet, hunting is a rite of passage for our warriors. They prove themselves by tracking and killing an *atura* beast."

"You killed this?" She wasn't sure if she was impressed or disappointed.

He didn't answer, only ran his hand over the fur.

"Davin?"

"No. I wasn't a part of the warrior cast growing up. These were a gift when I joined the cast."

"Which cast are—?"

He cut her off with a kiss. Unlike before, his kiss softened into a gentle caress. His lips suckled hers into his mouth as his tongue flicked across the captured skin. He was able to distract her completely with his mouth, so she didn't feel his hands on her uniform, opening the clasps that held it in place. The air in the cabin was cool against her heated skin, making her nipples pucker more than before.

Davin lifted his head and let his gaze travel over her exposed skin.

"You are perfect in every way."

"Shut up and kiss me."

Sara pulled him back down, holding his head with both hands. The spark of desire between them exploded into a full-fledged firestorm. Davin ripped at her lab coat and uniform, stripping her roughly, frantic to get to her skin. Sara groaned, ignoring what he was doing as she tried to undo the fastenings that held his pants closed.

In a matter of minutes, he was pushing her back against the furs on his bed, running his hands down her naked body.

"You're so tiny," he whispered, placing a kiss in the middle of her stomach.

Sara giggled and felt the blush creep across her face. "You say the sweetest things."

"You need to eat more."

"Davin!"

He nipped at her stomach. "You go days without eating. Probably forget. We need to change that."

"You brought me here to talk about my diet?"

"I'm scared I'd break you."

"If you don't stop talking and start fucking, I'm going to leave."

"We can't have that now."

Davin hooked his hands under her knees and pulled her thighs wide open. With a gasp, Sara looked down between them. His cock was hard, jutting straight up, pointing directly where she wanted it to go.

"Is this what you want?"

His question jolted her. Sara looked up and into his confused face. "Of course."

Davin didn't answer. The muscles in his jaw clenched as he thrust forward, filling her completely. His breath came out as a long, slow hiss, and when he finally opened his eyes, Sara swore she saw them glow.

"Do you trust me?"

He'd asked her this before. But this time it was different. Somehow *he* was different. Sara's heart began to race and her nipples began to ache.

"Yes." She wrapped up every emotion that was racing through her at that time in that one simple word.

A smile flitted across his lips before he nodded. Slowly, he pulled his gloves off, revealing the pale skin, covered in tattoos. Each time she saw them, she felt like she was seeing something, secret, forbidden.

"Give me your hands," his voice was low and it rumbled as he said those few words.

One by one, Sara laced her fingers through his before he held them down against the bed. He hadn't moved his hips, but she felt her desire building stronger than it had before. Davin leaned forward and rested his forehead against hers.

"Keep your eyes open. Look at me as long as you can." He let his lips brush against hers. "Can you do that?"

"Yes."

Davin pulled his hips back, nearly pulling his cock out of her before he slowly thrust back in. Sara had to concentrate to keep her eyes open and focused on him. Again he pulled back almost to the entrance of her pussy and, with a single thrust, filled her.

Every inch of Sara's body began to shake under the sensual pressure of his slow assault. She kept her eyes open, now unable to look away from the intensity of his eyes. Davin filled her once more, but this time he stopped. Every inch of her skin was touching his naked body. His cock stretched her, sending shivers through her.

It was then she felt it. Sara's hands began to tingle, lightly at first until the sensation traveled up her arms. Her eyes widened and she flexed her fingers. Davin's gaze never wavered, though the muscles in his jaw began to flex and she could feel his breathing increase.

"Davin?" her voice barely audible.

"Just feel."

The tingle crossed her chest, caressing her breasts and making her nipples harden. Her pussy began to tremble, the muscles tightening around his cock. Sara had to concentrate on breathing, her eye lids drooping.

"Keep looking at me," Davin whispered and ground against her.

Sara forced her eyes wide, focusing in on the war she saw Davin waging with his body. His golden eyes were growing large, wide, more like a cat's than a reptile's, as he trembled. Now everywhere he touched her she felt the buzzing, the growing connection between them increasing in intensity. Her clit felt like it was on fire and all it needed was a single touch for her to explode.

And then he moved. It couldn't have been more than half an inch, but the sudden, raw intensity was almost more than she could handle. Sara gasped and tightened her hold on Davin's hands. She knew she couldn't hold on much longer.

"I'm...Davin!"

She couldn't look away now even if she wanted to. His thrusts grew faster, erratic in his movements. Sara's pussy was drenched, her cream soaking both of them. Finally, Davin ground his hips hard against her clit and she shattered. She cried out as her orgasm exploded from deep inside her body. Davin's cries joined her almost instantly. Shaking and breathing hard he came deep inside her.

After that she couldn't see anything. All she could feel was the steady beating of their hearts.

"Oh my god," she tried to swallow past the rawness of her throat. "Oh my god."

"I've never...just amazing." He placed a kiss on her forehead.

Sara wanted to say something more, wanted him to know just how special he'd made her feel by sharing this, sharing himself. But the words that came to her mind were nothing compared to this.

Davin rolled to the side, keeping her locked tightly in his arms. With her head on his chest, she was lulled to sleep by the steady beating of his heart.

Somewhere in the back of her mind, she heard her communicator beeping. When she opened her eyes, she had Davin wrapped around her, but he was sound asleep. The steady beeping told her it was an emergency and she really had to get her ass out of bed and see what the problem was.

No matter how little she wanted to move, Sara somehow managed to extract herself from his iron grip. Davin moaned and reached for her, but she whispered softly in his ear and kissed his cheek, lulling him back to sleep.

Grabbing her uniform as she went, Sara prayed Silas and the rest of the crew had left the ship. The last thing she wanted to do was give them a free show. It only took her a minute to get dressed, slipping her boots on last and walking as silently as she could down the corridor and out of the ship. It wasn't until she was standing in the hangar bay that she flipped open her communicator.

"This is Fergus," she said into the small device. When static was her only response, she adjusted the frequency in case the metal of the ship was blocking the transmission.

"Med bay, this is Doctor Fergus. What is the emergency?"

"It's right here."

A large hand clamped over her mouth as a musty smell made her gag. The bitter sting of vomit rose in her throat and her last conscious thought was that Davin would think that she'd left him.

Chapter Six

Davin woke with a start and knew something was wrong. The bed beside him was empty and cold, though Sara's scent still clung to the furs. Ignoring his naked state, he went in search for her. She could have gotten turned around on her way to the lavatory or had been called to an emergency. The doors to his room slid open and he walked out into the corridor in search of her.

"What have I told you about walking around like that," Silas said, his hand covering his eyes. "It's not decent, man."

Davin walked past the engineer. "Have you seen Sara?"

"Well, that explains why you're naked at least."

"Silas."

"No, she wasn't out back. Think she got lost?"

Or ran away. "She might have gotten called to med bay. I'll check."

"Clothing first. You don't want to scare those poor Briel doctors."

Ignoring Silas' bark of laughter, Davin returned to his quarters. He quickly dressed before signaling med bay.

"Hello, Captain." Rachael, Sara's head nurse, smiled back at him. "What can I do for you? Need advice on things she likes?"

"Is she there?"

He didn't care that Rachael took a step back and raised her eyebrows. He needed to know where Sara was.

"I haven't seen her since before she left med bay this morning."

Davin didn't wait to hear anything else. He disconnected the call and quickly redialed, this time calling security.

"I'm trying to locate Doctor Fergus. It's an emergency."

"One moment," the young woman behind the desk said and typed into the computer.

Slowly one minute, then two ticked by, each second grating like claws down his back.

"I'm sorry, she's not responding."

"Do you know if she was called for an emergency?"

"Not that I can see, sir."

"Fuck."

He disconnected and redialed before the security guard could respond. When Kamran came online, his hair was disheveled and his clothing seemed unorganized. Davin couldn't see Haylie, but he knew she was probably naked and just out of view. At least he and Sara weren't the only ones who like a quick fuck in the daytime.

"Captain, is there a problem?"

"Sara's missing."

Kamran frowned. "You mean she left your company?"

Davin couldn't help but roll his eyes. "Is she normally the type to roll out of a man's bed without so much as a word, and there not be a medical emergency?"

"What!" Haylie said from off vid screen. "If something's happened to her I'll fucking wring your neck."

The sudden rustle of clothing and cursing almost drowned out Kamran's question.

"Are you sure?"

"Of course I'm sure. I wouldn't have bothered you otherwise. None of my crew has seen her and neither, has anyone out in the hangar."

Haylie's face popped into view beside her husband's. "Med bay?"

"I checked both there and with security. She's not answering her communicator for an urgent call. That doesn't seem like her."

"Shit, it isn't like her. The only reason she wouldn't respond to an urgent call is if someone was stopping her." Haylie turned away from the vid screen and muttered something, looking at Kamran.

For a minute nothing was said. Davin watched as they stared at each other in some sort of silent conversation. He'd never met a bonded Briel before, but it was a bit unsettling. From out of nowhere, Haylie threw up her hands and growled out of frustration. Kamran turned back to Davin.

"Give me a few minutes to take care of something. Taber and I will meet you at your ship in fifteen."

Davin nodded and the communication link was severed.

He spent the next fifteen minutes looking around his room for any sort of clue, something that would tell him why she'd gotten out of his bed after the most amazing sex he'd ever had in his life and walked into a trap. If it was even a trap. But the idea that she hadn't enjoyed their time together didn't seem plausible. Her lab coat was still on the floor in a ball where he'd thrown it. It wasn't easy to see at first and he knew she had probably been trying not to wake him up as she left.

Bringing the coat to his face, Davin breathed in deep. The mixture of vanilla, arousal and Sara washed over him, setting his heart pounding. He might not have been born into the warrior cast, but he'd learned many ways to kill a man over the years. Once he got his hands on the people who took her, he'd put those skills to good use. Unable to wait any longer, Davin grabbed his belt and his gun and marched out to the hangar bay.

He was standing, glaring at the door when Kamran, Taber and Sean walked in.

"That's a long, fucking fifteen minutes," he barked at them. "She could be halfway to Yardon by now! Where's your wife? I expected her to be here."

"I initiated a lockdown. No ships are getting on or off this planet until it's released," Kamran said in a calm voice. "And my wife has agreed to run the search from her office. She's asked Sean here to step in for her."

Davin had no doubt that in her office was the last place Haylie wanted to be right now. He couldn't imagine the conversation that had passed between husband and wife. Turning, he eyed the man he'd met only briefly in med bay. He looked as happy to be there as Davin was to have him.

"Taking her off planet isn't their intent." Sean spoke up and the group turned to stare at him. "They'd want her for the mine. A lot of men—"

Without thinking, Davin grabbed Sean by the front of his mining suit and hauled him into the air and gave him a shake. "You knew they were going to do this?"

Sean stared at him, a blank look that told Davin no amount of yelling or beating could scare this man. Without any care, he dropped Sean back to his feet and turned away, running his hands through his hair.

"No, I didn't. If I had, I would have been there to stop it. I owe her that much."

"We all want her back." Kamran stepped beside him, his quiet voice unnerving Davin's anger.

"It's my fault she's in trouble. I didn't know she'd left," Davin said in a quiet voice.

Again, he'd let someone down and they had to pay the price. His mother hadn't been strong enough and he'd been too scared to help her. Now Sara was in danger, all because he'd been lulled into a false sense of security. It was becoming a habit he didn't like.

Kamran placed his hand on Davin's shoulder. "I've known Sara for a little over a year and I have my wife's memories of her for the past seventeen years. If anyone will find a way to get into or out of trouble, it's our Sara."

Somehow, that didn't make him feel any better.

Davin looked hard at the three men and asked the question he knew everyone was thinking. "Do you think this is related to the bio weapon? Take her to use as leverage."

Taber looked at Kamran and then the floor. Sean crossed his arms across his chest and leveled his gaze at Davin. "If they did, then she's dead. We can't give them what they want, no matter the cost."

"We need to get her back before that happens," Davin said, unwilling to look away from Sean, despite the pull of the other man's wounded psyche.

"We'll have to move quickly if this is going to work." Sean stepped forward.

Davin eyed him, hoping he wouldn't get much closer. "Why do you care?"

"She's helped me." Sean took another step forward. "Why do you care?"

That was an answer he didn't have. At least one he didn't want to share. "She's nice."

Taber finally coughed, drawing everyone's attention. "I've secured you two enviro suits. Sean and Davin will be able to travel to the mines and find out where she is."

"Why not you? You're the Briel security chief," Davin said and waved a hand at the large Briel.

Taber glared at him but otherwise didn't show his annoyance. "I doubt my arrival would do anything but cause more problems."

Unfortunately, he was right. That didn't mean he trusted the human. Kamran must have detected his hesitation, stepped forward and drew Davin aside. The current administrator kept his voice low, but the intensity in his gaze told Davin as most as much as his words.

"Sean is...struggling with some demons. Sara helped him in the past and he owes her. He also helped me, saved my life. He needs to know that we still trust him despite what he thinks he's responsible for. I'm asking you, as a personal favor, let him come along and help."

Davin let his gaze slip from Kamran over to Sean, who stood calmly waiting for Davin's verdict. As much as he wanted to keep a wide distance from Sean, he wanted Sara back even more and if that meant enlisting the help of a man who made his skin crawl, he'd do it.

"Tell me where you need me to go and let's get moving."

* * * * *

The ride to the mines in the crawler was bumpy at best, fucking painful at worst. It had been a long time since Davin had traveled on a planet's surface this way, and it made him wonder why the colony hadn't built a better system before now. The loud crackle of the suit communicator in his ear made him turn to face Sean, who was driving.

"Only another minute and we'll be there. Let me do most of the talking until we figure out who has her."

"I thought you knew who was behind this." Davin ground his teeth in pure frustration.

"I know who sent the request for the bio weapon. Taking Sara feels different, unplanned. Besides, the last thing we need is for them to think my loyalties are divided. I'm going to bring you in and hope they buy your act. They'll know your relationship with Sara."

"We don't have a relationship."

"You're fucking her. That's all they'll care about."

Davin had to reach deep inside to keep himself from pounding the shit out of Sean. And while they were having sex, the crude way he'd described what was between them made his anger flare.

The crawler crested one final red dune before hitting the rock that led them to the mountain. Sean had given him a quick rundown of the layout before they'd left. The colonists had been digging underneath this mountain for the past twenty years. Most of the mines were secure, protected from the harsh planet's surface, but under the mountain was not a place for the weak.

Davin watched as Sean pulled the crawler into a dirty decompression bay that seemed attached to the rock face. A loud hiss of air from the door sealing and gust of wind from a fan sent the dust flying around them. Only after a loud beep echoed in the bay did Sean hop out of the crawler and yank off his helmet.

"Come on," he said to Davin before striding away.

It took a great deal of concentration to slip into his carefree attitude. Normally, he never let anything bother him, especially the disappearance of a woman he'd only met a few days before. But he couldn't get Sara out of his mind and it was scaring the shit out of him.

Careful not to look too anxious, Davin pulled off his helmet and set it in the crawler's seat as he climbed out. Next, he took his time to remove the enviro suit and tuck it away. He made sure his jacket wasn't in the way of his blaster and his gloves were on tight. He wanted to make sure anyone watching knew he was in no hurry to get where Sean was leading him. Sean seemed to pick up on what he was doing and by the time Davin reached him at the door to the complex, he was looking just as bored.

Two guards greeted them as soon as they passed through the inner airlock door. They searched them and took Davin's blaster and Sean's pistol.

"Who's this, Donaldson?" one of them gestured toward Davin with his chin.

"Friend looking for work. He's the idiot who crashed his ship and now can't afford to pay for the repairs. I was going to get him checked in."

The guard snorted, shooting Davin a sneer. "Find Grit and get him set up. We're under lockdown until further notice."

Sean frowned but nodded and led Davin away from the guards.

"Any chance we'll get our weapons back?" he muttered when they were a safe distance away.

"Not unless we steal them. Something weird is going on."

Walking through the narrow corridor, both Davin and Sean had to duck several times so to not smash their heads on rocks and beams that were jutting down. In more than one spot they were forced to walk single file until they made it out to a large cavern-like area.

"This is the work house. The miners report here for meals, breaks and to get work duties for the day. It was the first part they were able to open wide enough to accommodate the crews." As Sean spoke, he led Davin toward what looked to be an office.

"How long have you been down here?"

Sean turned to look at him and Davin could see a flash of something in his blue eyes. A deep pain Davin recognized instinctively. The cold numbness he'd felt the first time he met Sean in med bay ripped through him again. Only this time he could see there was more than loneliness. Guilt was tearing Sean apart.

"Long enough. Just follow me and we should have her tracked down soon."

They spent the better part of an hour talking to various miners as they weaved their way deeper into the mine. A few times they had to stop while Sean talked to several men about a variety of matters, more often than not explaining who Davin was and why exactly he was here. Each one he listened to, giving his undivided attention. For a moment, Davin saw a glimpse of the man Sean used to be.

A group of men passed by as he sauntered back over to Davin.

"This is a waste of time." Davin lightly pounded the rock wall with his fist. "We're never going to find her in this place."

Sean got right in his face so they were eye to eye. "I'll find her if you'll relax and let me do my job. Someone wouldn't risk kidnapping the colony's only human doctor if they didn't have a damn good reason. So calm your alien ass down."

"Fuck you, human."

"Donaldson!"

They both turned to see a pair of men walking toward them. The one in the front was a stout man with more than a few days old beard on his face. He wore the same gray mining uniform the rest of the men did, except his looked to be in far better condition. The man following him was clearly the muscle. Davin made sure to keep his eyes on the second man, just in case he needed to defend himself.

"I heard you've been looking for me." The stout man nodded toward Davin. "Who's this?"

"A friend. Someone *you* pissed off, Grit." I hear you've been busy. Looking for things you shouldn't have. Taking things that don't belong to you."

Grit eyed Sean. A deep frown filled his face. "What the fuck are you talking about?"

"Stocolran gel. Heard you wanted some."

Davin felt a measure of relief when the look of genuine shock crossed Grit's face. "Are you insane? Even if I could get the stuff, I wouldn't touch it. It could wipe out the entire planet."

Sean stepped closer to the man. "Glad to hear it. Where's Doctor Fergus?"

Davin didn't get any closer, instead hanging back with his arms crossed over his chest. He knew how intimidating he looked to the humans, relished that image because it got him what he wanted. And at this point, he wanted Sara.

Grit's gaze flicked between Sean and Davin and he swallowed hard. Good, Davin wanted him nervous. Grit looked over at the other man who simply shrugged.

"She's not hurt if that's what you're worried about," he said and smiled a bit too wide. "We needed to get her attention and this was the easiest way. We needed to keep the men up and running. There were too many injuries and we wanted her here."

That was all Davin could handle. With two steps he was in the man's face, his fists balled at his side so he wouldn't throttle the man. "Kidnapping isn't the *easy* way. And it's about to become the *painful* way if you don't take us to her—*now*."

Grit took a step back, his smile fading slightly. "Hey, now take it easy. Sean, we thought we could trust you."

"You can trust me. I could have brought Taber or Chief Bond. I didn't."

The cool, even tone in which Sean spoke seemed to reassure Grit enough. He nodded and motioned for them to follow. "You better keep up, alien, or you'll get lost."

They were led down a half-lit tunnel, one no one seemed to be using. Davin could only guess it was an older part of the mine, one that would be perfect for hiding guns, supplies or a feisty doctor. The maze of tunnels was getting challenging to remember. Davin hoped for his sake that Sean knew how to get the hell out of here.

"Why did you think I wanted the gel? It's not like you to jump to conclusions like that, Donaldson."

"Your name somewhere it shouldn't have been. Someone in the mine is playing rough. Be careful."

The tunnel opened up into another cavern. This one was half the size of the previous one but was filled with makeshift beds. Miners were everywhere, some lying down, some walking around with water buckets, offering drinks to their friends. The coughs and moans that echoed in the room were mixed with laughter and the threads of conversation. Davin realized it was the equivalent to med bay while they worked here.

"Did you know about this?" He turned to Sean.

Sean looked at him and nodded once but looked confused too. Like someone who was remembering something from a dream. "I've spend my fair share of nights here. But it's getting worse. Most I ever saw was half a dozen. There have to be at least thirty."

Davin walked into the cavern and some of the conversation died down. He could feel the pull of their injuries, their exhaustion, silently begging him to help. It would take nothing for him to pull off his gloves and begin, but he couldn't. It was too much.

"Davin!"

He turned to the side to see Sara standing over a man in one of the beds. She looked as tired as her patient. A wave of relief hit him hard and fast when he saw her smile.

"We needed a doctor," Grit said with a sigh. "They've increased our shifts to triples. That fucking Briel who took over is killing us slowly, and no one seems to give a shit."

"Who gave the orders?" Sean asked.

Davin didn't care about the why or who anymore. He was across the room and at Sara's side before anyone had time to argue. He was about to swing her up into his arms when he stopped short. She'd turned back to the patient and was finishing applying a bandage to his arm.

"Okay, Bobby, you're on bedrest for the next six hours. And no arguing or I'll have my medics haul your ass to med bay and you won't have a choice."

"Yes, Doc. I don't mind staying as long as I can stare at your pretty ass," he said grinning up at her.

Sara chuckled and patted his shoulder before standing up and facing Davin.

"Hi," she said and blew a piece of her hair from her eyes. "We need to talk."

At that moment, a surge of anger pumped him up. Anger at the people who took her. Anger at her for being okay. He grabbed her hand and dragged her away from the miners toward what looked to be a small supply shed.

"Davin!"

"Need a hand?" Sean called to them.

"Yes!" Sara said, pulling against his grip.

"No," Davin ground out.

Several men whooped and whistled as they passed them until he slammed the door of the shed, sending it flying open. The room was empty of supplies, and instead filled with three beds and two men sitting, playing cards.

"Out!"

They didn't bother to argue, grabbing their things and leaving as quickly as they could. Only once the door was shut behind them did Davin spin Sara around and force her to sit on the bed with a thump.

"What the hell's the matter with you! I have men out there who need me."

"You have a man in *here* who needs you. What the fuck is going on, Sara? One minute you're curled up in my arms and the next no one on the colony can find you."

She opened her mouth to say something, but nothing wanted to come out. Instead she shook her head and stood. When she reached for his hand, Davin didn't pull away. He'd been craving her touch since he realized she was gone. He'd known her only a short time and already she was becoming an important part of his life. Slowly, she slid her hand up his arm as she stepped closer to his body. Her scent filled his senses, making his head buzz. Leaning in, she placed a kiss on his chest.

"They were hurt. No one said a word to me when they first took me. Just brought me to this place and handed me a med kit. What the hell was I supposed to do?"

"Contact someone. Let us know that you were okay."

Davin hated that his throat was tight with emotions he'd long thought buried. Now they were pushing their way to the surface, threatening to tear down his defenses. All because of this tiny human doctor.

"They wouldn't let me contact anyone. They know I'm good friends with Haylie and they see her as a traitor. Married to the man who's making their lives a living hell."

"Kamran?"

"God, if he had any idea what was going on down here, he'd be furious."

"So why doesn't he? He didn't strike me as a man who would ignore a place like this."

In fact, the whole situation seemed bizarre.

Sara sighed. "I'm not sure, but I feel just as responsible. I sat in those weekly meetings listening to the reports of the mines. I had some of the miners show up in med bay, but I only treated the symptoms I saw. I could have done a whole lot more. Which is why I'm staying here until we can fix this."

Despite knowing she was right, that these men needed her more than anything else, Davin couldn't help but get the feeling this was a very bad idea.

"Did they say anything about the stocolran gel? About wanting to trade you for it?"

The look of fear flashed across her face quickly before she clamped back down on it again. "No. I doubt they would let me in on their plans even if they did."

Not surprising. Davin ran a hand down his face trying to wipe away the fear and exhaustion that had pounded over him for the last few hours. Sara was safe and with him now. Things would be fine.

"Well then, I'd best find us a few beds for the night," he said finally, looking up at her.

Her eyebrows shot up with surprise. "Us?"

He couldn't help but roll his eyes. "You think I'm going to leave you here alone with an entire cave full of men? Men who would gladly cut off their own hand if it meant having you hover over them, nursing them back to health."

"Oh come on. They wouldn't—"

"How old are you again? Because you're sounding like a *chatarn* right about now."

"I'm a cha...a what?"

He had to try hard not laugh at the angry expression on her face. She was very attractive when provoked.

"Like a child."

Sara huffed and crossed her arms across her chest. With her nose in the air and a blush on her cheeks, she looked more beautiful than he'd ever seen her. He really wanted to strip her out of her uniform and take her on the small bed behind her.

"Davin, I'm perfectly fine and I'm hardly a *child*. Besides, I need you to go back to the station and get me some supplies. The two med kits they stole are almost used up. And I could use Rachael's help."

"Sean can go."

Sara blinked and gave her head a shake. "Sean? He's here?"

"How else did you think I got in here?" When he saw her blush, he couldn't help but smile. "I see. You saw me and didn't have eyes for anyone else, eh? I think I like the sound of that."

"Not at all. I was with my patient and was distracted." Her face was flaming red now.

Sara tried to step away from him, but Davin grabbed her by the arms and pulled her close. Her body was crushed against his, which responded instantly. His cock sprang to life and pressed painfully against his pants. When she looked into his eyes, he could see she felt him. Her breath was coming out in shallow gasps as her gaze flicked from his eyes to his lips and back again.

"If you do *this* to me, imagine what you do to a bunch of sex-deprived miners. I'm not leaving you alone again, so don't bother to argue."

She ground her hips against him, her eyes half closing as she did. "The only deprived person I see here is you. Surprising considering what we were doing only a few hours—"

Three steps and he had her against the wall, his mouth covering hers in a deep kiss. He felt her tongue slip into his mouth, teasing him, stoking his need incredibly high. Her hands were all over his body, around his neck and in his hair. She pulled back, panting, and began to caress his face.

"When they took me, all I could think about was getting back to you."

"The second I woke up alone, I knew there was a problem."

"Really?" She was almost hopeful in the way she asked. "Were you scared?"

"I thought you'd gotten out before—"

Davin looked away, mentally cursing himself. This wasn't the time for baring his soul to her. Right now he needed her body. Needed to know she was his.

"Before what?"

"Before you knew how much of an ass I am."

Sara laughed and ran her hand down his cheek. "I knew that the second you poked your head out of your ship."

They stood there, pressed against the wall, looking at each other for what felt like eternity. His heart was pounding in his chest, making it hard to get a breath in. Right then, nothing else mattered except Sara. He didn't give a *friken* about the past or the future in that instant. She was everything to him. His one chance at happiness and redemption. All he had to do was reach out and grab it.

"I need you." The words were out of him before he had a chance to change his mind. But he didn't regret them — not this time.

Sara closed her eyes and tipped her head to the side, giving him complete access to her neck. He could see the fading circle where he'd bitten her before. His warrior self claiming her as his own, making sure no one touched her but him. Seeing the mark again fired him up and pushed him over the edge.

All he could hear was his brain screaming — *Mine!*

Davin didn't hold back — couldn't hold back — and began to lick her skin, tasting her salt and fragrance, stoking his need. Before either of them changed their minds, he began to pull at her uniform, exposing her creamy breasts to the dim light. Her aroused scent hit him like a slap to the face, dragging a moan from his chest. With a watering mouth, he bent his head and captured one of her dusty pink nipples lightly between his teeth, flicking the swollen peak with his tongue. Sara gasped, driving her hands into his hair and pulled him closer.

"I was so scared," she whispered, her body shuddering under his touch. "I didn't think I'd see you again."

He picked her up around the waist, letting her wrap her legs around his hips. Pushing her even harder against the wall, Davin was able to show her how he felt. His cock was near exploding from being so close to her cunt, so when he bucked his hips forward he had to bite down hard on his tongue to keep from coming. Sara moaned into his ear before she began to suck the lobe into her mouth. He could feel her dampness, smell her desire. He needed to fuck her now before he went insane.

Not wanting to lose another second, Davin carried her over to the closest bed and threw her down onto it. He should have been gentle, but that wasn't what either of them needed right now. Sara was pulling at her uniform, yanking it off with little grace, while he began to undo his pants. She was every bit as wild as he and he loved her for it.

"The door?" she asked in a breathless whisper, her eyes never leaving him.

"Fuck it. I'll kill anyone who comes in."

"God, I love it when you talk like that," she moaned, yanking off the last piece of her clothing.

Finally, she was naked before him, her skin a glowing beacon to him. Pulling his shirt off in one easy stroke, he tossed it to the floor and fell in between her legs. Sara cried out when he thrust into her in one easy stroke. They both held still for a moment before Davin began the steady, rhythmic thrusting. Sara clawed at his back as she wrapped her legs high around his waist. The angle of her hips allowed him deeper into her body, so much he was filling her completely. *Joural*, he could die right now and would be content with his passing.

The muscles of her pussy began to clench around his shaft wildly and he knew her orgasm wouldn't be far behind. Davin ground hard against her clit as he bent his head to torture one of her nipples with his tongue. Sara's back arched, pushing her breast farther into his mouth as she bucked her hips in time to his. Her taste filled him as his cock filled her body. Her scent was making him drunk, making his head buzz. Their energies were mixing together, adding to the power of their caresses.

Davin reached out with his body to touch hers on that basic, primal level. As before, the tingle started between them at a single point and radiated out. He knew she felt it, felt the pull between them. This wasn't merely a mingling of their bodies, but of their souls.

Instantly, Sara's body seized up and she cried out as her orgasm hit her. Davin covered her mouth with his in an attempt to dull the sounds. Quickly, he increased the tempo until he couldn't hold off the inevitable rush of release. Davin groaned loudly into Sara's mouth as his body thrust against her at a punishing pace. He felt every pulse of his cock as his seed spilled into her, filling her womb with his very essence.

He collapsed onto her, the small bed creaking in protest. The scent of sex and sweat filled the small room and Davin breathed it in deeply. For the first time in the past few hours, he felt at peace. Sara was safe.

And she was his.

Mine.

He hugged her hard, knowing he was probably hurting her but unwilling to let her go. She completed him like no other woman did, setting the ache in his heart at rest. How had she wrapped her way around his heart in such a short time?

A sudden knock on the door made them both jump. Davin couldn't help but let out a low growl. Sara smacked him hard on the shoulder.

"Yes?" her voice trembled slightly.

"When you two are finished, there are people here who need Sara's help," Sean's voice drifted through the closed door.

"Oh my god," Sara whispered, her face turning red.

"Give us a minute," Davin called out.

"I'm keeping an eye on the door. No rush."

Davin turned back to look at Sara and grinned. "Oops."

She smacked him on the shoulder. "How the hell am I supposed to go out there and face all those men now? What the hell are they going to think of me?"

"That you're off limits." He leaned in and nipped at her neck. "Which is exactly what I want."

"You are such an asshole, Davin."

Still, she giggled when she leaned her head back against the bed, her skin glowing from her orgasm and the blush that seemed to be permanently etched there. Davin brushed her hair away from her neck and placed a single kiss there. He could feel her exhaustion creeping into her body.

"If you're planning on staying here, I'll get Sean to grab some of your things. And get you something decent to sleep on."

"So you're going to stay?"

The disbelief in her voice made him look up. "I said I would. You'll need an assistant."

She frowned at him. "But you're not a doctor. It would be better to have Rachael here or one of the Briel doctors. They're used to working in harsh conditions."

"We don't need to put anyone else in danger. I don't buy that they brought you here simply to heal the miners. They could have contacted you in med bay, explained the situation and you would have come. There's something more going on here. Plus, they won't let us leave."

His heart began to pound as he stood up. He missed the warmth of her body and wished they could simply stay in bed all day and forget the world around them. But life wasn't going to make this easy on him. "I know a few things about healing. I won't be completely useless to you."

"Right, that thing you do." Then she stopped, sitting up and really looked at him.

Davin walked over to the pile of their clothing and began to get dressed. He'd left his gloves on this time and she seemed to be staring at them. When she let out a sudden rush of breath, he looked at her.

It was then he realized she was putting the pieces together. But she didn't know the extent of his abilities. Not yet at least.

"Back in your ship and back in your room on the station, what did you do to us? I mean when I was trying to get Rafe to med bay, you did something to him. With your hand. You said it was to buy him time. And then you healed my head. But no one else seems to know what you can do. Silas and Rafe didn't. I talked to them."

"Get dressed, Sara. We need to get out there."

"Can you only cure minor injuries? With the touch of your hands?"

"Sara."

"No this is important." She got up and walked over to him. "You have this powerful gift and you try to hide it."

Taking his gloved hand in hers, she turned it over and placed a kiss in his palm. Davin didn't move, scared something terrible would happen if he even breathed. No one knew, not even his crew, what he could do. His safety depended on it. But, somehow, he knew Sara wouldn't betray him.

"Why would I do something like that?" He flashed her a smile. "Seems a bit silly. Most people in this sector know what the Raqulians can do."

"But you said all your people can't do this." Then her eyes opened wide. "You said you weren't born into the warrior cast. Were you a doctor? A healer?"

"It doesn't matter, so please forget about it. I can help you now."

"Davin, you can trust me with this."

Her words sent a shiver down his spine. Her eyes were big, and for a moment, he thought, filled with tears. Davin bent down and placed a kiss on her forehead.

"Get dressed. People need you."

As he turned and walked out of the room, he swore he heard her whisper, "Like you."

Chapter Seven

Sara sat down on the closest thing she could find, some sort of crate, and tried to relax the screaming muscles in her neck and back. She looked up across the sea of beds for the first time since her arrival and wanted to curl up and die.

How the hell were they going to get through this?

The miners would rest after she'd patch them up, only to get up and take over for the next shift of men who were just as tired and injured. They seemed to be nothing but lifeless drones, focused on doing their job and nothing else. Her mind kept going over all the reports she'd sat through on the condition of the mines. That slimy weasel Grant had purposely misled the entire council about what was going on here. He'd been forcing the men to run triple shifts months ago, long before he ever thought of seeking consent from Kamran. But what really shocked her was the fact *none* of the miners had complained about the conditions they'd been working under. It was bizarre.

Even Sean seemed to be oblivious to the fact that this was what he'd been doing for three months. Either he'd been so engulfed in his own guilt over his part in the Ecada invasion last year or there was something else going on. Though she had to admit, he seemed better now that he and Davin were spending time together. She wasn't even sure if Davin had said anything about the attack, and maybe that was what put Sean at ease. Regardless, Sean was just as concerned about what was going on here as she was. They had to do something.

But it didn't explain everyone else. And then that ass Grant had the nerve to come here and tell these poor bastards it was *Kamran* who'd ordered the increased work. The first thing she was going to do when she got out of here was make sure that low-life, space-sucking asshole was thrown into the last prison cell at the bottom of the station. With no food, no medical care and an alarm that woke him up every four hours.

She'd like to see how he liked it.

But it was more than that. Talking to the miners made her uneasy. When they first arrived at her temporary med bay, they would barely notice her. Like they'd been sleepwalking their way through the shift and someone had herded them to her. Slowly, after she pumped their bodies full of fluids, protein supplements and forced them to rest, they seemed to wake up. Only then would they laugh and tease her like they would have back on the station, oblivious to how they'd been feeling or what they'd been doing only a few hours earlier. The cycle never seemed to stop.

She felt like she'd fallen into her own endless cycle too. Most of the past few hours were little more than a blur, the details blended and jumbled together. She'd tried to remind herself to check for microbes in the air, see if there was anything that could be causing it, but the thought never seemed to stick long in her head.

Sara looked up when she heard a familiar voice. Davin came from one of the side tunnels, his head moving from side to side as he scanned the area. He was talking to Sean, the two men pointing at part of the cavern. Somehow he'd managed to draw Sean out of his self-destructiveness and helped him focus. In the day and a half they'd been stuck here, Sara had watched her friend start to come around. Just one more reason she was falling for Davin a little bit more each day. Sara quickly pushed that thought aside, not wanting to see where it might lead.

It would have been fantastic if they were allowed to leave and they could celebrate back on the station. Sean tried to get through the lockdown that had been initiated a few minutes after he and Davin had arrived, but the guards wouldn't budge. They said they were under strict orders from

Administrator Kamran to keep everyone here. As if Kamran would ever do something like that. If they would only let them send a communication, she would be able to clear everything up. God, that suggestion nearly sent the guards into a fit.

Jerks.

Sara had no doubt it was that slimy, double-crossing asshole Grant. Probably knew she'd run to Kamran and report the horrendous conditions she'd seen here and get Grant's ass pitched out an airlock from a low-orbiting shuttle. Nothing brought out her mean streak like preventable injustices.

The only bright point was that Kamran, Haylie and Taber *knew* Davin and Sean had come here. If they didn't check in soon, Taber would come running with the cavalry and get them out. God help Grant when that happened because she was going to make him pay for everything he'd done here. The man must be insane to think he could get away with it.

She sighed, pushed away the nasty thoughts of what she would do to her new adversary and watched Davin walk past several of the miners who were lying down. He'd been by her side for most of the day and into the night. Shit, she didn't even know what time it was anymore. As they worked she kept watching him, trying to see if he'd use his ability to heal people. Not once did she see him press his hand to someone's chest or hold on to an injury longer than normal. Not that anyone was dying, but she was hoping he'd help by using his gift. She wasn't sure why, but she knew it was important that he stop ignoring his abilities, what he could do for the people around him. The things she could do with a gift like that! Instead he'd been by her side, handing her bandages, scanners and anything else she'd needed.

But he'd been there. And that was more than she had the right to ask of him. This wasn't his planet or his people.

He moved closer to her, his attention still locked deep in conversation with Sean. It was the first time she'd been able to really watch him. His body was a bit larger than Sean's, more bulky muscle compared to Sean's lean, athletic build. Davin's brown hair had fallen down to frame his square jaw, giving him a hungry look. His every move was exact, sharp, like a warrior.

A quiver of desire began to pulse through her body, despite her exhaustion. Watching him now brought back images of what they'd done earlier in the shed. God, *everyone* knew what they'd done, a few had even teased her when she was making her rounds. Mostly once Davin was out of earshot—no one was brave enough to do otherwise. Her breasts tingled and her nipples tightened as if they remembered his touch, craved it again. She'd never been with a man like him before. Someone who was strong, sure of himself, a warrior. But he had a vulnerable side that he kept buried deep. She could tell, could see it when he looked at her a certain way, only to turn his head to hide it when she caught him looking. He was a contrast of cold strength and warm heart.

The idea of making love to him again sounded good. Too bad she could barely keep her eyes open.

He turned and saw her watching. His slow smile slid onto his face and he ran a hand through his hair, pushing it away from his face and giving him a mischievous look. Davin sauntered over to where she sat, his belt riding low on his hips. God, she wished she could see his ass right now.

"Did you eat?" he asked when he was close enough. He gave her a onceover, checking to make sure she was still in one piece.

"Yeah, I had some of the rations. When we get out of here, I'm seriously going to kick someone's ass. These conditions are crap. And the food sucks. They need hot meals and a freshwater supply."

"You should see things lower. Sean took me down to where they are actually blasting." Davin shook his head. "I don't know how they can work here."

"They're survivors—that's for sure. Did you learn anything about the stocolran gel? Who's after it?"

"No. No one would talk to us, especially the deeper we went into the mines. Have you noticed how they act? Like they're..." He shrugged, giving up on finding the right word.

"Like they're sleepwalking. It's creepy weird."

She realized looking up at him that she wasn't the only one who'd been pushed past their limits. Sara scooted over to make enough room for him on the crate beside her. When he didn't move at first, she patted the wood plank beside her.

"You look like you're about to collapse. I promise I won't bite."

"That's not much of an incentive," he drawled.

Davin grinned and took the spot beside her. They stared at each other for a moment before Sara felt a yawn erupt from her. Her eyes watered and burned at the same time, the dust from the mine covering every inch of her now.

"You should sleep," he said, his finger brushing the side of her thigh.

"I tried a while ago. I'm not sleepy so much as worn out." Sara dropped her chin to her chest and rolled her head from side to side. "I wish I could get out of here just for a little while. I'd feel like I could focus again."

"I might be able to help with that."

Sara looked up into his face and saw the small smirk on his lips. "Dare I ask?"

"I have a surprise for you," he said and bumped her shoulder with his.

"Gourmet meal? Cause I don't know about you, but those rations sucked ass."

"Better than that. Up for a little walk?"

She leaned close and squinted her eyes. "Why do I get the feeling you are up to something."

"Because I am. But you'll have to come with me to find out exactly what that is."

He didn't wait for her to respond, instead sliding off the crate and walking back in the direction he'd just come. Sara managed to hold herself back for four or five seconds, ample time to inspect his ass, before giving in to her curiosity. As she walked, she heard several of the men chuckle and wish her luck.

Catching up to Davin wasn't that difficult. He was taking his time in the tunnel that served as the main artery between the makeshift hospital and the main meeting area. When she came up beside him, she kept her eyes forward and her hands clasped behind her back. They walked in silence through the twisting tunnel until Sara wasn't sure exactly where they were any longer. It seemed to be away from the current dig area, in a part of the mine that wasn't being used.

"You know, these miners are quite an industrious bunch," Davin said after a few moments of silence.

"Oh?"

"They have the most amazing things smuggled into this place. I've seen food and pictures of naked human females, even heard music. Sean doesn't even know where half of it came from. Though he admits he doesn't remember much from the past year or so. I get the feeling he was trying to bury himself here."

That caught Sara's attention. "Did he tell you what happened?"

"No, but I can feel the guilt coming off him. You know?"

She nodded. Sean had been coming to see her over the past year, but he talked very little about his experience with Ray. "Someone he trusted messed with his mind. Made him do some nasty things."

"He wasn't in control?"

"God no. But he's one of the reasons I'm here to talk to you today. Saved Haylie and Kamran and helped stop the

Ecada attack. Not that he sees it that way. He blames himself for not being strong enough to fight the influence of the Ecada and the crazy Briel who was trying to take over the colony."

Davin looked at her sideways. "I'll have to thank him later then. This trip would have been far less entertaining if you weren't around."

"You would have crashed into an Ecada-infested planet. More likely you'd be dinner." When they turned another corner, Sara sighed and crossed her arms. "Where the hell are we going?"

"Are you always this impatient?"

"Just when there are surprises involved. You should see me on my birthday."

Davin snorted and shook his head. "Thankfully, we don't have much farther to go. It's right through here."

Sara followed his lead through a small hole in the side of the wall. It was barely big enough for Davin, but she fit through easily. What she wasn't expecting was the large, open cavern they walked into after a few steps. There were three large flood lamps set up around the cavern, casting just enough light so Sara could look around. Large stalactites hung from the top of the cave, funneling drops of water downward into a large natural cave spring.

"Holy shit," she whispered, stepping around Davin to get a better look.

"Sean found out that a group of miners discovered it a few months ago and they'd been trying to keep it a secret. Apparently someone smuggled in a testing kit and the water is safe and clean."

"This could really help the station and maybe ease some of the water reclamation concerns. This is amazing." She turned and smiled. "Why haven't they told anyone about this? Sean knows what this type of discovery would mean to us."

"Sean said he just found out today while we were patching our friends up. He plans on bringing Kamran here as soon as we get out."

Sara's heart was pounding from the rush of excitement. Turning around, she tried to take in every detail of the cavern.. They were about five feet above the lake, which looked to be very deep. Grabbing her flashlight, she squatted to point it into the water. She could see the bottom, which was free and clear of anything that looked to be alive. It was perfect.

"Amazing," she whispered.

Sara stood up too quickly, sending her head spinning. She was overcome by a wave of dizziness that had her reaching out blindly before she passed out. Her hands found Davin's arm and grabbed ahold for dear life. It was just enough to throw them both off balance and send them tumbling into water below with a crash.

Sara came sputtering to the surface, her body shocked by the cool water. She looked around for Davin but didn't see him. Spinning around as best she could while treading, she tried to find him in the dim light.

"Davin?"

After a second, he broke the surface with a huge gasp and began coughing. He managed to make his way over to the side of the rock wall and held on tight.

"For the love *nusda*! Are you trying to kill me!"

She knew she shouldn't do it, but Sara couldn't help the bubble of laughter that popped from her. "I'm so sorry."

"I can't swim," he said in between coughs.

It took her only a minute to swim over to where he was clinging, a murderous look fixed firmly on his face.

"I was hoping you wouldn't see this side of me," she said as she desperately tried to wipe the smirk off her face.

"What's that supposed to mean?"

"I'm known as a bit of a bad-luck magnet. Haylie has been hurt by my clumsiness more times that I can count over the years. At least you didn't land on a rock."

"Instead I almost drowned." He frantically looked around while his knuckles went white from holding on to the side. "Do you see a way out of here?"

They both tried to see if there was a ledge they could use as a boost to get themselves up and out. Sara even swam around trying to find a spot that would make their ascent much easier. While the water was shallower on the far side, the ledge was several feet higher, making it impossible to climb up. It turned out their best option for escape was the ledge Davin was holding on to.

"We'll have to try from here." He motioned with his chin when she got back to him. "I can boost you up, but you'll have to haul yourself over the edge. Think you can do that?"

As much as she wanted to get out of here, there was something thrilling about swimming in the water. She hadn't been in a pool, natural or otherwise, in years. There was something about it that made her want to strip her soaked clothing off so she could feel the water on her naked skin.

"Come on, Sara. I can lift you."

"Do we have to?"

Davin turned to her, a look of shock on his face. She didn't wait for him to ask any questions and began to undo the opening of her jumper. The water was cool on her skin, but she quickly adjusted to it. The black tank top she'd put on underneath clung to her like a second skin, accentuating her puckered nipples. With her boots on, it was hard to kick or swim around easily. Lying on her back, Sara kicked her way over to the shallow spot. From there she was able to stand up, the water coming up to her neck.

With her feet planted firmly on a large flat rock, she shrugged out of the uniform and got her boots off. Clad only in her underwear, Sara felt like a kid again, free to do something a little wild. From across the pool, she heard Davin groan.

"Did I mention I can't swim?"

"Call this incentive to learn. I've managed to get my pants off."

She tied the laces of her boots together so they'd be easier to hold. She threw a boot over one shoulder, and her wet uniform over the other. Then, with her eyes locked on Davin she began to swim over with long leisurely strokes. When she got a little closer to him, she could see his golden eyes glinting in the pale light, fixed on her every motion.

"You're going to kill me, Sara."

She laughed and ducked her head under the water, her uniform and boots pulling tight against her body. Kicking close to Davin was easier without the extra drag from her clothing. Popping out right in front of him, she couldn't help but grin in his face.

"Hi," she said and set her wet uniform over his shoulder. "Mind holding this?"

Davin reached out with his free arm and circled Sara around the waist, pulling her tight to his body. He'd managed to wedge his boot into the rock, giving him lots of leverage. Sara halfheartedly struggled, more in an attempt to get closer to him than to get away. When she felt him let out a low growl again, she stopped and instead looped her arms around his neck.

Davin's eyes were barely slits as his gaze traveled over her face and down to her chest. His breath was heavy and Sara could tell he was trying to keep his reactions under control. With his hands busy keeping his grip on both her and the ledge, Sara was free to explore.

She pushed his dripping brown hair from his cheek and tucked it behind his ear. He looked like an alien pirate, missing only the eye patch. His jaw was clenched, the muscle dancing in his cheek as he ground his teeth. Sara leaned in and placed a kiss there, letting her tongue dance out to taste his skin. The water tasted almost sweet, so she gave his face another little lick, lapping up several more drops.

"Yummy," she whispered.

Her fingers traveled down his chest to his belt. She didn't dare take it off, but that wasn't going to stop her from teasing. Despite the coolness of the water, Sara could feel Davin's erection. When she wrapped her fingers around the bulge pushing out the front of his pants, Davin sucked in a breath.

"Are you smuggling something in there, Captain Jagt?"

"I'll never tell," he said as he finally let a small smirk play on his lips. "Too bad you can't inspect me."

Sara gave him a squeeze. "What makes you think I can't?"

His golden eyes narrowed. "I'm afraid to taunt you."

She didn't wait and opened the fastenings of his pants to pull out his cock. She felt him shudder when the cool water hit his exposed flesh before she palmed him with her hand. The action made him loosen his grip on her waist enough to give her the freedom to move. Sara took a deep breath and ducked her head under the water.

The need to keep her eyes closed didn't cause her any problems. It wasn't difficult to find the head of his cock with her mouth by feel alone. She popped it in, letting her tongue swirl around the swollen head. The water gave her buoyancy, so it made the bobbing motions smooth and easy. After a minute, her lungs were screaming at her for air. She released his cock from her mouth and popped her head up to the surface to suck in a breath.

Davin's head was thrown back and his eyes were closed. The corded muscles in his neck were strained and his arm was shaking as he clung to the side. Not wanting to stop for long, Sara took another breath and returned to her task. This time when she sucked him into her mouth, she used her hands to seek out his balls, rolling and teasing them with her fingers.

The muscles in his legs began to shake when she raked her nails of her free hand down the inside of his thigh. His free hand reached for her head, tugging her toward the surface. Not quite ready to release him from her sensual torture, Sara gave him one last, hard suck before letting him go and coming up for air.

Davin half pulled her the rest of the way out of the water up to his mouth. His kiss was scorching, driving out what little air she had left in her lungs. There was nothing gentle in his touch, only the painful, blinding need that she'd driven him to. Shit, she loved him crazy like this.

When he pulled back, he was at her neck, licking and nipping the still-sensitive spot on her neck where he'd bitten her days before. Every time he ran his tongue over that spot, Sara's pussy clenched and her cream began to flow.

"Fuck me," she managed to say in a harsh whisper.

Without a word, she reached up and above him and grabbed a part of the ledge. From that position she was able to wrap her legs around his waist to grind her cunt against his rock-hard cock. Davin used his free hand to push her panties aside, giving him access to her pussy. Needing to carefully balance their position, he thrust into her with a slow, precise thrust.

That one motion was almost enough to push Sara to the edge. Her head was buzzing madly, her skin tingled as if it were electrified. It was different than before, different from when he'd done that thing to her back in his ship. She felt like she'd been oxygen deprived and this was her first breath of air. She needed him more than that.

Pushing back as far as she dared go, Sara relished the full feeling of his cock buried deep inside. The water once again made things easier for her, allowing her to bounce easily up and down on him. Davin's eyes were two narrow slits, his intense golden gaze fixed on her. She tried to look away but couldn't. Risking their precarious balance, she reached down with one hand and caressed his cheek as she rode him hard.

His hand was at her back, holding her in place as he guided her hips.

"I want to touch you," he said in a whisper that was more of a hiss.

"Where?"

"I want to suck your nipples hard. I want to lick your cunt until you scream my name."

Sara gasped and ground her swollen clit against him. Her leg scraped against the rocks the faster she moved. A dull ache began on her outer thigh, but she ignored it, instead concentrating on the intense buzz in her head. Her orgasm was close, so close.

"What else would you do to me?" Sara leaned in and sucked his earlobe. "Tell me what you'd do."

"I'd teach you a lesson for throwing me in the water. Maybe I'd give you a spanking. Maybe I'd fuck your ass just to see what you'd do."

Sara gasped before she buried her face in his neck. The sensation of the cool water mixing with her hot juices teased her clit to near bursting. The image and sensations of what he'd do to her were wild.

"You'd like that?" Davin cooed against her ear. "I'll have to remember that, wild one. I won't forget that you like this."

Before she realized what he was doing, the hand that was at her back slid down to cup her ass. His finger began to explore the crack of her ass, teasing her puckered entrance. It was too much for Sara. She drove her body down on his cock and her orgasm exploded from her body. Not wanting her cries to echo in the cavern, she buried her face in his neck, her mouth clamped shut.

Davin moved his hand to her ass cheek again and squeezed it hard. He began to pound into her pussy as hard as he could. It only took a minute before she felt his cock swell and, with one final thrust, shoot his cum deep inside her.

She felt his arm shaking under the strain of holding both their bodies still. Missing their closeness but not wanting to hurt him, Sara pulled back and dropped her legs from around his waist. They stayed there panting and staring at each other for a few minutes before she began to grin.

"We better suggest they don't drink the water for a while."

"Poor bastards," he said and winked at her.

The crazy buzzing in her head wasn't subsiding now that she'd had her mind-blowing orgasm. She was about to say something to him about it when they heard voices coming their way. Sara was about to call out to them when Davin pulled her close and placed a finger over her lips.

She gave her head a shake. "But we need help."

This time he put his hand over her mouth and yelled at her with his gaze to keep quiet. She stopped moving as she heard the men shuffle into the side room, their voices low.

"No one is aware of what's going on. We are not concerned."

The voice sounded familiar to Sara, but the buzzing in her head was making it difficult for her to place it. Afraid of attracting attention, she didn't want to move too much, but she needed to know who was talking.

"Look, with Donaldson and that alien asshole poking around everywhere, they're going to find something. I think this is a bad—"

There was a soft gagging noise and Sara recognized it as someone who couldn't breathe.

"Fuck...you," the choking man gasped.

"We are aware of all who are here and what they can do. There are no problems. If you cannot help us, we will have your body brought to us and we will enjoy it."

Sara felt her eyes go wide as she kept her gaze locked with Davin. The way the second man said *enjoy* sent chills down her back. Davin gave his head a single shake to keep her quiet. They were in no position to do anything about these two. If only she could place that voice. And why the hell was he talking about himself as a plural?

"Do you understand us?"

Sara could only imagine he nodded yes because after a few more seconds of silence, the man started gasping and coughing.

"Jesus."

There was a brief scuffle and she heard someone get thrown against the rock wall. The second man's voice came out as a slow drawl. "We are glad you understand us."

"Look, someone is bound to come looking for them. They've been gone too long as it is. I need to get ready."

There was a slight pause. "Very well. Report back to us when you have completed your task. We expect you to find us what we need. The gel is important."

Another round of rustling clothing before she heard someone leave. The quiet chirp of a communicator was answered, the man walking to the edge of the pool. Sara didn't dare look up for fear of attracting his attention.

"Yes? I'll have the payment. You just make sure you have my product. My boss has high expectations. Two days. Out."

The man snapped the communicator closed and paused long enough to kick a rock into the pond. It landed a few feet away from where they stood. With a little grunt, he turned and walked out.

Sara tried to move, to say something, but Davin held her still. They stayed that way for so long she thought he'd forgotten how to move. Not able to take the inactivity any longer, Sara pushed his hand away and reached to the ledge.

"What the hell was that all about?" The words sounded loud after their extended silence.

"Nothing that concerns us. I'm going to try to climb out of here."

Sara smacked Davin's arm. "What do you mean it doesn't concern us? They are trying to get a biological weapon. Most likely to use on my home. We need to do something to stop them."

"No, we need to get out of here. If you want to tell your Briel security *daeu* and your pregnant friend, fine with me."

She had to give her head a shake. "My what? What the hell's the matter with you?"

He tried to pull his body from the water onto the ledge but couldn't. She could see his muscles shaking from the strain of having held on for so long. Not only that, he was shaking his head, as if there was something stuck there he was trying to get out.

"There's nothing wrong with me. I don't give a fuck what happens on this colony. I'm not staying forever."

His words hit her like a slap to the face. The buzzing in her head grew louder and it was becoming hard to concentrate. Davin was going to leave. She hadn't considered it a possibility until now and it suddenly pissed her off. A lot.

"Davin?" Sean's voice drifted down to them.

"Donaldson! Down here."

Sara wasn't even happy to see him when Sean poked his head over the ledge and looked down at them.

"I'm not even going to ask," he said with a straight face. "Are you hurt?"

"We're fine. Can you get a rope or something to haul us up with?"

Sean nodded. "I'll see what I can find. Sara, are you okay?"

She started to nod but then quickly shook her head. The buzzing had grown so loud it was starting to hurt her head.

"Sara?" Davin reached out for her arm.

The Bond that Heals Us

Pushing her feet against the rock, she managed to avoid his grasp. The last thing she wanted right now was to get closer to Davin. Not if he didn't care about the colony and what happened here. Especially not if he was going to leave her.

"Let me get that rope," Sean said before disappearing once more.

"You okay?" The concern in Davin's voice was clear.

"Fine. I'm just ready to get out of here."

"Sara, come here."

"I don't think so."

She ducked her head under the water and swam around for a bit, hoping the tears that were threatening to spill would simply get washed away. Breaking the surface again, she watched Sean come back in with the rope and something that looked like a gun.

"I'm going to spike this into the wall. It should be secure enough to hold your weight."

"Should?" Davin asked flexing his fingers on the ledge.

"Best I can do. Ready?"

"Let's get out of here," she piped up.

Sara was far enough back from the ledge she could watch Sean walk over to the rock wall with the spike gun. He placed it into a divot, turned his face away and pulled the trigger. The small explosion from the cartridge drove the spike into the rock, securing it for their ascent.

In a blink Sean had the rope attached and was feeding it over the side to them.

"Sara, come out first," Davin beckoned. "Just in case this thing can't support my weight for long."

Past arguing, she swam over to him and took hold of the rope. Before she started to climb, she grabbed her boots and uniform from around Davin's neck.

"I'm going to need these," she said without looking him in the eye.

"See you up there." His words were soft.

Not meaning to, she looked into his eyes and saw his confusion. He didn't have a clue what his leaving would do to her. Probably never cared that much to think about it. She was another quick fuck he could add to his list.

Pushing those thoughts away, she carefully walked her way up the rocky five feet to the top. Sean was there to grab her around the waist and pull her close. For a fraction of a second, their bodies were close, her wet shirt and taut nipples pressed against him. Sean quickly but gently set her to the side, far enough from the edge so she wouldn't fall in again.

"I grabbed you a dry uniform too. It might be a bit big." Not once did he look at her directly, instead pointing blindly at the pile of clothing. "I set it there."

"Thanks." She tried to smile but instead turned and walked over to where the uniform was.

Not that she was attracted to Sean, but his rejection stung after Davin's. She knew she wasn't the first person most men thought of when they envisioned a wife, but she wasn't a hag either. Men either ignored her completely or they turned out to be psychopaths.

"Getting cold down here." Davin's voice floated up to them from below.

"Rope is coming now."

The splash of the rope hitting the water seemed to echo in her head as she got dressed. It took her a while to maneuver her body into the too large miner's uniform and begin to fasten the clasps. By the time she was half done, Davin was out of the water, dropping the rope to the ground with a wet thud.

"Thanks. How did you think to look for us in here?" Davin asked as he walked over to grab the second, even larger uniform.

Sean shrugged. "I checked the shed first, but it was empty. I figured you'd bring her here soon enough."

As he spoke, the words started to sound hollow to Sara. She had to give her head a shake, like she had water in her ears and couldn't get it out. The buzzing was there too, and her skin suddenly seemed to prickle as the uniform rubbed against her skin. To make matters worse, her thigh where she'd scratched it began to burn. She tried to dig at it, but when she bent forward to do it, she stumbled against the wall.

Both Davin and Sean were at her side in an instant.

"Sara, sweetheart, are you feeling well?" Davin whispered.

"What the hell is that noise?" She gave her head another shake.

Davin and Sean looked at each other for a moment before both of them flanked her sides. Despite still being angry at him, Sara reached out and tried to hold Davin's arm. Her vision blurred for a second as she tried to look into his face.

"I've got you. You're going to be fine," Davin said as he wrapped an arm around her waist.

She tried to answer him but instead felt the pull of unconsciousness and promptly passed out.

Chapter Eight

Davin didn't remember much of the last several hours. When Sara collapsed in his arms, all his annoyances and frustrations vaporized. Even the buzzing in his head had quickly disappeared. He didn't even remember carrying her, still dripping wet, down the tunnel and back to the shed she'd been using as a base while she was helping the miners. All he could focus on was her overheated body lying on the small bed in front of him.

Sean had disappeared in search of Grit in hopes of getting some medical supplies and fresh water. They'd used what little was left in her medical kit when they'd gotten back. It seemed to help things for a while, but then the fever hit her harder than before. Davin would have gone himself, but that would have meant leaving her side. And there was no way that was going to happen.

Sara moaned and kicked the sheet that was now bunched around her feet. At least she wasn't tearing at the uniform anymore. For a while, he was scared she would claw herself to pieces trying to get it off. It had taken all of his strength to hold her arms at her side so she wouldn't hurt herself for the twenty minutes it seemed to take for her fit to pass. Reaching out, Davin placed a hand on her forehead, her hot, sticky skin burning up beneath his fingers.

He'd taken his gloves off a while ago, long past caring if anyone saw the tattoos that covered his hands. It was doubtful that any of these humans understood the significance of them, of how much more than a simple healer he was. Not that he was acting like much of one right now.

His father's voice had been screaming in his head, chastising him for just sitting by while Sara was fighting for her life. The internal battle of his emotions—the desire to help her versus the fear of what reclaiming his birthright would mean—raged on. He had the ability to do something, so why the fuck wasn't he helping her?

Because deep down, he knew this is how it started. This is how his mother had gotten pulled into being a healer. One person, one life that had to be saved. All it meant was giving up everything that made him the man he was. He'd turned away from this and had chosen the life of a warrior. To protect rather than heal. To kill rather than save.

But losing Sara wasn't an option.

Looking from his hands to Sara's flushed face, Davin wasn't sure if he could call on his long-forgotten healing abilities. But he knew he couldn't just sit by and watch her die. Not when she was starting to become important to him. Davin rubbed his hand down his face and across the tight muscles in his neck. His body had already recovered from the strain of holding on to the rock in the pool. Maybe he'd also recovered from whatever it was that had gotten a hold of Sara. His body could be the key to saving her life.

The creak of the door opening caught his attention, and he looked up in time to see an exhausted Sean walk through the door. Empty handed.

He took a seat opposite Davin. "What little medical supplies we have left won't do her any good. Best keep them for the miners."

"The guards?"

"Short of killing them with my bare hands, we're not getting out of here."

"That sounds like a good idea," Davin grunted. "At least it would be better than sitting around here doing nothing. Your *buddy*, Grit?"

Sean shook his head. "I can't find him anywhere. And I even tried to find a short-range communicator to try to get in touch with Kamran or Taber. They're all apparently busted or have gone missing."

"*Friken*. Any good news?"

"The miners all love her, so if there is a chance they can help, they will. For now, we have to hope she can pull out of this."

Davin reached out and smoothed down her hair with his hand. "I don't think she can."

They sat there in silence for several minutes. Davin couldn't stop caressing her damp hair and face. She looked so small, so fragile, it broke his heart.

Sean motioned to Davin's hand. "That must have hurt. I assume they mean something."

He almost wanted to laugh. Instead Davin sat back and looked at the other man. They'd both been running from their personal demons. Sean all the way under a mountain, just as he'd run all the way to the far reaches of outer space. Davin turned and showed Sean his arm. He placed a finger on the *Veran* symbol that covered most of his biceps. The long curves spiraled around the muscle and snaked down his arm.

"This shows me which cast I was born in. While most people stay within their preordained profession, it is possible to move. I was born into the healing cast."

Sean sat up straighter, the muscles in his jaw flexed. "Healer? Can you help Sara?"

Davin ignored him and pointed to the next symbol that covered his forearm. "This is this *Macha* symbol. It's from our warrior cast. I joined when I reached the age of maturity. I was a young, angry man who desperately wanted to kill something. Unfortunately for me, we weren't at war."

Sean nodded and Davin knew he understood.

"Anger is a very powerful thing," Sean said quietly. "It makes you want to do terrible things. Mostly to people who you care about."

"I haven't been that angry in a while. This symbol is a constant reminder to be careful never to let myself get that out of control again." Davin sat back and crossed his arms across his chest.

"What about the symbols on your hands?"

Davin and Sean stared at each other. Both wounded soldiers of pointless conflicts. For the first time in a long while, Davin was tempted to tell the truth. With the exception of removing the weight from his shoulders, it wouldn't help them. Sara's healing was not in her mind. Sara moaned again, this time coughing harshly. Both men were by her side, holding her still.

"I'll get her some water," Sean said and stood up. As he was about to open the door, he stopped and turned back to Davin. "You may have run from the person you were, but she could really use your help right now. If you care for her even a little, you'll consider moving past your anger and helping."

Davin swallowed past the tightness in his throat. "Those are wise words, my friend."

"It's something Sara said to me not that long ago." He then stepped out and shut the door softly behind him.

Davin's heart was pounding in his chest as he stared after Sean. Other than the occasional quick burst of healing he'd do in an emergency, it had been years since he'd treated a patient. It was like asking someone who'd only used bandages for years to perform an operation. He honestly didn't know if he'd be able to do this, to save her.

And he no longer had the excuse of his mother's death to turn away from what he could do. Even though he hadn't spoken to his father in years, had done his best to drop off the edge of the galaxy, he couldn't say he was still that bitter young man who'd learned to take the lives as a warrior that his father had so desperately tried to save as a healer.

His decision to ignore his ability to heal was for revenge. Nothing more.

Another look at Sara told him he had no choice. Her eyes were flicking madly back and forth beneath her eyelids. At the same time her skin, pale and flushed, told him she was losing the fight against whatever was attacking her body. Regardless of how cynical he'd grown since fleeing his home, he couldn't sit by and watch her die. Not when she'd given so much to so many people.

Not when his heart had finally let her in.

Davin stood up, his legs and hands shaking slightly as he removed his belt and boots. He needed to feel focused, grounded, if he was going to make this work. He needed to ignore everything in the outside world and concentrate on Sara, on making her better. Rubbing his hands together, he brought the blood to the surface, warming his skin, sensitizing it for what he was about to do. Davin dropped to his knees and moved as close to Sara's bed as possible. He closed his eyes and let the world around him drop away into the blackness.

He let out a deep breath and focused all of his concentration on pushing every last molecule of air from his lungs. Then, slowly, he sucked in a deep breath, feeling every particle as it expanded the sacs of his three lungs. The air moved in and out of his body, expanding and contracting, filling his body with life. Mentally, he retreated to that part of his mind that allowed him to connect to the outside world, to the hurts of others. It was difficult, his mind refusing him entry, straining against his attempts. Another deep breath had his body relax more, his mind following suit. Mentally, he stood in front of that large black wall he'd erected to keep his abilities tucked away. A faint glowing light bled from around it, the small currents that allowed him to lightly heal others. He reached out, hand trembling, and touched the barrier. An electrical charge prickled at his skin until it traveled up his arm and into the rest of his body. With Sara's face floating in his mind, he pushed hard against the mental barrier, as hard as he could.

A blinding white light seemed to explode behind his eyes. The rush of long-ignored power seemed to fill every cell in his body. He was suddenly aware of his hunger, the pain in his arms and the itch on the back of his neck. It was as if his body had been numb for years and only now had come roaring back to life. As he focused his attention on each spot, he could feel his ability explore the damaged area, diagnose the problem and quickly heal it. It was painful for him at first, but as it touched each successive spot, Davin felt it increase in power and ability. The rush of energy was almost too much for him, threatening to overtake his mental control. Faster and faster the healing power surged to various spots in his body, inspecting and healing where necessary, before it moved on. If he didn't get control over his ability soon, it would overpower him. Davin retreated back to the quiet spot in his mind, just as his mother had shown him as a child. The blackness began to seep out, calming the surging power now flooding his body.

His heart rate slowed beat by beat until it reached a normal rhythm. When he opened his eyes, he could see Sara, but it was if he were looking at her through a vid screen. Her image looked odd, detached and distorted. Like a curiosity that needed to be explored. He was dispassionate and disconnected, the perfect instrument for healing. A small voice in his head started to scream at him. *This is Sara! You care about her!* Davin squashed that voice, focusing his attention solely on her illness. On how to make her better.

When he touched his hand to her head, he instantly felt her illness. The fever was caused by some sort of parasite in her blood stream. He could feel them eating away at her cells, consuming them from the inside out. They were relentless in their hunger and Sara was an unlimited food source. But when he went to find them, Davin found he couldn't locate isolate them. The parasites were small, so much so it had the ability to elude him, ducking and hiding in cells and organs. As he went, he was able to heal the damage done by the hungry bastards, but it wasn't enough. He tried to concentrate, focus his attention, but the more he tried the harder it was to find the tiny beasts. Davin sat back on his legs with a gasp, his body shaking from the effort. Sweat covered his face, dripping down his chest and back. His muscles ached from the tension and the weight of his defeat. He'd lost the them.

Friken!

It was only then he realized he wasn't alone in the room. Looking up he saw that not only had Sean returned, but he was accompanied by Kamran and Taber. A flash of panic raced through him, at what they'd seen him doing. He didn't want them to know of his failure. It hit him hard, like a punch to the face and Davin dropped his chin to his chest.

Sean stepped forward and placed a hand on Davin's shoulder. "Were you able to help her?"

His heart sank as he shook his head. "There are parasites in her, causing the fever. But it's been so long… I couldn't stop it. And they're multiplying."

Sean helped him stand, but his muscles felt weak, underformed and almost unable to support his own weight. Davin fell back onto the other bed and let out a shaky breath. Failure was never an option for a healer. People died—Sara would die if he couldn't stop this thing from eating her alive. The rising panic threatened to choke him off as his father's voice began to ring in his ears.

"How long?" he asked, his voice little more than a croak.

"Did you start right after I left?" Sean said walking back to Sara.

"Yes."

"Forty minutes."

"Fuck." He rubbed his eyes with his hand

Kamran walked over to Sara and placed a hand on her head. "You did your best. Let's get you over to med bay so one of the Briel doctors can take a look at you."

"Glad you finally came looking for us," Davin said as he rose once more to his feet. The muscles in his legs were shaky, but he could feel his strength start to return. He'd be fine in a few minutes.

"We would have been able to get you out sooner if the guards had believed our communication. It seems someone used an active high-level security code to transmit the order," Taber said, clearly annoyed.

"I've been meaning to visit the mines for a while now," Kamran said frowning. "Now that I'm here, I can't help but wonder how long things have been like this. We have our work cut out for us to get this mess straightened out."

Davin heard the men talking, but he lost focus on the words. The only thing that concerned him at that time was Sara. His eyes were watching the steady rise and fall of her chest as she drew shallow breaths. There was a little more color in her cheeks, but he knew it wouldn't last. He needed more time.

Walking over to her, he bent and slid his arms under her head and knees. She barely weighed anything as he lifted her up and into his arms. When she sighed and draped her arm around his neck, Davin's heart did a small flip. No, he couldn't afford to get attached to her, couldn't afford to fall in love, no matter how much she was starting to affect him. Not if he wanted any chance of saving her.

"We need to get her back to med bay now. I can't help her here."

The other men stopped talking and all looked at him.

"What makes you think you can help her at all?" Taber's question was clipped. "Your first attempts weren't successful."

Davin stood there and glared at the other man. The Briel warrior didn't look away, his cold, blue eyes transmitting silent threats. Not that it mattered to Davin. If anything happened to Sara, he'd punish himself enough for both of them.

The tension was broken when Kamran stepped between them, his steady, calm gaze traveling between the two warriors.

"He's a healer. I thought I recognized those markings." Kamran nodded. "Other than Sara herself, I doubt there is a better physician in the quadrant at the moment. That is, as long as you feel up to this?"

"I have to try." And next time he wouldn't stop until he'd succeeded.

Kamran nodded. "Let's move quickly and get her back. Haylie is already off to let med bay know. They'll be ready for you when you arrive."

Davin nodded and made his way to the door. He paused, waiting for Taber to move aside, allowing him passage. Their gazes locked for a moment as they came to a silent understanding—Sara wouldn't die. Taber finally nodded and stepped back and to the side, opening passage. As Davin walked out of the small shed, many of the miners were standing around, each staring at Sara in his arms before looking down at the ground. Davin couldn't help it—he walked slowly past them, giving each man a chance to wish her well, and prayed she heard each and every one of them.

"See that, wild one?" he whispered. "Everyone wants you to get better. Don't let them down."

Kamran, who'd come out with him, stopped to talk with several of the miners as Davin carried Sara out.

"Medical staff are on their way and shifts are to be cut starting now." Kamran's voice drifted over the group. "My lack of knowledge of what was going on here isn't an excuse. I will do what I can to make things right."

A smattering of applause went through the crowd behind them as Sean fell into step with Davin. Together they navigated her limp body through the narrow tunnels, careful not injure Sara further. After what seemed like an eternity, they reached the doors to the rover bay. The guards who'd been there earlier came over to help, bringing two EV suits with them. The look on their faces was nothing short of painful.

"We'll get the crawler ready for you," one of them said.

Davin nodded as he squatted on the ground, careful to keep Sara's body held high as he fumbled with the suit, not wanting any part of her body to touch the red dirt.

"I'll help you get her suited up. Then take the crawler and get her back to the station," Sean said as he grabbed the EV helmet.

"You're not coming?" Somehow, Davin had grown to like the man over the past few days. He felt a little more secure with him at his side. It had helped that Sean's inner guilt seemed to have lessened as he worked to make things right in the mines.

Sean smiled faintly but shook his head. "Kamran asked me to stay and coordinate things here. Seems I'm useful again." The faint trace of bitterness undercut his sincerity.

Davin stopped and squeezed Sean's shoulder. "I don't think there was ever a question of your usefulness. Everyone respects you."

"We'll see."

The two men worked to get Sara suited up and into the crawler, careful not to jostle her too much. The seat strap held her in place, but Davin knew it would be a hard ride on her body. Before climbing into the seat beside her, he gripped Sean's forearm below his elbow, saying goodbye as he would to a fellow warrior. Davin pulled his EV helmet on and signaled for the chamber to be decompressed and the doors opened as soon as Sean was clear. As the large metal doors creaked open, Davin gripped the controls tightly, his foot hovering expectantly over the throttle. Sara didn't have time to wait. Before they were fully open, he slammed the crawler forward and scraped through the still-rising door.

The ride over the sand dunes was rough as he pushed the crawler full throttle. The wind had picked up, beating against them and blowing clouds of dust up into his EV mask. Davin kept one hand on the controls with the other across Sara's chest. Whether it was because he'd managed to slow the parasite's progress or that simply moving her around managed to settle her nerves, Sara wasn't as restless. If she could stay that way for the remainder of the journey there, it would be a blessing.

They crested one of the larger dunes, bringing the colony into site. Davin felt relief rush through him just as his communicator chirped in his ear.

"Captain Jagt, come in. This is Chief Bond."

"I'm about fifteen *mics* from the station. You have that medical team ready?"

"They'll grab her the second that chamber decompresses. They wanted me to ask you if she's stable."

"Yes. Tell them it's some sort of parasite. I can track it down better once I get her to med bay."

There was a brief pause and he could hear the muffled voices chattering in the background. "Problem?"

"Nothing I can't straighten out for you. Just get her back here in one piece."

He smiled and snuck a look at Sara's unconscious form. Somehow he wasn't surprised she had such loyal friends.

"We'll be there shortly. Thanks…Haylie."

"You're welcome, Captain. Oh," her chuckle crackled through the com. "Kamran says don't even try flirting with me."

"Wouldn't dream of it. I don't have a death wish."

The silence that followed the soft click of the com turning off was soon replaced by a moan from Sara.

"Wild one? Its okay, I'm getting you some help. Hang on."

"Davin?" her weak voice was barely a whisper.

He gave her arm a hard squeeze through the EV suite. "Hold on."

"Not feeling good," she muttered and tried to roll over toward him.

His heart began to pound as he tried to fight a powerful blast of wind and sand against the crawler and hold her in place. "Sara, listen to me. Lie still. I don't want you to get hurt."

"Cold."

"Haylie will have a nice warm blanket waiting for you. Just stay still a little bit longer. Can you do that for me?"

"Okay."

Davin slammed his foot against the accelerator again and pushed the already speeding crawler even harder. When the open door of the station crawler bay was finally within sight, he felt a sudden release of built-up fear. Help was there.

The door and decompression took longer than he was able to wait. Hopping out, he lifted Sara into his arms and carried her across the bay to the closed inner door. He could see through the window Haylie waiting with a team of medics. Some of them wore EV suits, and all were weighted down with several med kits.

The hiss of the seal cracking as the door opened was the best sound in the world. Davin walked up to Haylie and bent his head down.

"Get this fucking thing off me."

Haylie pressed the clamps with a pop and yanked it off. "The stretcher is over here. They'll get her strapped in and we can—"

"No time, I'll carry her."

He looked into Haylie's hazel eyes and saw the concern he felt reflected in her eyes. She gave him a good long look before passing some silent judgment on him. Haylie nodded, "I'll escort you in case I need to yell at someone."

"Don't..."

They both looked down at Sara, who had her eyes open a tiny bit. She was looking at Haylie as she tried to lick her lips. The EV helmet made her soft voice seem hollow and distant. With a limp hand, she motioned toward Haylie's stomach.

"We're taking you to med bay now." He pulled her as close to his chest as their suits allowed.

"Don't upset the baby," she muttered as she wrapped an arm around his shoulder.

"Shut up, you, and get better. Or who will be there to keep me in line?"

Sara mumbled something else, which quickly turned into a moan

"Let's go." Haylie spun and pushed past another group of medics who were on their way to the mines.

The station was as bright and cheerful as it had been when he'd first arrived. The bazaar was loud as humans and other species shouted, talked and laughed as they conducted business. Under different circumstances Davin would have joined them, bought a drink and tried to broker a deal. One that would take him far away for a long time. He clutched Sara a little tighter to his chest as they pushed through the crowds, Haylie clearing a path for them as they went.

When they passed the corridor that led to the bars, images of their one date filled his mind. Their ground-moving kiss in the hall that led Davin to her bed, still fresh as ever. He needed her back and was going to do whatever it took to fix her.

The sterile air in med bay sent a rush through his body as he marched Sara through one of the doors Haylie held open and over to an isolation bed. Rachael was at her side as she and Haylie began to work off the EV suit. Davin made short work of his own, tossing it into a corner behind him. His feet had been bare in the suit's boots and now as he kicked off his boots and stepped onto the med bay floor, his skin seemed to absorb the cold, sending a chill through his body.

Rachael tried to shove him out of the way as she moved around the table. "Thanks for helping, but we've got her now. One of the Briel doctors is on his way."

"I'm not going anywhere," he said in a voice that felt foreign to him. Looking at Haylie, he tried to keep all uncertainty from his voice. "I'll need something to sit on if I'm going to do this properly."

"The only thing you are going to be doing is taking a seat out in the waiting room. Now move!" Rachael gave him a light shove.

"Please get him a stool." Haylie's voice was steady, a voice in command.

Rachael gaped, her gaze passing between Haylie and Davin. "You can't be serious. He's not a doctor."

"Actually he is and he's here. The other doctors aren't. Now please, Rache, get him something to sit on so we can save our girl."

For one tense moment, Davin didn't think she was going to help. Finally, Rachael let out a long sigh, nodded and disappeared behind a curtain.

"Do you need anything else?" Haylie asked, one hand resting on Sara's shoulder, the other on her stomach.

He brushed a piece of hair from Sara's cheek. "Make sure no one touches us. Not until I find this thing in her system. I'll have to concentrate to find the little fucker and it will take a while. "

"How long?"

Davin looked into her hazel gaze and held it until he knew she knew how serious this was. "Long."

Haylie swallowed hard and nodded. "Then get your ass to work."

Chapter Nine
ೞ

Sara hurt. Not a shallow ache or a cramp, but a severe pain that pulsed through her in waves. She was getting buried by it, losing her identity with each successive wash of discomfort. The small reprieve between waves was getting shorter and shorter in duration. Soon she wouldn't be able to keep her head above the surface any longer and she'd sink. And she didn't want to sink, wasn't ready to give up and die. God, she'd just begun to live her life! It wasn't fair.

The pain rolled over her again, sucking the air from her lungs. She wanted to scream but knew she couldn't afford that luxury. She had to fight. Keep ahead of it, refuse to give in.

When the next reprieve came, something strange happened. She felt something, a presence that hadn't been there before. She looked around in the dark, trying to see something, anything, that would offer her hope. But the next wave of pain came instead. This time she felt her head dip below the surface and she almost let it take her. But she felt the pull of that presence again, encouraging her to kick to the surface.

This time when she looked around, she was surprised to see a light. It was faint at first, so much so she wanted to discount it as a trick, something her mind was conjuring up to offer her broken body hope. But soon she realized it wasn't a trick. It grew stronger, chasing the blackness away and making it easier to breathe.

It took some time, but she finally felt she could control the pain. A soft buzzing in her mind told her she was going to be okay, that she had to help it fight. She didn't know what she was combating, but she trusted that voice. So she fought for all she was worth.

When the light was finished healing her, Sara finally felt at peace. The hurt was gone, replaced with a soft ache she knew meant she was on the mend.

Thank you, she whispered in her mind. She swore she felt a soft caress on her face like a hand. The touch of the fingers was replaced by a gentle kiss.

Sleep, Sara.

And she did.

* * * * *

The first thing Sara realized when she opened her eyes was that it was very dark. The soft beeping of the heart rate monitor threatened to lull her back to sleep. It wasn't until her brain caught onto the reality of what she was hearing that she started to pay attention. The patient's heart rate was a bit slow but stable. Probably indicating they were coming out of surgery.

What she couldn't remember was performing the operation. Frowning, she tried to recall anything from the past few days, but every time she thought she had figured it out, the memory slipped away. Her stomach growled, which encouraged Sara to flip over to her side and draw her knees up to her chest. A dull ached pulled at the muscles in her back, and for the first time in her life, Sara was tempted to administer herself some pain meds.

Why the hell was she sore anyway?

The blinding realization hit her like a blow to the head, sending Sara bolt upright in bed. She'd been sick, stuck at the mines. Her hands went to her temples and began to massage the skin, hoping the massive headache that pounded beneath would stop. What the hell had happened to her? One minute she had been flirting with Davin and the next thing she knew, pain was pounding her into submission.

Davin…

Sara looked around the room. She was definitely back at the station and in med bay. The isolation room by the look of the equipment. God only knew how long she'd been out of it. Had she infected anyone else? Was that why she was here?

"Computer, time and date?" Her voice was barely a hoarse whisper.

"Twenty-three hundred hours, six minutes. Eighth day, second month, 2328."

"About time you woke up," a gruff voice spoke softly.

Sara leaned over and pulled the curtain that hid her bed from the rest of the room. She gasped when she saw Davin slouched in a chair tucked in the far corner of the room. He had well over a day's worth of growth of beard and she couldn't help but think how sexy it made him look. He was wearing a dark blue shirt that could barely contain his massive biceps and was pulled tight over his chest. His shoulder-length brown hair was a mess, as if he'd been running his hands through it over and over.

He was the most beautiful sight she'd ever laid eyes on.

"Hi." She choked on the word.

Davin didn't move, his gold eyes locked on her body. Sara felt pinned in place, naked under his gaze. He looked her over clinically at first, passing over her in long sweeps. But after a few minutes, his gaze slowed and locked on her neck, her breasts and the swell of her calf that poked out from under the hospital gown.

Sara felt her face flush and did her best not to squirm. She reached up and touched her hair, finding several knots in her long strands.

"I must look terrible," she chuckled, not quite able to meet his gaze.

"You're perfect."

He said the words with such intensity, such absolute sincerity, Sara didn't know how to respond. This wasn't the Davin she'd met last week, was it? He'd been all smiles and jokes then. He'd played and teased as he kissed her, as they made love with the passion of a rocket blasting off. She'd felt light and happy when she was with him, relaxed for the first time in a very long while.

Looking at him now, she could tell things were different. That somehow, he'd changed in the time she'd been sick. Sara shifted her body so her feet now hung over the side of the bed. Her legs felt stiff and more than a little underused, but that wasn't about to stop her from doing what she wanted to do. With slow, deliberate movements, she eased herself off the bed until she was standing shakily on the floor. It took her a few minutes to steady herself enough that she felt able to attempt to walk.

Davin didn't move but she knew he was holding his breath. Not wanting to look into his beautiful golden eyes, Sara concentrated all her attention on the floor in front of her. It really was a short distance, but when she could barely lift her foot off the floor to take a step, she knew it would be a painful journey. One foot after the other, she made her way to the halfway point between the bed and his chair. Really, with only a few more steps his outstretched legs would come into her field of vision. As long as she ignored the shooting pains in her legs and lower back, she could do this.

Suddenly, her bare foot refused to cooperate and she stumbled forward. Sara's arms whirled madly around as she tried in vain to catch her balance before toppling forward. She squeezed her eyes shut in an attempt to block out the imminent pain of impacting with the floor. It never came.

Large, strong arms were around her back and waist, catching her in mid fall. The air in her lungs rushed out as her body impacted the solid muscle wall of Davin's chest. Sara couldn't stop the trembling that shimmered through her. His wonderful masculine scent wrapped around her like a blanket, chasing away the rest of her fears. Sara breathed in deep, enjoying the soft buzz that filled her head.

"Open your eyes." His words were soft, heavy in the silence of the room.

How could she resist him? Sara opened them, but didn't meet his eyes. Instead, she did her own inspection of his body. Her fingers followed her gaze as she took in his every detail. The muscles in his neck were tight, corded as if they'd been strained from overuse. She touched the base of his throat when he swallowed hard. His skin was warm under her cool fingers and she absorbed his heat. When he swallowed again and his grip tightened around her waist, she felt a sudden rush of fear.

"Am I okay?" She couldn't look at him, instead focused on how his pecs pushed up against his shirt.

"You will be. We got the parasite out of your system."

This time she looked up into his eyes. "We?"

Davin scooped her up in his arms and carried her back to the bed. He set her down gently and pulled her blanket up to cover her legs. She thought he was about to return to his chair when he climbed up and joined her. She was able to move just enough for them both to fit. He rested his head so it lay on her stomach, her breasts brushing against him.

"Davin?"

"Close your eyes and try to rest. We'll talk later."

"How long was I out?"

"Rest."

"Davin…"

"You are the most stubborn woman I've ever met," he growled against her.

Her heart began to pound and the increased rhythm was picked up by the computer. Something was wrong and he was keeping it from her. Probably didn't want her to worry and was trying to shelter her from the bad news. Anxiety clawed at her chest, making it hard to breathe.

She was about to argue with him, demand the truth when he slipped his hand around hers and began to stroke the inside of her wrist with his thumb. That simple action took all of the fight from her. Her heart rate dropped back to normal, the pressure in her lungs eased and she suddenly felt very tired.

"What did you do to me?" Her voice was soft and sleep filled as she spoke.

"I couldn't stand the thought of something happening to you. So many people here need you. Care for you."

"I don't understand."

She wanted to focus on him, what he was saying, but his steady caress of her wrist was making it impossible.

"You're perfectly healthy, wild one. You'll be fine in a day or two."

"Then why are you so sad?"

He didn't answer her before she drifted off to sleep.

When her mind stumbled back to consciousness, Sara was afraid to move. Scared that Davin would have left her alone, not wanting to disturb her. But when she tried to move her arm, she couldn't. Opening her eyes, she looked down to see his long, hard body still resting in the same spot where he'd climbed up. She could tell by the steady in-out of his breathing that he'd fallen asleep too.

Somehow her short nap had done wonders for her body. Her muscles didn't feel the same overwhelming exhaustion they had when she'd first woken. In fact, she almost felt ready to go for a run around the station. And that type of exercise was normally the furthest thing from her mind.

Instead she kept her gaze locked on Davin's body. He really was the perfect man. Tall, broad shoulders, tight ass and a cock that could pleasure her until she didn't have the energy for another orgasm. He didn't take life too seriously but had been there for her when she'd needed him. How else would she have gotten out of the mine and back to med bay in one piece? He was her knight in shining armor.

As she shifted her body, Davin groaned and pulled her closer to him. The wonderful weight of his body sent a shiver of desire straight through to her pussy with such an alarming speed that Sara gasped. She'd been stuck unconscious in a bed god knew how long, weak from some sort of illness, and right now all she wanted to do was strip his body bare and ride him until she screamed from multiple orgasms.

Not really a bad idea.

Her body must have still been stuck on overload because another surge of arousal moved through her, this one so powerful she arched her body off the bed. The motion stirred Davin but didn't wake him. When he shifted, she felt his massive erection pressing against her leg. He moaned and pulled her even tighter against him.

"Davin?" Her voice was husky as his name rumbled from her.

He moaned, his hand sliding up her body to her breast, where he kneaded her sensitive skin. Her nipple instantly sprang to life, pebbling against his heat. As his touch brought her body to life, Sara began to feel a tingling building between them. It was different from before when they'd made love in his ship. The warm buzzing now held a degree of power to it, one that hadn't been there before.

"Wake up." She gave him a gentle shake and prayed he could hear her.

"No."

Relief was mixed with arousal when he shifted, lifting his handsome face to look at her.

"I think I'm ready to check out of here." She offered him a small smile. "I'm feeling better."

"Your doctor will be the one to make that decision. Not you." As he spoke, he flicked her nipple with his finger.

Sara closed her eyes, soaking up the erotic sensations he was sending into her. When he rolled her nipple between his thumb and forefinger, she let out a low moan.

"Who's my doctor? Get them the hell in here so I can leave."

"That would be..." He dropped his mouth to her breast and suckled her through the thin fabric for a moment before lifting his head again. "That would be me."

The shock was almost as powerful as her arousal. Davin slipped an arm around her waist and pulled her down on the mattress until his body hovered above hers. Heat was rolling off him and Sara felt it cover every inch of her. She gasped when he rolled his hips against her.

"But you're not...a doctor." She gave her head a little shake. "You wouldn't help back at the mine."

"I had a change of heart."

"Why?"

"You were sick."

It was then Sara felt her world begin to spin out of control. Davin lowered his head, inch by inch, down to her. His golden eyes were wide, steadily locked onto hers. She bit down on her lower lip, sending a small pulse of pain which did little to counteract her arousal.

"You seem different," she whispered when his mouth was only an inch from hers.

"I am different. It changes you."

"What does?"

"The gift."

Davin brought his mouth to hers, but neither of them closed their eyes. Their kiss was gentle, as if they were testing the feel of each other for the first time. And somehow it was different. Davin felt harder, somehow older than he was. She could feel him holding himself back.

They both stopped at the same time, Sara's mind spinning madly. She reached up and caressed the side of his cheek.

"Thank you."

Davin closed his eyes and smiled his lopsided smile. Sara ran her hand into his long hair, relishing the softness of it. Complete contrast to the feel of his body hard as steel.

"Now what happens?" she asked, almost afraid of the answer.

"We get you out of here. Then I finish the repairs on my ship and leave."

He said the words with such certainty, Sara would have accepted them as absolute if it wasn't for the fact he was breaking her heart.

"Why?" She leaned up and placed a single kiss on his closed lips. "You can stay here with me. I could use the help in med bay."

His hair fell over their faces, blocking the outside world from their view when he shook his head no.

"Why not?"

"It's complicated."

"Try me."

"Sara."

"No. You crashed into my life and turned it upside down. I'm doing things that I would never have done in a million years. Feeling things…and you're just going to walk away?"

His eyes were calm, steady and didn't betray a shred of emotion. "Yes."

The pain in her heart began to spread to the rest of her chest, squeezing the tears to her eyes. She tried to swallow past them. "Why?"

"I told you it's complicated."

"That's not an answer, Davin. Why the hell did you bother to save me if you're just going to fly out of my life again?"

He opened his mouth as if to answer but closed it. Instead he reached over, caught a curl of her blonde hair and twirled it around his finger. She waited, refusing to make this easy for him. He leaned forward and brushed his lips against her temple, placing light, feathery kisses along her cheek and along the ridge of her ear. When he finally spoke, Sara shivered as his hot breath teased the skin along her neck.

"I saved you because I couldn't imagine what the universe would be like without you in it."

A sob escaped her and Sara had to clamp her lips shut to stop any more from bubbling out. Her lips began to quake, so she closed her eyes and concentrated on keeping her emotions in check.

"You care so much for everyone around you. Do you know what the last four days have been like for me, sitting here waiting for you to wake? A constant flow of people coming in, making sure you're okay. People who love you, care for you as much as their own family. All because you give and give and never expect anything in return. And there I sat, never asking to be born a healer, never wanting this curse. I sat there and felt ashamed of myself for not being more like you."

She couldn't hold it in any longer. Sara sucked in a long, shuddering breath and let out a small cry as the tears slid down her cheek.

"I don't want you to go," she said in a tiny voice. "You can find another job. Work with Kamran. Just don't leave."

"I got word from Silas a few hours ago. My ship will be ready to fly in two days. I'm yours until then. Then I have to go."

"But I—" She stopped herself before she said the words. He didn't want her love, never told her that he did. She didn't want to trap him, guilt him into staying with her. There'd be no point.

She wanted a real relationship, not a hollow pretext of what their lives could be like.

"I wasn't going to leave until I knew you were better. But now…no, it's better this way," he said and pulled his face back so he was looking at her. "You'd grow to resent me over time. The fact I have this healing gift and won't use it."

"I wouldn't—"

"You would. I've seen it happen. My father never understood. Always pushed… You'd resent me given time."

"Davin. Please don't do this."

When he lifted his body from hers, Sara immediately missed his warmth. Her body still wanted him too, craved his naked skin against hers. He didn't look much better, his breath coming out in short, shallow puffs. His eyes did a final quick pass over her before he leaned down and kissed her forehead.

"I promise I'll give you everything you want for the next two days. Everything. But then I have to leave. Okay?"

She couldn't say anything, so she simply nodded.

"Good." He still didn't turn to leave. Instead he stood there, his hand balled at his side.

It wasn't until they heard the gentle hiss of the isolation door opening that they looked away from each other.

"I thought I heard talking in here," Haylie's happy voice seemed too loud in the small room. She strode over to Sara and clamped her arms around her in a fierce hug.

"I'll leave you to your visit," Davin said, his voice emotionless.

"I didn't mean to interrupt," Haylie started.

Davin held up his hand and smiled. "Enjoy your visit. I'll let Rachael know you're ready to go home."

"Thanks, Davin." Haylie grinned at Sara once he left. "Who knew our shady captain was a gentleman. No wonder you're…hey what's wrong?" Haylie reached out and brushed the stream of tears from Sara's face.

"He's leaving in two days." Sara was surprised when her voice came out steady, almost calm.

"What? We figured with everything that had happened, I mean he's been here day and night…" Haylie's words trickled off and she shook her head.

"He's promised me two days of whatever I want. Two days of bliss until he steps back on his ship and flies the hell out of here."

Haylie sat on the edge of her bed, grabbed Sara's hand and gave it a squeeze. "That's two days you can use to change his mind."

"He said I'd resent him because he won't use his gift."

"Ah."

"The sad thing is, he's probably right. To have that kind of ability and never use it, to watch people die when you had the power to save them. After a while, I'd get tired of it all and ask him to help and then demand it. He'd grow to hate me."

"Sara, you wouldn't do that."

"Wouldn't I? Wouldn't you? What if it was Kamran lying there dying or your baby? Wouldn't you want Davin to save them if he could? Wouldn't you hate him for not trying?"

Haylie sighed and nodded. "You're right, I probably would. But he can't run from who he is. I tried that myself, remember."

"Trying to hide a photographic memory isn't the same thing as being able to cure a dying person."

"No? How many times would people get nervous around me when I would visit them? I couldn't read anything without people wondering if I was going to use it against them later on. No, it wasn't life or death, but it took me a long time to see it as a gift. Especially when every instinct out there told me it was a pain in the ass I never wanted."

Sara looked at her friend who was more of a sister and sighed. "So what do I do?"

"It seems he needs you. It's your turn to save him."

Chapter Ten

The quiet in Sara's living quarters was starting to get on her nerves. She'd been free of med bay for little more than four hours and the inactivity was already pushing her limits of self control. Her uniform was sitting on the bed behind her, but she had no intention of putting it on today. Going back to work was the last thing she planned to do. No, sitting on the floor, trying to figure out what the hell she could do was the only thing she wanted to concern herself with right now.

Two days to change his mind.

She'd tried to sleep when she'd first returned to her quarters, get some much needed rest. But it had completely backfired. She'd dreamed about Davin. When her mind had finally drifted off, she realized she was standing back on the beach on Earth. Her fantasy lover had come up behind her, wrapped his arms around her waist and pulled her back against his chest.

Closing her eyes now, she could hear his private whispers.

"I want you so bad," his deep voice purred in her ear.

Sara had moaned and stretched her arms up to circle his neck. Rubbing her ass against his hard cock drew a moan out of both of them.

"Fuck me," she whispered.

His firm hands slid up her body to cup her breasts through the thin fabric of her dress. In a blink, her clothing was gone and his rough fingers captured her nipples between them.

"Turn around and face me," he said, tugging at the swollen nipples.

A thrill raced through her body and she pressed her ass even harder against him. "I can't—"

"Sara."

He tugged at her breasts once more before turning her around. Instinctively, she closed her eyes. She didn't want to see the face of her fantasy lover, needed to keep her dream safe from the reality that threatened to take it over.

His breath was warm and smelled of exotic spices as it tickled her cheek. When he chuckled, she could feel the deep rumble against her breasts. Sara tightened her grip around his neck, pulling herself up, closer to his face.

"Kiss me," she begged, needing to feel him.

"I can't. I'm not real."

"Please."

"Open your eyes and then I'll kiss you."

When she didn't do as he asked, her fantasy lover chuckled again. "Coward."

Annoyance flashed through her, even asleep, and Sara knew she couldn't give in. Slowly, she opened her eyes. Instead of looking directly at his face, she focused her attention on the hollow of his throat. She watched as the powerful muscles moved when he swallowed.

"Look at me," he said again.

Unable to put it off anymore, Sara shifted her gaze up. Over his chin, along his strong cheekbones and nose, to look into a pair of eyes that reminded her of a reptile.

Davin's.

"That's my girl," he whispered.

But when he bent his head to kiss her, Davin suddenly faded from her. Sara immediately missed his warmth, and let out a cry. She'd kept crying until she woke from her sleep.

Two days.

Stretching out her legs proved to be more of a challenge than she'd anticipated after sitting there for so long. Her muscles were still constricted from having been in bed for three days, and being immobile on the floor wasn't helping.

God, what a waste. That was time she could have had with Davin, used it to change his mind about staying with her. She let out a sigh and tried to lean forward enough to work out the kinks in her back.

Sooner or later she was going to have to get dressed and find him. And while she had no doubt that seeing her in her undergarments would be a turn-on for him, that wasn't how she wanted to start things. Oh no, she was going to go slow, drag things out until he was begging for it, begging for her. So much so that by the time he was ready to leave Eurus, he wouldn't be able to do it.

With deliberate, easy movements, Sara pulled herself up to her feet and had to wait for a minute until a wave of dizziness passed her. Once it did, she took careful steps toward the large mirror that hung along the side wall of her bedroom. Her body was thinner than it had been the last time she'd looked, and not in a good way. The parasite in her system had invaded her body through cut on her thigh and proceeded to eat its way through her body fat and start in on her muscles. Rachael had said they couldn't pick it up on any of the med bay computers until Davin had managed to lead them to it. She would have died within hours if he hadn't have helped her.

She pushed aside thoughts of his healing gift and started to get dressed. Ignoring her bra, Sara slipped a blood-red, tight-fitting sleeveless top over her breasts. The collar covered her neck, framing the V that exposed an ample amount of cleavage for Davin to drool over. Next, she slipped into a long black skirt that clung to her hips and ass, accentuating the few curves she had left.

She wanted her hair down and had to fight the brush through the tangles that had developed since her shower. When she was finished, the long blonde strands shone as they hung in loose curls on her shoulders and down her back. This was as good as things would get.

Two days.

Sara slipped on a pair of sandals she'd brought with her from Earth but hadn't had an opportunity to wear at this point. They felt odd on her feet after having worn nothing but boots for a year. Before she had a chance to chicken out, she marched out of her quarters and made her way down the corridor to the section where Davin's guest quarters were located.

The bright morning sun shone through the corridor windows, fueling her body for the mission she'd set out to accomplish. She wasn't about to let him get away from her that easily. As long as her body cooperated, Sara planned on showing Davin exactly what he'd be missing if he left her.

But when she finally made it to his door, she couldn't move. The muscles in her arms refused to cooperate, paralyzed by uncertainty. Wasn't she being selfish? He had his reasons for turning his back on this gift, and regardless of what she thought of them, they were valid.

Fuck it.

The computer made a soft chiming noise when she tapped her fingers over the key pad. The silence that seemed to stretch forever was only a few minutes. She tapped the key pad again, and tried to ignore her frustration and growing doubts. Finally, a muted rustling sound reached her as the doors whooshed open.

She could tell by the look on Davin's face he had been asleep and was about to yell at the person who'd disturbed him. But the look on his face softened when his golden gaze touched her face. Sara stood with her hands clasped behind her back as he inspected her outfit.

"You look beautiful," his gravelly morning voice rumbled out of him.

"You look like hell," she said and tried to keep the grin from her face. "I'm assuming I woke you."

"Haven't slept much in the past three days."

She ignored the hot flush that crept onto her face. "I suppose I should thank you for taking such good care of me."

Davin shrugged and leaned his large frame against the open doorway. He wasn't wearing a shirt and the tight-fitting black shorts highlighted every muscle and bulge on his lower body. It made her mouth water for sex, knowing that when they came together it would be explosive. A shiver of wanting passed straight through to her pussy and the wetness began to pool between her thighs.

"May I come in or do we have to have this conversation in the corridor?"

His cock clearly twitched in his shorts as it began to grow. Davin kept his eyes locked on hers as he leaned forward, hanging the weight of his body from either side of the doorway with his hands.

"You know where this is going to lead if you come in here."

She raised her eyebrows and gave him what she hoped was a bored expression. "Do I look like I was anticipating another outcome?"

Sara felt her nipples tighten when his gaze moved to her breasts. And unlike before, she did nothing to hide her obvious signs of arousal from him. Taking a step, she moved into the circle of heat his body was projecting, moving her face very close to his. Instead of kissing his full lips, she turned her head and placed a kiss on the inside of his biceps. She traced the line of the muscle with her tongue, savoring the flavor that was uniquely Davin as she went. When she turned her face back to his, she could see he was grinding his teeth, his body shaking from the strain of controlling his body.

"Can...I...come...in?"

Sara let out a yelp when his arms came around her waist and Davin yanked her into the room. He held her arms high above her head, pressed her whole body flat against the wall. His thigh went between hers, pressing her long skirt in so it pulled tight against her hips and ass.

Their breathing came out in gasps, matching their frantic rhythm until they were sharing the same air in the small space between them. Davin's cock was fully erect and pressing into her stomach. Knowing how aroused he was only served to ratchet her body higher.

"Sorry I woke you up," she whispered before she leaned in and swiped her tongue over his closed lips. "But I really didn't want to waste any of my time with you."

"You still haven't recovered fully. I don't want—"

"This has nothing to do with what you want. You gave me a deadline. Two days. I plan on making the most of the time I have with you. So if you don't shut up and kiss me—"

Davin crushed his mouth to hers, sucking the air from her lungs. Sara sighed and tugged against his iron hold of her wrists. She wanted to touch him, taste every part of his body. She wanted him to fuck her so hard she'd scream herself raw from the force of her orgasms. But he wouldn't let her move. His tongue invaded her mouth, mimicking what she wanted him doing with his cock. She squirmed against his thigh that was pressed against her cunt. She was so wet she could feel her juices flowing down her thighs, only to be absorbed by her skirt. When he finally pulled back, Sara moaned, panting as she tried to stop her world from spinning out of control.

"Do you want this?" His harsh tone was undercut by the grinding of his cock against her belly.

"Oh god, Davin, yes"

He moved his hand so both her wrists were held by one, freeing the other to explore her body. He traced a gentle path with his fingers down her cheek and along her shoulder. When he reached her hair, he captured a long strand and brought it to his mouth. She watched as he rubbed it against his lips and over his chin.

"So soft. Just like your sweet body."

He took the hair and rubbed it against her throat, teasing the skin above her cleavage. Getting close to his destination, Davin dropped the curl when it no longer reached and let his fingers continue their exploration.

"You wore this for me. You know how much I love your breasts. Don't you?"

Sara didn't answer, instead closing her eyes and reveling in the sensations of her body. His fingers were wicked as he teased her. Tiny electric pulses moved through her, making her grind her pussy hard against him. When he suddenly stopped, Sara moaned.

"I asked if you wore this for me."

"Yes. Just for you."

His hand was back, this time slipping under the edge of her shirt collar to caress the warm skin underneath. He trailed light touches along the top of her breast, and with each pass got lower and lower, closer to her painfully erect nipple.

"Fuck, you're so wet for me. If I put my cock in you right now you'd come, wouldn't you?"

Sara bit her bottom lip and nodded frantically, her eyes squeezed shut.

"That's my girl. I bet I could make you come without my cock. I bet I could suck your beautiful breasts until you screamed my name. Should I? Should I do that for you?"

She couldn't think anymore. Her brain had shut down while her body ran on instinct. So when she felt his hand reach for the hem of her shirt and tug it up until her breast was exposed to the cool air of his quarters, all she could do was hold on for her sanity's sake.

Davin's hot tongue darted out and swiped over her nipple. Her whole body jolted, but he kept her from moving too far. After a few seconds he repeated the motion and Sara thought she would die from the contact. Her body began to tremble as she tried to anticipate when he'd touch her next. Again and again his tongue darted out, licking and teasing her senseless. Finally, his fingers reached out and gripped her breast, pushing her erect bud even farther out. When he moved his face closer this time, Davin sucked her nipple hard into his mouth and Sara cried out.

"Too much," she gasped and ground her clit against his thigh.

But he pulled his leg just far enough away so that she couldn't ease the burning in her pussy. Instead, he increased the pressure on her nipple and madly flicked his tongue over it.

"Not enough," he spoke the hot words against her breast once he lifted his head. "You need more."

"Your cock, please."

He chuckled but moved his head to her other breast. His mouth and tongue increased in speed on the fresh nipple while his fingers rolled the wet one. Sara couldn't breathe as her cream flowed out of her body, the scent of her arousal permeating the air around them.

His expert touch and unrelenting attention were more than her overcharged body could handle. She felt the orgasm start low and deep in her body, like a trickle of water that preceded a dam break. The rush of pleasure quickly overwhelmed her senses, blinding her sight, making her deaf until all she could feel was the rip of pleasure through her body. Sara cried out his name as her body thrashed, caught between his body and the wall. As the last wave rolled through her body, she lost the ability to stand and fell limp against him.

Davin lowered her arms and draped them lightly on either side of his head. He buried his face in her hair and drew in a deep breath of his own.

"You are so beautiful," he said on a sigh.

Sara let her hand slide down the front of his body until she found his rock-hard erection straining through the front of his shorts. He was so big, she couldn't stop the shiver of anticipation that shimmered through her, knowing how fully he filled her body.

"You're not so bad yourself," she said and chuckled when his cock twitched in her hand. "Do you plan on keeping me against the wall for two days or would you like to find the bed?"

Davin let out a low growl that seemed to echo deep inside her body. When she lifted her head to meet his eyes, they seemed to be glowing.

"Davin?"

His hand captured the back of her knee and pulled her leg up, opening her body to him. Sara felt her skirt slide down her leg, exposing her bare skin and giving him a perfect view of her soaked pussy. Not that he was looking anywhere but her eyes at the moment. Davin leaned in, pressing his powerful cock against her, with only the thin barrier of her panties and his shorts between them.

"Right…here." He said the words with deliberate slowness, his hand flexing against her leg.

Before she had a chance to react, Davin used his other hand to pull at the thin fabric of her panties. The tearing of the cloth was an instant turn-on and Sara felt herself gush with anticipation. After several tugs, he ripped through one side and let the panties slip to the floor. With her now completely open to him, Davin took advantage and slid his fingers along her warm, inner thigh.

Sara couldn't believe her body's reaction to his touch. She was already wet again, another orgasm threatening to push through her body again. *Too soon.* As Davin's fingers teased the curls of her pussy, Sara moved her hand inside his shorts so she could feel the hot length of his cock in her hand.

This time when she touched him, Davin closed his eyes and moaned his approval. His groin thrust against the palm of her hand, mimicking what he wanted to do to her. And holy fuck if she didn't want him inside her now. No, she needed to go slow. Enjoy each and every touch of his body. She had no time to waste.

Leaning in, Sara licked his earlobe and around the ridge of his ear. "I want to taste you."

Davin pushed his fingers against the opening of her cunt, wetting them with her cream. When he brought them out, he licked every drop of her wetness from his fingers. Sara sucked in a breath and couldn't believe how erotic it was to watch him do that.

When he finished, he grinned at her. "Seemed only fair."

He dropped her leg slowly to the floor but didn't move his hand from her inner thigh, teasing her. Sara wasn't about to let herself get distracted by his wicked hand. Instead, she grabbed him by the arms and spun him around so his back was pressed against the wall. As they stopped moving, she reached in and licked his nipple.

"Fuck!"

"It's only fair," she chuckled and repeated the motion.

"You're going to kill me."

"You'll enjoy it, then."

Sara dropped to her knees in front of his black shorts. The material was form fitting, so his swollen cock was held tight against his body. Inhaling deeply, she enjoyed the rush of his scent as she gently pulled his shorts down.

His cock sprang free and Sara caught herself moaning. His balls were pulled tight against his body and she could see they were a dark gold color. With her head buzzing, she leaned in and ran her tongue along the bottom of his balls, enjoying the feel and taste of his hairless sac. She paid particular attention there, lapping up every inch of skin while ignoring his pulsating shaft. It wasn't until she felt his hands come into her hair that she knew it was time to move on.

She ran her tongue up the length of his cock until she reached the tip. The satiny skin was amazing in her mouth, tasting like a bittersweet spice. Sara couldn't stop, didn't want to give up on the heady sensations that were running through her. Leaning forward, she took as much of his shaft into her mouth as she could manage while gently massaging his balls with her hand. Davin's grip instantly tightened as his body shook. He was so close, she could feel it.

"Sara…"

He tugged at her head, but she refused to move. Increasing the pressure of her fingers along his balls, she picked up the pace of her sucking. She wanted to taste him, all of him. Wanted to swallow the most intimate part of his body, his very essence and keep it with her forever.

"Sara, I can't stop," he said in a shallow gasp as his thighs began to twitch uncontrollably.

Rising up high on her knees, Sara began to stroke his shaft in time with her bobbing head. Somehow, his cock seemed to thicken in her mouth and Sara knew what was about to happen. Davin roared as his hot cum flowed into her mouth with powerful spurts. Sara swallowed repeatedly, savoring the spicy taste of him until she'd licked him dry.

With a surprise rush of energy, Sara gasped when Davin picked her up and carried her over to the bed. He dropped her down on the mattress before reaching down and yanking her skirt all the way off.

"More," he growled.

"We can wait. If you need to rest—"

"More."

She lay still as he stripped the rest of her clothing from her body, watching the intense expression on his face. His golden gaze flying over every inch of her skin, his fingers touching everywhere his eyes weren't. Sara couldn't stand it, her body shivering from the heat her body was producing. When he pushed her thighs wide apart and buried his face between her legs, she cried out.

"Tastes amazing." He said the words against her clit and licked again, only slower.

"Davin."

A final lick and he began to kiss his way up her body, across her belly, along the edge of her ribs, over the tips of her breasts until he reached her neck. She could feel his heavy cock was already growing stiff again as he humped her thigh. When his hot mouth reached her neck, she arched her back, giving him complete access. He opened his mouth and nipped at her shoulder, sending a jolt of electricity to her cunt. Her hips jerked in response, her hands clawing at his wide shoulders.

"With my people, sex is…frantic." He nipped at her again. "I've been holding back."

She shivered, remembering the few times they'd made love. If he'd been holding back, then she wanted to see everything.

"Don't," she whispered. "I want to be everything for you."

His heavy head pressed against her shoulder. "I don't want to hurt you."

"You won't."

"You don't know that."

"You only gave me two days. I want to know everything, be everything for you. Don't…hold…back."

Davin gripped her wrists and held them out to her sides. His body weight was supported on this knees and forearms. Without touching himself, he maneuvered his cock at the opening of her damp pussy but didn't thrust forward. His gaze trapped hers and she suddenly felt a low burning deep in her belly. Unlike the warm buzzing last time, the heat began to pulse from the very center of her womb, jacking her arousal as high as it could go. Her heavy lids slid shut as her body melted with pleasure.

"I can feel you. Your whole body, inside and out. You're so beautiful." He thrust forward and swallowed her cry of pleasure with a deep kiss.

The burning desire crept into every cell in her body. She could feel the heat as it moved along with her blood, bringing light to the dark parts of her body. Relaxing, she let the sensations fill her. The tingle combined with the steady thrusts of his cock in her cunt took Sara to new heights of pleasure. The simple act of breathing was arousing.

"*Joun talla*, you're amazing."

"Just...don't stop."

She relaxed even more, feeling the pulsing heat move through her chest and up into her neck. A million tiny invisible fingers caressed the skin of her back, touching her from her shoulders down to teasing the puckered entrance of her ass.

When she opened her eyes, she realized with a sudden jolt they weren't working. But the terrifying blackness was suddenly replaced with a crystal clear image of what she wanted Davin to do to her. His body slamming into hers from behind, her back pressed firmly against his chest. It wasn't like any thought she'd had before, but rather like watching a vid screen. Sara sucked in a shuddering breath and arched up so hard against him that Davin cried out.

"My God, what is...what am I seeing?" she said as she clawed at his shoulders.

"Your desires. Is that what you want, Sara? You want me to fuck you from behind?"

Her blood pounded in her ears at the thought of him doing exactly that. "Oh yes."

Davin was off her and pulling her to her knees in a heartbeat. She had to give her head a shake to clear the mental image of what he was about to do to her from her mind. It was then she realized he'd positioned their bodies so she could see their reflection in the long mirror on the opposite wall.

Her pale white skin and blonde hair were in stark contrast to Davin's dark gold complexion and long brown strands that framed his face. She watched as he pushed her thighs apart so he could settle his long, thick cock at the entrance of her pussy. Sara couldn't look away, memorizing every detail of how their bodies fit together. When he thrust deep inside her, Sara could see her body shudder, watched her nipples tighten even more and saw the dark blush as it spread from her face down her neck to cover her breasts.

Davin caught her gaze in the mirror and leaned down to whisper in her ear. "You are the most beautiful woman I've ever seen. You have nothing to be ashamed of."

As if to drive his point home, he ground his groin to her, pushing into her pussy with hard, sure strokes. The rush of excitement at watching her body get thoroughly fucked was more than she could handle. His grip was firm as he pulled at her nipples. ‚Pleasure mixed with pain, overwhelming and pushed her over the edge into oblivion. Sara reached up and held on to Davin's neck for dear life as the orgasm took over. When she didn't think she had anything left in her, Davin's body shuddered as he cried out before he bit down on her neck again. His frantic thrusts as he came, and the now familiar sensation of his bite, sent another ripple of pleasure through her until there was nothing left.

Unable to hold her body up any longer, Sara let Davin pull her body down to the bed. The air in his quarters was cool but felt nice on her sweat-slicked skin. She snuggled in close to his body and hoped this was only the beginning of their pleasure for the next two days. With her energy reserves quickly spent, Sara drifted off to sleep.

* * * * *

Davin knew the moment Sara was asleep. It wasn't because her body relaxed against his or even the deep, steady sound of her breathing. No, he knew because he'd been able to slip into her mind when they'd made love. And a connection like that was a hard one to break.

Pulling her even tighter against him, he tried to ignore the guilt that began to gnaw at the edges of his mind. Of all the people out there, Sara was the last one he wanted to hurt. And while she wouldn't feel any ill effects from his invasion, he knew she would be angry.

But by *Maltil,* she had a beautiful mind. To actually see images like he had was rare. The few times he'd entered another's mind to help them heal, the mental pain and anguish had been black, cold, not a place he wanted to be again. Repairing another's mind, the ability to fix the dark places in their soul, were gifts according to his people. Not that Davin considered them such. So many of the healers in his cast wanted the gift, would do anything to be branded with the sacred tattoos on their hands that acknowledged the power. And he'd been the one *blessed.* The marks had burned as they'd been permanently inked onto his hands when he'd first displayed the ability. A fucking curse. One he'd been trying to run away from since he reached the age of maturity.

Now that he'd opened the barrier that kept his abilities back, there'd be no stopping it. The urge to help others would be overpowering and soon people would seek him out, begging him to assist. And after time, there'd be little left of him. His mind would be consumed by the darkness of others until he was a breathing shell.

Just like his mother had been.

Sara sighed and snuggled deep against his chest. He picked up a strand of her hair and twirled it around his finger. He couldn't do that to her. She'd figure out what was going on and would want to try to save him. But she wouldn't be able to and she'd die a little more every day she watched him fall apart.

At least his father had been cold enough, removed enough from his emotions that when his mother died, he'd considered it an honor. Fuck, he'd been proud of the fact his dead wife was a *Mise*—soul healer. That's why Davin had run. He knew his father would push him to the same fate.

Well, fuck that.

He'd give Sara her two days and then he'd find a job that took his crew to the edges of the galaxy where he could fade away.

Chapter Eleven

Sara's growling stomach was the first thing she heard when she returned to the land of the living. But moving was the very last thing she had on her mind. Davin's arms as well at his heavenly scent were wrapped around her, better than the best blanket in the world. Being this close to him was a powerful temptation. His brown chest hair seemed even darker against his golden skin, giving him an exotic, definitely alien look.

God, she loved him.

The realization was painful, considering that he continued to push her away. For the life of her, she couldn't figure out why. If she knew, there might be someway she could convince him it didn't matter. She wanted him regardless of what problem he thought they had.

She was tired of being alone.

"We need to get some food into you, wild one. You're going to need your strength."

When he kissed the top of her head, she sighed. She reached in and kissed his chest, rubbing her nose against his skin as she did.

"Too bad we can't get delivery. I really don't want to move."

"Delivery? You think I'd let anyone but me see you naked after what we just did? I'd be forced to kill them. And I don't think Haylie would approve."

"Oh my god, poor Haylie. She's pregnant and I've barely had time to run a scan on her and the baby. I need to get to med bay soon and look after her."

The fact she'd forgotten, even for a moment, about Haylie made her feel guilty.

"I wouldn't worry. Your friend is strong. I don't think there is much out there she can't handle."

"True. And now that she's bonded to Kamran, I don't have to worry about her quite so much."

Davin brushed her hair away from her face and placed a kiss on her temple. "You do that a lot."

"What?"

"Worry about other people. It will kill you if you let it rule your life."

Something about the way he said it made Sara cock her head back so she could look at his face. "Sounds like you're speaking from experience."

She felt him grind his teeth for a minute before he took a breath and forced his body to relax.

"My mother was a healer, like me. She pushed herself too much, taking on everyone's ills as her own. It was too much for her and she died."

"I'm sorry," she said and placed a kiss on his chin. "Were you very young?"

"I hadn't reached the age of maturity. I'd spent my youth idolizing her and her death...hurt."

"Both of my parents are alive and kicking back on Earth. But I haven't seen them in years. We moved to Luna when I was a kid for my dad's job and I stayed for medical school. Haylie was the first person I met."

"Your parents must miss you."

She shrugged. "When I got this posting, they were very proud. My dad had something to brag about and my mom knew I'd found a purpose. They're older and were worried that I'd be left alone if anything ever happened to them. At least I've made a life for myself here."

Sara hadn't talked to her parents in over a month now and she suddenly missed them very much. She couldn't imagine what it would be like to lose one of them now, let alone as a kid.

Her stomach chose that moment to let out another loud grumble. It was accompanied with a twinge of pain and she knew she wasn't going to be able to ignore the sensation much longer.

"Food," Davin said in a teasing voice. "My primal warrior instincts are kicking in. My mate needs me to hunt for sustenance."

Her giggle shook them both. "Well, this is one girl who can help with the gathering. But it means we need to get up."

"And get dressed. Remember the murder thing."

"Yes, we don't want to put Haylie to work. Though I think she'd enjoy it."

When Davin released his grip on her, Sara rolled away from his body and instantly missed it. They'd get some food and eat on their way back here. She didn't want to move from this bed for the rest of the day. Davin must have been thinking the same thing because when he met her eyes, they flared with lust.

"Just like a supply drop on Tannas. In and out before anyone knows we're there."

"And then back to bed?"

"We'll bring supplies back with us."

Sara shivered but made sure to grin back at him with as much desire as she felt at that moment. "I think I like that idea."

They both dressed quickly, Sara enjoying the privilege of watching him choose his clothing. Who knew that simply watching him do such a simple thing would mean so much to her.

He finished dressing, sliding his belt over his black, form-fitting pants and pulling a tight blue sleeveless shirt on. Only then did he turn to her and grin. "Doctor, might I have the honor of escorting you to lunch?"

He waited, holding out his arm while she stared at him. What the hell was she going to do when he left?

"The honor is all mine, Captain."

They walked out together toward the bazaar, arms linked. It was strange, but she felt completely at ease at that moment. The parasite might have threatened to kill her, but in the end it had given her a great gift. As her thoughts drifted back to the mine, she found herself frowning.

"Did they ever figure out where I picked up that parasite? I'd hate for anyone else to catch it."

As she said the word "parasite", Davin tugged her arm a bit closer to his body. "We're not sure. But where it entered your body through a cut in your leg, it means they'll have to keep a close eye on everyone. The medics who conducted the physicals on the miners didn't detect any further infections but that doesn't mean much. Mind you, it might have been bad luck that it happened to get into your system."

"Let's hope. Did you talk to Kamran about the men we heard talking?"

Davin stopped walking and looked at her. "It didn't cross my mind to mention it."

"They were obviously doing something illegal. Maybe even had something to do with the stocolran gel. Kamran should know."

"At the time I was a bit preoccupied with you being sick. But I promise you I'll let him know as soon as we get back to my room." He gave her arm a tug. "Are we going to eat or do you want to interrogate me further, Doctor?"

"Sorry. I hate not knowing what's going on." She gave him a shy smile. "I've always been nosy."

"And clumsy. Haylie and I shared some entertaining tales. She wasn't at all surprised to hear you knocked me into the water."

Sara felt a blush heat her face. "You didn't tell her about what we did, did you?"

He gave her a wide grin. "We best get you some food."

"Oh I hate you," she muttered as she let him continue to lead her toward the bazaar. "She'll never let me live that down."

They continued their banter as they waited in line at one of the booths. One of the humans had set up a Luna Cuisine shop and Sara picked out several dishes she figured Davin would enjoy. All spicy with added kick. Sara didn't wait for them to get back to his room before she started eating. So when Rachael found them in the hall, she had to swallow a large bite before she could answer.

"What's up?" Sara managed after a minute of intense chewing.

Rachael looked between Davin and Sara, looking like she was about to ruin their day.

"I know you're still not fully recovered, hon, but I think we have a major problem."

Sara's hunger was instantly forgotten. "What's wrong? Haylie?"

"No, she's fine. But I think the miners aren't. I re-ran some of the blood work the medics took two days ago. It's contaminated."

"The parasite?" Davin asked, clearly not happy about where this was going.

"I ran it twice. The parasites have doubled since the initial sample was taken. And it's just not one or two of them. Everyone."

"Oh my god," she muttered.

"Show us." Davin took Sara's arm as they made their way to med bay.

* * * * *

When Sara lifted her face from the cell scanner, she bit back a curse. It was exactly what Rachael had said, the parasite was consuming the blood. And the more it ate, the faster the process.

"These men are going to be dead if we don't do something," she said as she turned around.

Kamran, Haylie and Sean were standing around all looking as if someone had died. Which would soon be the case if they couldn't figure out how to stop this.

"I want to run a full workup on you, Sean." She brought over a needle and motioned for him to sit on the bed. "Have you felt anything odd? Dizzy?"

Sean sat down and rolled up his sleeve. "Nothing. I feel the same as the day I went in there."

"So why the hell did it affect Sara so quickly?" Haylie blew out a breath. "You'd think we'd have seen a pile of cases before now."

"Depends on the source," Kamran said and looped an arm around Haylie's waist. "Maybe Sara went somewhere in the mine that Sean hadn't. Came into contact with it there."

"Or came into contact with someone," Sean muttered.

Sara's gaze flew to his when she recognized what he was implying. "Davin has nothing to do with this."

"He's an alien. There could be something about his body chemistry that started this."

"It's not me," Davin said as he strode into the room.

Sara saw that he had his gloves back on covering the tattoos on his hands. He was dressed much as he had been on the day he crashed, except now his hair was tied back at the nape of his neck.

"He's right," Sara said as she finished drawing blood from Sean's arm. "We ran tests on Davin. The parasite hasn't appeared in his system at all. Which is odd because we were in most of the same places together."

"I have a natural immunity to most diseases. I doubt it found my blood tasty."

Davin walked over to Sara and stood close without touching. She felt her body instantly react, a painful reminder that he'd be leaving as soon as Kamran lifted the quarantine.

"Sit here a minute until I check this out." She patted Sean on the knee.

"I'm all yours, Doc," Sean said on a sigh.

Walking over to the cell scanner, Sara tried to push away the torrent of emotions that had built up in her. Just seeing Davin, knowing that their relationship was about to fall apart was killing her. She silently cursed when her hands shook as she placed several drops of blood on the glass slide and pressed it into the scanner.

"This will only take a minute."

Kamran walked over to one of the chairs, Haylie in tow, and sat down. He pulled her into his lap despite her weak protest struggles. Sara heard her friend's contented sigh as she dropped her head to her husband's shoulder.

"This is going to take a minute," she said on impulse. "Haylie, why don't I run a quick scan on you since you're here? Just to see how things are progressing."

"I'm fine," Haylie shrugged. "I've just been a little tired."

"Humor your doctor. Now get your ass in the other room so I can run my tests."

Haylie rolled her eyes. "I hate physicals."

"Too bad. Move your ass, Chief."

Kamran chuckled and gave her a little push to get her going. "Never argue with your doctor."

The two women went into the side room and Sara pointed at a small bed. "Up you go."

"Did I mention you are as bad as Kamran?" Haylie sighed and hopped up.

"And lucky for you that I am. I want to make sure this little one is going to be okay. Lie down."

Haylie swung her legs around and settled her head on the thin pillow. For no reason, she let out a giggle before she managed to get things under control.

"Tell that husband of yours to behave."

"Oh believe me, I've tried." Haylie took a deep breath, closed her eyes and seemed to go into a little trance. When she opened them a minute later, she looked at Sara and smiled. "There. I've bought us a little privacy."

Sara smiled, shaking her head. "Nice trick."

"When you're sharing head space with another person, you have to learn to put a little wall up." Haylie reached over and squeezed Sara's hand. "I figured from the look on your face there was more to this than you wanting to check out the baby. Am I right?"

The sudden sting of emotion as it bit the back of her throat and burned her eyes was almost too much for Sara to hold back. A quick look over her shoulder and she caught Davin talking quietly to Kamran and Sean. She pulled the privacy curtain blocking him from sight.

"What's wrong, hon?" Haylie said sitting up. "Did he do something?"

Sara turned back and smiled as a single tear rolled down her cheek. "He's leaving tomorrow. As soon as his ship is ready and Kamran lifts the quarantine order."

"Oh sweetie. Come here."

Haylie wrapped Sara in a hug and she couldn't stop the tears. Silently they poured out of her and onto Haylie's uniform. After a minute she pulled back, wiping the tears from her face.

"Sorry," she said in a choked whisper.

"For what? I think you're allowed to be a little emotional." Haylie shook her head. "But I doubt he'll be out of here tomorrow. Not until you can figure out how this parasite is spreading. Kamran won't risk it getting passed on to another colony."

"So it takes another day or two. Maybe a week. He'll leave as soon as he can." Sara turned and picked up the medical scanner, running it over Haylie's body. After a minute it chirped, indicating everything was fine with both Haylie and the baby. "At least you didn't catch it."

"Sara, look at me," Haylie squeezed her hand. "What happened between you? I thought you were going to try to convince him to stay."

"I think," she swallowed past a lump in her throat. "I think he's scared of his ability to heal. His mother could heal others and she died."

"Shit." Haylie sighed. "I can appreciate how much that will mess you up."

"But I think it's more than that. I just haven't figured it out yet."

"Well talk to him. Kamran can keep the quarantine in place for a while at least. Maybe we can buy you some time."

Sara leaned in and gave her friend a fierce hug. "I appreciate that."

"Anything for you. I know what it's like to love someone and feel trapped by circumstances you can't control. And you do love him."

Sara pulled back and nodded. "Everything just seems to be happening so fast."

"At least it's been a couple weeks for you. I only had a few hours to figure things out when they happened between me and Kamran." Haylie pushed a strand of Sara's hair away from her face. "Look, let's figure out about this parasite first. Then we can beat some sense into your captain after."

"Yes, Chief."

"Excellent. We better get back out there. My mate is getting impatient with me blocking him from my mind."

When they emerged from the side room, Kamran immediately stood and made his way to Haylie's side. Before he had a chance to do anything, Sara wrapped her arms around him and gave him a hug.

"Thanks," she whispered.

"For you, anything. Now," he looked at Haylie and smiled when he was finally able to put his arm around his wife. "I believe the scanner is done."

"Thanks."

Sara walked over to the cell scanner only to find Davin quickly at her side.

"What was that about?" his whisper was harsh at her ear.

"What?"

"Hugging Kamran."

"A personal matter." Her whisper took on a hard edge. "You don't want to be a part of my life so what does it matter to you?" She pounded her fingers hard against the computer panel. "Sean, you're infected too. But only a few of the parasites seem to be there. Like you only recently came in contact with the source."

"Probably at the same time you were hit." Sean ran his hand through his hair. "It could be fucking anything in that place."

"Or they could have been dormant until recently. Or simply dying out. God only knows at this point."

"This is going to take a while," Davin said, his voice grim.

"First thing, we need to get them out of your body before they start to spread. It won't take them long to multiply." She picked up a syringe and walked over to where Sean sat. "Based on the tests I've run, I think this might help. But I haven't tested it on a sample yet, let alone a living person."

"Shoot me up." He held out his arm.

"Are you sure?" It didn't feel right to her testing a theory on Sean before knowing the side effects.

"There are men in those mines who could be dead before those tests are done. Just shoot me up and we'll deal."

She felt Davin suck in a breath, as if he was about to say something. But when she looked up at him, he closed his half-open mouth and shrugged.

"Okay, Sean. I want you to lie down."

Sara took a breath and pressed the syringe to his arm. She hoped the amber-colored antibodies produced by the computer would take care of the parasites. They all stood there waiting as Sean lay on the bed staring at the ceiling.

"So how will we know if it's working?" Davin asked after the silence seemed to fill the air.

"I'll run some blood work again in twenty minutes. That should give it enough time to reach most of the parasites." Sara turned to look at Haylie and Kamran. "Why don't you head back? I'll let you know once we have some news."

Kamran nodded and looked directly at Sean. "Get better. I have a feeling I'm going to need your help with this one."

Sean didn't respond verbally but nodded once. Once they left, Sean let out a long breath.

"No pressure there, man," he muttered.

"I think he wanted you to know he still trusts you," Davin said sauntering over to the chair. "Not a bad thing, is it?"

She didn't quite hear what Sean muttered, but it sounded something like, *I don't deserve it*.

The trio waited in relative silence for time to pass. Sara did her best to ignore Davin's gaze as it followed her around the isolation room. She was acutely aware of him, how he held his body, his scent as she moved around him. This was going to drive her crazy. Needing something to do, Sara grabbed the syringe and drew some of Sean's blood.

"It hasn't been twenty minutes," Davin said in his teasing voice. As if he knew what was putting her on edge.

"This will give me something to compare. Hold still, Sean." Looking down into his eyes, she noticed they were staring blankly into space. "Sean?"

"What's wrong?" Davin was on his feet and beside her in a heartbeat.

"Sean? Come on, you, talk to me."

She gave him a hard shake, but nothing happened.

"Oh no, don't do this to me. Sean?"

"He's gone into some sort of shock." Davin grabbed the back of Sean's head as Sara removed the pillow. "Did you get some blood?"

"Yes. I'll run it."

"Sean? Hey, buddy, don't give up on us now. You haven't learned how much of a pain in the ass I am yet," Davin said with mock teasing voice.

Sara barely saw the glass slide as she smeared several drops of blood on it and jammed it into the cell scanner. Punching the keypad didn't help her frustration and it didn't make the computer complete its analysis any faster. Her heart was racing and she had to force herself to calm down enough to keep perspective on what she needed to do.

"Sara, he's getting pale. His breathing is shallow." Davin's voice was strained, his words coming out clipped.

"I need another five minutes before this is done. Heart rate?"

"Ah…sixty beats per minute and falling. That bad?"

"Shit. BP?"

"What?"

Sara pushed away from the computer and raced to Davin's side. Sean's face was more than pale—it had taken on a distinct gray tinge and he was barely sucking in any air.

"He's going to have a heart attack. Get me the defib unit." She raced around to the other side of the table and pulled Sean's shirt open. "Davin, get it now! He doesn't have time to wait."

Davin didn't make a move toward the kit. Instead, he pulled off his gloves and slipped off his utility belt.

"What the hell are you doing?" She heard the panic in her voice and quickly quashed it. "Never mind, I'll get it."

Just as she picked up the defib unit from the table, the computer let out a warning sound. Sean's heartbeat was becoming erratic. Sara tore the sensors out of their wrapping and started to head back to the table when she stopped dead in her tracks.

Davin was standing with his back to her, but even still she could see the faint glow coming from his hands. Her gaze flicked between him and the computer monitor and she hoped he was going to be able to pull this off.

"Davin," she whispered, coming up beside him.

Sara didn't want to disturb him, but she needed to know that they were both going to be okay. Davin's eyes were closed, a deep frown etched on his face. He had one hand hovering over Sean's chest, just above his heart, and the other one gripping the edge of the table. He didn't seem to be aware of what was happening around him, even of the fact his body was beginning to sway. Sara slid her arm around his waist to steady him.

"Sara," he said her name so faintly it barely left his lips.

"I'm here. Tell me what I can do to help."

"Analysis complete," the computer's sterile voice filled the silence of the room.

"Computer, relay analysis," Sara said from over her shoulder as she tightened her grip on Davin.

"Parasite designate PH5-98 is multiplying in subject's blood. Estimate total hemoglobin consumption in three minutes."

"Oh shit," she whispered. She swallowed hard and gave him a gentle squeeze. "Davin, did you hear that? The antibodies the computer manufactures only sped things up."

"So many."

"I know, baby. Can you get them all?" When he didn't respond, she gave him another squeeze. "Davin, can I help?"

The hand that he was gripping the table let go and rose slowly until it came in contact with one of hers. He barely touched it, tugging it in the direction of his outstretched hand.

"Help," he whispered.

"You want me to put my hand on yours?" She couldn't figure out why, but really she didn't completely understand what Davin did anyway.

Without further argument, Sara reached out and gently rested the palm of her hand on the back of his. The contact sent a pulse of energy charging through her body. Instantly she became aroused and didn't think she'd be able to focus, when everything went black.

Med bay faded into the distance until she found herself standing in a cold, dark space. Buzzing around her unseen were some sort of insects. They would come within a short distance of her but would suddenly veer away. Panic began to build in her and Sara had to fight the urge to scream. How the hell did she get here?

"Davin?"

"It's all right." His deep, rich voice was beside her.

She felt his arm come around her shoulders and the panic fizzled as quickly as it had arrived.

"Where are we?" she asked, purposely keeping her voice low. While she didn't know what the hell those insects were, she knew she didn't want their attention.

He chuckled, his body brushing up against hers. "I'm not sure if you'd believe me if I told you."

"Of course I...wait, we're in Sean?"

"I knew you were smart, wild one."

"How is this possible? This shouldn't be—"

Davin reached up and brushed a strand of her hair, wrapping it around his finger. "This is how my people heal. We are able to project ourselves into the patient's body."

"Why is it so dark? I can't see you." she shivered as she said the words.

"Sean is...dark inside. He's been through hell and still holds a part of that time inside him. Punishing himself."

"Oh god."

"I can help him but not until we get his body healed."

"All your healers can do this?" Sara asked in awe. The implications were staggering too.

"Not like this, no. I'm...special. I'll tell you about it after we fix our friend up."

A thousand questions were bouncing in her head, but she knew Sean didn't have that kind of time. "What do you need me to do?"

"There are so many parasites, I don't have enough energy to kill them all."

"The antibodies I gave him seemed to act as a stimulant. They are eating the hemoglobin in his blood."

"That explains a lot." Davin sighed. "It's been so long since I've had to do this. Now with it being so close to me having healed you..."

Sara turned against his body. Feeling for his face in the dark, she reached up on her tiptoes and placed a gentle kiss on his mouth. "I'm here to help. Please just tell me what to do."

Davin's hands captured her face as he brought his lips hard against hers. Sara felt her body respond to his kiss, how his tongue teased her mouth. Wave after wave of arousal began to circulate through her body, all pooling at her pussy. His hands found her nipples and began to tease her into a frenzy. He tugged and rolled the sensitive tips while continuing to kiss her deeply. Sara's head was spinning when he suddenly pulled back. *Fuck, she'd almost come!*

"That's it," he sighed. "I need you charged up. I need your energy."

"You needed me horny? Well, I've got you covered." She licked his bottom lip. "Can you heal him while you do this to me?"

She felt him shake his head.

"I can come back once the energy is drained. Charge you up again. But when I'm healing I need to concentrate."

"So you just need my sexual energy?" *Fucking weird.*

"Normally no. But it's the fastest, strongest thing we have. And Sean is running out of time."

Sara couldn't believe she was about to suggest this. She took a deep breath and tried to relax her body. "Go heal, Sean. I can take care of keeping my body charged."

Davin's body stiffened. "What?"

"I can arouse myself. You just do what you need to do."

"But—"

"Now, Davin!"

She felt him step away and wished he could have stayed beside her. It would have made what she was about to do easier. Sara slid her hand over her breasts and to her nipples where Davin's fingers had been only a short time ago. They were still erect and begging for her to touch them. She drew a lazy circle around her nipple and felt the shiver of pleasure pass down her back.

"God, I can feel you," Davin ground out. "Tell me what you're doing. I can't see."

"I'm touching my breast, pulling my nipple with my fingers."

Davin cursed in his own language. "Stop, I'll never be able to heal him."

But it was too late for her to turn back now.

"I'm so horny. If I just touched my clit, I'd come." She moaned as she slid her hand down the front of her body until she reached her damp pussy.

"Yes. Come for me." Davin said the words, his voice strained.

Sara dropped to her knees, knowing her legs wouldn't be able to hold her up once she got started. Her fingers found her clit easily, and somewhere in the back of her mind she realized she wasn't wearing any clothing. She pushed through the damp curls, slick with her own juices, and slowly circled her clit. A moan escaped her lips, but she didn't stop. Sara pictured Davin's hand teasing her body.

When she pushed two fingers into her pussy, she felt her muscles clamp around them. She imagined it was Davin's cock thrusting into her. Everything else around her was gone. The only thing she could focus on was reaching that peak, blessed release.

"That's it," Davin's voice broke through the darkness. "Just a bit more and I have what I need."

"So close," she whispered. Her fingers were thrusting into her, her cream flowing down her hand as she felt the orgasm approach.

Brushing her thumb across her clit as she moved her hand was the edge she needed. Sara cried out as the first wave of pleasure pulsed through her. Her body was shaking, but she didn't stop moving her hand. Each wave brought her higher than she'd ever been before. When she couldn't take anymore, Sara slumped forward, her hand bracing her body, keeping her from lying on the floor.

She was about to speak when she heard a triumphant shout and a blast of light and heat that made her fall. Sara squeezed her eyes shut and prayed everything would be okay.

Chapter Twelve
෨

Davin didn't know where he was when consciousness finally returned to him. He shook his head a few times until his vision clearly returned. He was looking down and realized he was holding Sara's hand. Her body was pressed hard against his and her breathing was shallow.

The feel of her beside him was heavenly. He could still feel the surge of power she'd released, the power that had helped cure Sean. Davin looked over at Sean and felt sudden relief when he saw his breathing had returned to normal and his color wasn't gray any longer.

"Sara," he croaked out, his voice weak from the strain on his body. "*Jalla*, are you all right?"

He ran a hand along her shoulder to her neck where he massaged her tense muscles. He shouldn't have used her the way that he had, but there wasn't any other way to save Sean. Finally, her body shuddered as she awoke from the healing trance with a deep sigh. Sara's body tensed as she clawed wildly in the air.

"I can't see!"

"It's okay. Your sight will return shortly." He held her close and kissed her temple. "The first time is always hardest."

Her body shook in his arms, but he was surprised at how well she controlled herself. He'd seen many of his cast panic and injure themselves and others when they emerged the first time. But not his Sara. Davin whispered softly against her temple, absorbing her scent and her heat. It was amazing in some ways that this was the first time he'd healed another and didn't resent what it meant—being forced into a life that had destroyed his family.

"Is Sean okay?" Sara asked after a few minutes. Her voice was calm even though her body still trembled.

"I think I was able to kill all of the parasites. The computer says everything is normal."

"Thank god. I thought I'd killed him." Her body sagged against Davin. "I think my sight is coming back, but I could use some help to get to the chair."

He led her across the isolation room to the chair and once she was sitting comfortably, he knelt in between her legs. "How are you feeling?"

She smiled and shrugged. "Like I stuck my finger in a power outlet."

"Do you remember what happened?"

Her smile quickly turned to a frown as she concentrated. "I…I remember coming over to you, putting my hand on yours and then it gets a little fuzzy."

Davin rubbed his hands up and down along the length of her thighs. "I'm not surprised. Very few people do the first time. I needed your help to boost my own natural ability. How are you feeling?"

When she blushed, Davin couldn't help but chuckle. Her gaze snapped to his face and she punched him lightly on the shoulder.

"Why the hell are you laughing at me? I haven't even answered you yet."

"Well?"

"I'm…shit. Now I know how Haylie felt," she muttered the last.

"What's that mean?"

"I'm horny, okay. Happy? I'm horny!"

"Horny?"

Sara grabbed him by the shirt and pulled his face close to hers. "I really want to rip your clothing off and screw your brains out right now." Her face was bright red by the time she finished.

"I'd rather you wouldn't do that."

They both turned around to see Sean's face turned toward them.

"Sean!" Sara was on her feet and practically stepped on Davin to get over to the bed. "How are you feeling?"

"Like I got hit by lightning and then run over by a crawler. What happened?"

When Sara reached out and pressed her hand against Sean's cheek, Davin had to fight the urge to snatch it away. She was a doctor—she had to touch the other man, had every right to. It's not like they were mated.

The idea of spending the rest of his life with Sara was immediately appealing. When Sean had grown ill, her first reaction was to try to save him. Not ask for his help or try to use guilt or bully him into using his gift to help. She probably wouldn't have thought of it at all if he hadn't intervened when he did. And if he hadn't, Sean would be dead.

"The antibodies I gave you had the opposite effect of what I'd hoped. It sped up the growth rate of the parasites." She reached down and squeezed Sean's hand. "I'm so sorry."

"But I feel fine. A bit sore, but I don't think I'm about to die on you." Sean managed to pull his body up to lean on his forearms as he spoke.

"That was thanks to Davin. I thought we were going to lose you for a minute."

Sara moved out of the way so Sean and Davin were side by side. When Sean looked at Davin, he smiled faintly and held out his hand. Davin could feel the other man's gratitude as he clasped his hand. Their connection still strong after the healing.

"I guess that's twice we owe you, Captain."

"I'm just trying to buy enough favors to be able to smuggle some nice shit from Eurus."

"Don't let Taber or Haylie hear you say that. They'll throw you in the brig." Sean's smile brightened a bit more.

"I wouldn't give that Briel *rakel* the pleasure of catching me. Besides, I don't plan on going anywhere until we figure out what is going on with this parasite."

Sara straightened. "Really? I thought you needed to leave."

Only a fool could miss the note of hope in her voice. And Davin was far from being a fool. When she broke contact with his gaze, he knew she didn't want to pressure him to stay. She was so different from any other woman he'd ever been with. But he couldn't be the type of man she needed. Not really.

"I have a feeling Kamran won't be letting anyone on or off this planet until we get this situation under control. So I can either sit around and torment your Briel friends or I can help."

"I know I'm happy as hell you're here to help," Sean said and let his body fall back against the bed. "If I'm this bad, I can only imagine what the other miners are like."

"You rest up. We'll come check on you in a bit." Sara patted his shoulder. "Davin, can I talk to you in the office for a minute?"

He nodded a quick goodbye to Sean and followed Sara out into the hallway that led to her office. When they came in, she shut the door behind her and didn't move until he flopped into her chair, spreading his legs in a relaxed pose. His body was still humming from the power he'd taken from her in the healing. Sara's body seemed to glow, her erect nipples pressing hard against her uniform. His cock noticed too and he had to push aside the thoughts of what he wanted to do to her.

"What did you want to talk about?" He swung his leg so his ankle rested on the opposite knee, blocking her view of his crotch.

"Why haven't the other miners gotten this sick?"

Not exactly what he thought she was going to say. "Something in the antibodies ramped the parasite's growth?"

"But until I was ill, we didn't know a thing about them. Probably wouldn't have either. And Sean was fine until I tried to get rid of them. Why did they go from barely registering on the computer scans to almost killing him in a matter of minutes? That shouldn't be possible."

Sara pushed away from the door and sauntered over toward him. He could tell she was mentally engaged, trying to solve this issue. But he also knew she was still aroused from the way she touched the side of her neck, played with a lock of her blonde hair. Without thinking, he grabbed her by the waist and pulled her onto his lap with a yelp. She only struggled for a moment until her round ass came in contact with his stiff cock.

"If there is something in the mines that is keeping the parasites from taking over the host, then that means we have time to figure things out."

"Davin, we shouldn't—"

"Oh I think we should." He leaned in and licked a trail along the side of her neck. "I really, really think we should."

"Someone might come in," her words came out as a breathy sigh and she dug her nails into his arm.

"You don't remember what you did for me when I was trying to heal Sean, do you?"

"No." Her body shivered.

"Oh I think you do. Your body does even if your mind can't recall. I needed energy, power. I'm out of practice when it comes to healing."

Davin nipped at her shoulder and felt his cock twitch in his pants. There was something about Sara that set him off every time. Her scent and taste fired every drop of his blood, making him want to eat her alive.

"And you took power from me?" Her hands had come alive on his chest, clawing and rubbing his muscles.

"You gave it to me. You touched yourself here," he said and reached down between her legs. When his fingers pushed against her clit he felt her suck in a breath. "And you came for me. That energy helped save Sean's life."

"The healing power of orgasm. That's a new one." Her chuckle turned into a gasp when Davin pushed a bit harder against her clit. "If I came then, why the hell am I so fucking horny?"

"It didn't really happen." Davin reached and cupped her breast through her shirt. "But I plan on thanking you properly for your help."

"Oh," she sighed.

Sara tipped her head back, thrusting her breasts close to his face. Davin's mouth began to water as he pushed her shirt and undershirt up exposing her breasts to the air. The pink nipples taunted him, begged him for his mouth. Something he was more than happy to help with.

He sucked the nipple closest to him and began to flick his tongue over the swollen tip. Sara's hips bucked up and her legs clamped around his hand. When he rubbed against her this time, he could feel her wetness.

"I want to taste you," he said against her nipple.

"Someone might—"

"Now."

He stood up, a rush of energy filling him as he lifted her up. It took him only a minute to pull her pants free of her legs, opening up her body to him. Davin picked her up by the waist, walked her over to the wall and lifted her so high her head almost touched the ceiling.

"Legs over my shoulders."

"Davin!"

She didn't protest any further when he licked a circle around her bellybutton. One, then the other leg was draped over his shoulders, putting her pussy right in front of his mouth. He took another step closer to the wall, making sure she had enough support before leaning in and licking a path up from her cunt to her clit. Sara's nails dug into his scalp and her body shook violently from that one touch.

"You are amazing," he whispered and licked her again.

The sweet and spicy taste of her cream covered his tongue, making him hungry for more. Davin thrust his tongue into her pussy and mimicked what he would soon be doing with his cock.

Sara's head was thrashing from side to side as her muffled cries reached his ears. He could picture her biting on her lower lip trying to keep quiet. But he didn't want her quiet. He wanted her crying out, yelling his name. He moved his face back to her clit and sucked it into his mouth. Her body tensed as she cried out, her cream covering his face from the force of her release.

Davin let her body slide down the wall until one of her legs reached the floor. He kept the other leg bent, her body open to him as he kissed her deeply.

"Can you taste yourself? See why I love it?"

"Davin." She pulled him back down for another kiss as one of her hands found the opening of his pants. "I need you."

"You have me."

As soon as her fingers freed his shaft from his pants, he began to buck his hips forward. Her long fingers wrapped around him, pulling him into position at the opening of her pussy.

"Make me come again." Sara's words were hot against his cheek.

Davin's brain shut off and he let out a string of curses as he pushed into her warm cunt.

"You're so wet. Do you feel what you do to me?" Davin pressed his body hard against her, contacting with as much of her body area as possible.

Releasing his mind, he let loose the healing power his body connected to, let it out to mingle with Sara's energy. Now that they'd healed Sean together, they had a connection far deeper than what a normal couple could experience. Their bodies merged, sharing and amplifying each other's pleasure.

With each thrust he tried to keep a firm grip on his control, but the temptation to let go was so great. Sara arched her back against him, her breasts thrusting up toward his face. He cupped her and reveled in the feeling of her hard nipples poking against his palms.

The mingling of their energies increased, sending a constant stream of pleasure swirling between them. Davin closed his eyes, unable to keep them open against the power of their mutual arousal. The barriers of his mind were gone and all he could feel was Sara. There was no darkness, only joy and love all solely directed toward him.

Davin and Sara gasped at the same time. Davin felt as if he was falling forward, diving into a deep pool of pleasure and Sara was right beside him. He felt her inner muscles clench around his cock seconds before he came hard into her. Their cries mingled before being smothered with a long kiss. He couldn't stop. Davin licked and tasted Sara's mouth, cheek and neck, breathing in her sweet scent that gave him a sense of peace. His thrusts slowed to become a gentle rocking until they both leaned against the wall, kissing and caressing each other.

"You are so…perfect," he said before leaning in and placing a kiss on the end of her nose.

Sara opened her mouth to speak but closed it and instead rested her head on his shoulder. He knew what she was going to say, despite the words not coming out. She wanted him to stay. Wanted him to work with her and be a part of her life. Give up his ship and crew. Stop traveling from station to station dodging local authorities to drop off supplies and other black market goods.

And for the first time in seventeen years, he was tempted. Really, honestly tempted.

Sara lifted her head, looked into his eyes and smiled. "We should get dressed. I'm sure Rachael is wondering what the hell we're doing in here."

"I think it's very obvious what we're doing in here. Unless you have a soundproof office."

"Shit," she said and immediately turned red.

"I think your friend would be very happy for you."

"My friend will tease me mercilessly once you leave." Sara looked suddenly very uncomfortable. "Not that you'll be going anywhere until we figure out what's going on with those damn parasites."

Davin lifted his body from hers and Sara straightened. She didn't move away from him immediately, instead pushing against the wall to wrap her arms around him. Locked in her embrace, Davin felt his heart soar and cherished the gift she'd given him.

It took them a few minutes to get cleaned up and straighten their clothing. Sara tripped over her desk and jumped around, massaging her smashed toes.

"How have you survived all these years?" He chuckled as she bent down to massage her wounded foot.

"Why do you think I became a doctor? Between always hurting myself or causing one of my friend's injuries, I figured it was time to do something about it. I can't imagine doing anything else, to be honest." Sara gasped, her hand going to her mouth. "I'm sorry. I didn't mean to imply you should be a doctor, healer too."

Davin laughed a bit harder and brought her foot up to his mouth. He placed a kiss on the top of her toes before sliding it into her shoe.

"I would never assume you'd mean anything like that. You're too concerned with making everyone feel better to cause harm, wild one."

"Sometime I say stupid things. Haylie always laughed too." She smiled down at him.

At that moment, there was nothing he wanted more than to take her back to his quarters, throw her onto the bed and not let her get up for the rest of the day. Instead, he stood up and pulled her tight in his arms.

"Stupid isn't a term I'd associate with you." He brushed his lips against hers before running his tongue over the seam of her lips.

"Oh." She smiled as her gaze roamed over his face. "And how do you think of me?"

"A brilliant, caring doctor."

Sara blushed again and Davin loved seeing the color spread across her cheeks. "And how do you see me, wild one?"

"The rogue alien captain wants to know what a simple human doctor thinks of him?" Sara leaned against him and mimicked his earlier action by running her tongue over his bottom lip. "I think you're very exciting and fucking sexy."

"That kind of talk is going to get you in trouble again. And you have patients to cure."

"Yes, I do." With a sigh, Sara stepped out of his embrace and moved around to the computer. "I need to go back to the mine to see not only where the parasites are coming from, but what is keeping them from killing the miners."

The thought of Sara going back to the mines, even if she was healthy, sent Davin's internal warning sensors into overdrive. Walking up behind her, he slid his arms down along her shoulders and arms.

"I'm sure there is another way. We can get the medics who are there to bring you some samples. You'll have all of the equipment you need here to run your tests."

Not looking back at him, Sara shook her head and bent over to pick up a data pad on the desk in front of her.

"I need to retrace my steps. Somewhere I got infected. That's where I'll find the solution. It will take too long to get someone else to go where I was and even then I can't guarantee they won't miss something."

"Sara, you've barely been out of isolation yourself. You're not honestly going to put your body back through that."

That got her attention. Sara spun around, her mouth open with a look between shock and anger on her face.

"That's my job. I'm perfectly fine now, thanks to your help. I have to do everything in my power to make sure no one else suffers. I can't afford to have a whole station full of Seans out there."

"And they can't afford to have you get sick and unable to help. I'm not a doctor, just a healer. I can't solve this, I can't save all of them. They need you."

Sara gave him a shove strong enough to send him staggering back a step. "Who the hell asked you to save them? I've never asked *anything* of you, Davin. Not even to help Sean. So don't get a martyr complex on me. This is my job and I'm damn well going to do it!"

Davin found his teeth grinding together and he had to take a deep breath to keep from snapping at her. Didn't she realize how important she was to this colony?

"I'm simply asking that you let someone else collect the samples. You can still do your job."

"What do you care anyway? As soon as Kamran gives you the all clear you'll be out of here. You've made it no secret that you don't want to stay."

"Just because I don't want to give up my life doesn't mean I don't care about you!" he roared.

They stood there, panting and staring at each other. Davin's heart was pounding madly in his chest as he stared at her. Sara's chest was rising and falling as fast as his, but her eyes were wide and locked on him.

"What did you say?" she whispered.

Fuck. "That I care about you."

She swallowed hard. "Do you love me?"

By Ralla *yes!* "No."

"I see."

Sara picked up the data pad, slipped on her medical coat and walked to the door. Davin fought every muscle, every impulse to keep his body still. He couldn't go after her. If she stayed with him he'd use her. More and more he'd drain her energy, healing the people she'd never ask him to heal. All because he wouldn't want to disappoint her.

No, it was far better for her if he cut all ties now and let her live a full life. It wasn't like they'd formed a permanent attachment. It had only been a few weeks. Not long enough to give up everything he'd known to stay with her.

Sara turned once she opened the door to the office and stepped outside. "You know, I thought I cared for you too. I can't get you out of my mind. Damn near obsessive. I thought there was a time when I might even love you. But I see that really wasn't the case. Take care of yourself, Davin."

"Please don't go back to the mine." His throat was tight and the words were painful to say. The ache in his throat spread to his chest, squeezing his heart.

"I don't have a reason not to. It's my job and it seems that's the only important thing I currently have in my life."

Without another word, she turned and walked away.

Chapter Thirteen
ೞ

Sara took a long drink from the canteen that held her water rations, enjoying the sensation of the cool liquid filling her stomach. When she looked around the area that they'd set up as a makeshift med bay, she felt a sudden wave of exhaustion pass over her. She'd been struggling to deal with the parasite infection for the past two days and hadn't made any progress.

One of the medics who'd been here since Davin had gotten her out walked over with a man draped around his shoulders. "We have another man who's showing symptoms, Doctor Fergus."

"There is a free bed near the back, Marc. If you can take a blood sample and put it into the scanner, that would be great."

"Got it."

She watched as he helped fill one of their last three empty beds. Since her return, more and more men had started to show signs of the parasite infection. Shit, she had to rush one man to the station because she didn't have the resources she needed here to help him. Last she'd heard from Rachael, he was in stable condition but barely holding on. Maybe Davin had been right about her coming here and things would have been better if she'd stayed on the station, doing her analysis there.

No! The last thing she wanted to do was second guess herself. Davin was nothing but an ass. She needed to be here to help. These men needed her. Everything else was irrelevant. And his fears that she'd get sick again were unfounded. There wasn't a single parasite in her blood and she felt great.

Totally, ass-kicking exhausted, but great.

"Doctor Fergus."

Sara looked up and tried not to groan out loud when she saw Grant walking toward her. It was hard to believe he hadn't put in an appearance long before now, considering the impact this parasite infection was having on production.

"Mr. Grant." She stood up to face him. "What can I do for you?"

"I want to know when the hell I'm going to have my mine back under my control." His red face somehow grew redder. "This foolishness has been going on long enough."

"What foolishness is that, sir? The total infection of every miner in this facility or the fact that you're still insisting on working the miners during this crisis?"

"With the exception of a few, most of the men are fine. As I said before, they are taking advantage of your bleeding heart."

Oh this guy was really pissing her off.

"Please take a seat," she said, and pointed to the small chair she was using as an exam area. "And roll up your sleeve."

"There is nothing at all wrong with me. This is ridiculous." He stood and crossed his arms across his chest.

"Well, unfortunately for you, I'm the judge of that. I have orders from the administrator himself that anyone who enters this place must undergo a full blood scan and physical to see if they are showing any signs of distress." Sara took a step away from the chair and pointed at it without breaking eye contact. "Sit."

Grant huffed a few times and looked ready to snap at her again, but he finally plopped his heavy frame into the small chair.

"Completely unnecessary," he muttered.

"As I said, I'll be the judge of that. Now, when was the last time you were here?"

"Last week. I came for my meeting with the shift leads to get my progress report."

"And have you noticed any strange feelings or sensations? Dizziness, shortness of breath, that sort of thing?"

Grant stared at her, the cords in his neck tensing and relaxing and he ground his teeth. "No."

"Good. Then your blood test will most likely be clean and you'll have nothing to worry about." Except the fact that Kamran was going to kick his ass back to Earth for screwing with the wellbeing of the miners.

Sara gave the needle an extra firm jab into his arm and a small, vindictive part of her enjoyed the small twinge of pain on his face. The rest of her felt guilty.

"Sorry. I'm a bit tired."

"There's no reason for you to be here at all. These men will be perfectly fine."

Tired of hearing other people's opinions as to whether or not she should be here, she felt her entire body tense, wanting to retaliate. Instead, Sara closed her eyes and somehow managed to push her annoyance away. "I'm doing my job. Nothing more. Now I'm going to run your blood sample. It should only take a minute for me to get the results."

Standing in front of the cell scanner seemed a blessed relief. The quiet hum of the motor as it did its work lulled her into a state of peace. For a moment, she could almost believe her heart hadn't shattered.

Davin didn't love her. Despite all of the feelings she had and all of the signs she thought he'd given her, he didn't love her. But that didn't make sense! The way he'd touched her, the passion with which they'd made love all told her he cared. Fuck, even the fact he hadn't wanted her to come back here proved he had feelings for her.

Though he admitted to caring for her, he just didn't love her.

"I can't sit here and wait around for your tests." Grant stood up so fast his chair nearly fell to the floor. "I'm leaving to attend to my business matters here in the mine. If I'm about to die, please find me."

Before she could argue the matter, he stomped off in the direction of the lower drilling cavern. Sara wanted to scream but somehow managed to keep it inside.

"Grant is a fuck-up," a voice behind her muttered.

Sara turned and saw one of the miners she'd treated yesterday lying on a cot, his head propped on his hand. He winked at her when she smiled.

"I'm not the nicest person to deal with these days either."

"You're a saint, Doc. Don't let that ass make you think otherwise."

She couldn't stop the small smile that leapt to her face. "Thanks. It's nice to know someone appreciates what I'm doing."

"Do you think you'll be able to figure out what's causing this? I haven't felt this shitty since I did a tour on an ore hauler ten years ago."

"That's what I'm hoping to find out," she said and ran her hands into her hair and pulled it back into a fresh ponytail. "Do you remember when people started getting sick? My records in med bay don't really show an increase in patients."

The miner rolled onto his back and pursed his lips. "Must be about a month or more now. Just after the order from that alien asshole came to shut us in and run triple shifts."

Sara took a step closer to the man, her hands placed firmly on her hips. "Kamran did no such thing. Chief Bond and Taber are trying to find out what happened, where the order came from. The last thing Kamran would want to do is harm anyone."

"I didn't mean to upset you, Doc. But a lot of us down here don't really know the administrator. Your friend Grant there told us the orders came from him. Most people still belive him."

"Well Grant is full of shit."

No wonder Grant had wanted Kamran's approval so badly at the last board meeting. He'd been throwing his name around down here at the mines. He was probably scared the miners would stop believing his stories and contact Kamran directly.

"I was at the meeting where it was discussed. Kamran most certainly *didn't* give his approval."

The cell scanner dinged, indicating it was done with its scan. Sara punched the buttons on the keyboard, annoyed with the whole situation. Why did things always seem to go to crap at this place? When the computer displayed the results, she thought it was her annoyance that was making her see things.

"Computer, please confirm results."

After a few minutes of running a silent check, the computer beeped again. "Confirmed."

"Holy shit," she whispered.

"Problem, Doc?"

"Ah no." Not one she was about to share with anyone but Haylie and Kamran. "Are you going to be okay for a few minutes? I need to get in touch with the station."

"A mandatory rest? I'm in heaven."

Not wanting to wait any longer, Sara downloaded the test results onto a data pad and practically ran over to the utility shed that they'd transformed into a makeshift office for her. Only once she'd secured the door did she hit the data pad and checked the results again. There had to be a mistake.

It only took her a few minutes for the call to reach Haylie, who grinned when she saw Sara. "Hey, you. Still feeling okay?"

"I'm good. How are you feeling? Still have the morning sickness?"

Haylie stuck out her tongue. "Kamran likes to tease me. Says Briel women don't normally get sick. So I had Taber lock him in the brig for an hour." She frowned and leaned forward. "Now that was funny, so why aren't you laughing."

"I think I have a problem here. Grant came by. Said he had some things to check on."

"Pissed you off again, did he?" Haylie grinned. "Doesn't sound like anything you can't handle."

"I made him submit to a blood scan."

"And?"

Sara took a deep breath as she slid the data pad into the portable communicator. "I'm sending you the results right now."

It took only a few seconds for the data to transmit and for Haylie to open the file. She frowned and looked up at Sara. "Am I reading this right?"

"He's totally infected with them."

"Is he sick? I mean, you only had a fraction of this amount and it damn near killed you."

"Doesn't even look tired. The parasites may be what make someone sick, but there's more to it than that."

"I'm going to let Kamran know what's going on. He'll want to haul Grant from active duty until you figure out what we should do next."

"I'm going to get you to send a few extra security personnel too," Sara piped up. "I'm guessing Grant was the one who imposed lockdown on the mine and he blamed Kamran, even though we can't prove it. God knows what he'll do when I confront him with this."

"I'll have a team there in twenty. I want you to stay away from him until they arrive. The last thing we need is you getting kidnapped again and having an accident. I don't trust that man as far as I can throw him."

"Do you want me to see if Davin can tag along?" Haylie asked in an even voice.

Sara looked at her friend, knowing her emotions were clear on her face. Not that she could have hidden how she felt from her best friend anyway.

At the mention of his name, Sara couldn't help but think of Davin. This is where they'd made love when he'd found her the first time. God, she'd actually been excited beyond belief when she saw him walk into the cavern.

"No. He doesn't want to be with me. Dragging him back here is only going to make him feel guilty. Best to keep away. Just send that security detail so I can get Grant back to med bay and find out what's going on."

Haylie didn't respond for a minute and Sara thought she was going to argue. She really didn't need a lecture from her blissfully happy friend right now.

"Haylie, hon, just let this one go. It didn't work out. Davin's not the first man and he won't be the last."

"Did you know that I'd given up on Kamran? It was right before the Ecada attacked and he was in the brig." Haylie took a breath and smiled. "I thought we'd finally connected. Not just the bond, but something deeper. And then he pushed me too hard the wrong way and blocked me out. I thought he was rejecting me."

Sara shook her head. "I can't imagine. He's crazy about you."

"Sometimes that's not enough for things to work. And sometimes men think they are protecting us when really they're scared. I've seen the way Davin looks at you. I wouldn't give up on him yet."

"But he doesn't..." She took a breath and tried to relax. "He said he doesn't love me. And while the sex is fantastic, I need more than that."

Haylie sighed. "Look, we'll talk about this when you get back with Grant. That security detail is on their way."

"Thanks, hon."

Sara sat in the silence of the shed and felt sorry for herself. She brushed a tear from her cheek, her thoughts drifting back to Davin. She really did wish he'd come, but not because he was asked to. Not to act as her protector because it was what he thought he should do. She wanted him to come because he loved her, was worried about her. But the chances of that happening were nonexistent.

A loud knock had Sara on her feet and yanking the door open in an instant. "What's wrong?"

Grit, the miner shift leader she'd met when she'd first been kidnapped, was standing there. His face was pale and he looked like he was about to collapse. He grabbed her by the wrist and dragged her out of the shed.

"Doctor Fergus. Man down. I think he's dead."

"Show me."

Sara ran after him, grabbing one of her med kits as she rushed past the patient area. Grit led her down the tunnel that she and Davin had traveled only the week before. When he pulled her into the cavern with the underground pool, they had to push past two men who were standing there looking down over the bank. Sara gasped when he finally saw what they were staring at.

"Oh my god. Go get one of the other medics. Now!"

Grant was floating face down in the water. Not thinking at all, Sara dumped the med kit on the ground and dove in after him. She managed to flip Grant over and pull him back to the bank.

"Help me pull him up."

Somewhere from above, two sets of hands pulled Grant's body from her grasp. Within a few seconds, another set of arms were extended down to help Sara up. She fell to her knees by his body and yanked his shirt collar open.

"My kit," she barked out the order without looking at the men. When the strap hit her open hand, she yanked it open and grabbed her scanner. "Didn't anyone think to pull him out!"

No one answered and Sara was too busy to look. When the med scanner didn't show any life signs, she began CPR and mouth to mouth resuscitation on him. Looking up, she glared at the men who were simply standing there watching.

"Where is my med team? This man is dying."

"No, he's dead, Doctor," Grit said to her, stepping forward.

Sara was about to yell something at him when the words died in her throat. There was something in the man's eyes that looked dead, like he wasn't there at all. The flat tone of the med scanner told her Grant hadn't stood a chance. He was gone and there wasn't a thing she could do about it. Slowly she turned the device off, keeping her eyes locked on Grit and the too silent group of men standing around her.

"What do you want from me?" Her voice shook as she asked the question.

All the men grinned as Grit took a step forward.

"Time to find out."

* * * * *

"Okay, try it now, Silas."

Davin barely managed to pull his head out from under the bulkhead before the power surged through the circuits. The console held on to life for a few minutes before it blinked, sparked and went dead.

"Great," he muttered.

"Did it work?" Silas shouted from the crawlspace below. When Davin didn't answer him right away, he poked his head up from the floor. "Well?"

"It's blown. We'll have to get a replacement." Davin tossed aside the welding gun and burned-out drive crystal and sat down on the floor with a thud. *Great fucking day.*

"It will take us a week at least to get a new one. Unless you can do some fancy trading out at the bazaar. Though I doubt they have much in the way of Raqulian engineering parts," Silas said as he hauled his heavy frame out from the crawlway. "At least you can spend some more time with your doctor friend."

Davin winced. He doubted Sara wanted anything to do with him. He knew he was a fool for letting her walk away, but he just couldn't figure out how to make things work between them.

"I'm going to go up front and contact some people. I might be able to get something here sooner."

"There a problem, Captain?" Silas reached out and grabbed Davin's arm. "I thought you'd be all over wanting to spend some more time with Sara. She's a sweet thing."

"I'll be up front." Davin pulled his arm away and moved through the door.

He knew Silas was following him but refused to look around. The last thing he needed was the human's advice.

"You bastard. You're just going to walk away from her, aren't you?"

"I don't see how this is any of your concern."

Davin stepped over a large cord of cables that were lying in the middle of the corridor. They were coming out of his bedroom and he saw his unmade bed as he passed. He remembered Sara's naked body splayed out on it, his face buried between her legs, licking her sweet pussy, and it made him grind his teeth.

"The mood of my captain is most certainly my concern. The last time you got pissed, we spent a year and a half on the rim. Damn near fucking killed us."

Silas had chased him all the way to the drive pit. The door had been repaired since the crash and now slid open easily when Davin hit the sensor. He was about to walk in and shut the door on Silas' face when the other man grabbed his arm.

"How long have we known each other?" Silas kept his gaze fixed on Davin.

"Nine years."

"Have I ever once disagreed with any decision you've ever made?"

"You did punch me when we crashed—"

"That's because you trashed my ship doing something stupid. Now answer my fucking question."

Davin sighed. "No, you haven't."

"Then it's a first. You're a fucking fool if you walk away from her. You've been different since we landed here. Happy, if I had to guess." Silas dropped his arm and took a step back. "Don't be an ass and go find her. Life is meaningless if you can't share it."

Silas turned and walked away. Davin stared after him only for a second before closing his eyes and leaning his head back against the doorframe. Maybe he was being an ass. But he didn't want to hurt Sara either and he wasn't sure he could give her what she deserved. A partner who would be there no matter what.

"Did I come at a bad time?"

Davin opened his eyes to see Kamran standing there. Davin couldn't help but stare at the man. He'd never seen someone so comfortable in their own skin before. He looked relaxed, in control and something that Davin hadn't really picked up on before now. Kamran was a very happy man.

"How could you do it?" The question left Davin's lips before he had time to think about it.

Kamran raised a single eyebrow. "Do what specifically?"

"You were a powerful ambassador for your people. Or so I've heard since I've been here. And you gave that all up. For a woman."

A very slight smile played on Kamran's lips. He came into the ship and sat down on the edge of a desk. "As an ambassador, I had to learn to weigh all aspects of a dilemma. Looked at what each party brought forward and was forced to evaluate the importance. Many times I had to choose between impossible options."

Davin didn't move. He waited as Kamran tipped his head to the side, reached up and touched his neck. The gesture was so intimate and unconscious, Davin wasn't even sure if Kamran realized he'd done it. When Kamran returned his gaze to Davin's he could see the change in the other man.

"You asked how I could do it? I'm not as familiar with your people as I'd like to be, but on Briel, being with your mate is the most important thing. They complete us in a way nothing else could. If I was told I had to choose between this colony and Haylie, I wouldn't hesitate. She's my life."

The words struck Davin deep inside. To be that committed to another person, to be willing to give up everything to be with them, was hard to accept. But in another way it made sense. Silas had been right about one thing—he had been happy since crashing on this planet.

"The people in my cast, the healers, our relationships can be all consuming. We can connect to others on a physiological level. Use their body's energy to heal." Davin took a deep breath and looked away from Kamran. He'd never said these words out loud before. "There are some who can use that energy to heal a person's mind as well as their body."

When he looked back at Kamran, he didn't see the censure he'd expected. Instead, the administrator looked curious. "This is a rare ability?"

"Those who have it are marked. Their skills are in great demand and they are usually taken from their homes to work in *daaten*, special hospitals."

"It sounds like you are very familiar with these *daaten*."

A long-buried ache stretched across his chest, and Davin had to fight past the emotions. "My mother had this *gift*. It was one of the reasons my father mated with her. He pushed her to use those skills to help others. He was a healer there and he wanted to save everyone. What he didn't realize was that he was killing his wife."

Davin remember the last time he'd seen his mother alive. She'd been only a shell of a woman then. Her frail body refused to accept any of the healing energy he'd tried to push into her. She'd given up. Too many horrific images were seared into her mind, tormenting her.

"And you're scared Sara would do the same thing to you, knowing you could help others?"

Davin's head snapped up when Kamran chuckled. "This isn't funny, Briel."

"How many human women have you dealt with in the past?" he asked, still chuckling.

"I have two humans on my crew. They're all the—"

"Human *women*?"

Davin ground his teeth for a moment. "None."

"Then you need to learn one thing. They will surprise you every day with the things they are willing to do to protect the ones they love. If Sara knew how you felt about this, she wouldn't put you into a position where it would cause you harm. She's very much like my wife that way."

And Davin knew he was right. She'd never once asked him to help save another, even knowing he could. It would be no different with his other ability. Being away from his father, he'd have the control over his skills, to use them as he saw fit. He'd been running from who he was since his mother's death. Maybe it was time he stopped running.

He looked down at his hands and saw the black gloves that covered his hands and wrists. Slowly, he pulled them off and tossed them aside. The black tattoos that covered the skin over his hands, curled down over his fingers. So few of his people had this skill, it had seemed a curse to him. But maybe with someone like Sara, he could do some good without losing what it meant to be him.

"It seems like you've reached a decision," Kamran said and stood. At his full height, the Briel's head almost reached the ceiling in the low corridor. "If you are up to it, Doctor Fergus could use your assistance."

After their little talk, Davin guessed helping her had nothing to do with healing patients. The warrior in him reared up, protective instincts kicking in. "What's wrong?"

"One of my staff, Grant, is infected with the parasites but isn't showing any symptoms. She asked for a security detail to help bring him back."

Davin pushed away from the wall and stepped past Kamran. "I'll go."

"The rest of the team is suiting up. Taber and Sean will be going with you."

Davin nodded and jumped out of the ship. If Sara needed him, then he'd go to her. And with any luck she'd be happy to see him.

Chapter Fourteen

Davin, Sean and Taber stepped out of the second crawler once it pulled up behind the rest of the security detail. Unlike the last time he was here, there were no guards posted at the door. In fact, there was very little activity at all.

"I don't like this," Taber said, removing his blaster from his holster as he tossed the EV helmet aside.

"There should be at least an engineering crew here this time of day," Sean said, tossing his helmet to join Taber's. "You don't think Grant would have done anything to prevent normal operations? The miners couldn't stand him for good reason."

"Maybe *they* did something to Grant," Davin said, yanking his blaster and a knife from his belt. "Let's find Sara and the other medics."

"Rachael said there were three of them plus Sara. Let's stay together. I don't want them to take us one by one because we've separated." Taber stepped into the corridor and motioned for the security guards to bring up the rear.

Sean fell into step behind them. "Agreed. We'll start with the area they set up as a med bay and expand the search from there."

The three of them led the security detail through practically abandoned corridors, passing only the occasional man. The miners they questioned seemed disoriented, like they didn't know where they'd been or what they'd been doing. By the time they reached the med area, Davin's warrior senses were screaming at him that something was wrong. There was no one there and Sara's med kit was gone.

"What the fuck is going on?" He growled and kicked an empty bed. "Where is everyone?"

Taber came up beside him. "We'll find her. There must be some sort of emergency for everyone to be gone."

"The men we talked to didn't know a fucking thing. I'm surprised they knew they were in the mine." Davin ran a hand through his hair, pushing it back from his face. "*Ruian* help them if they've done anything to her."

Turning around, Davin was about to say something to the others when he noticed Sean. His face was pale and his hands were clenching and unclenching by his sides.

"Sean?" he walked over beside his friend. "What's wrong?"

"This isn't right," Sean whispered. "This shouldn't be happening."

"What isn't right?" He placed his gloveless hand on Sean's shoulder.

The second he came in contact, Davin felt the surge of cold push through him. He knew it was coming from Sean's mind and whatever it was pulled at him, trying to bring Sean into a dark place.

No! Davin closed his eyes and dove into the black, yelling for Sean. *"Don't give in to it. Stay with me!"*

"So cold, so dark," a frightened whisper echoed around Davin.

"Let's give them some light then."

It had been a long time since Davin had attempted to heal another's mind, but he didn't hesitate. Sean didn't have time to waste. Letting his defenses down, Davin let a blast of healing light sweep from him and into Sean's mind. They both gasped at the force of the mental surge and were left shaking.

The darkness receded for a brief second before pushing forward again. Davin could sense the return of the parasites as well. Not coming from a wound but rather being placed in

Sean's body by a powerful outside source. It was this connection to Sean's mind that was causing the problems. If he didn't seal off the hole, there wouldn't be anything left.

"I'm going to help you, Sean, but you have to trust me."

"I…I do. So cold. Like before."

"Before when?"

"Please help me."

Davin projected himself even further into Sean's psyche and stood in front of the breech. The cold pounded into him, trying to push past his barriers and infect him as well. Taking a deep breath, Davin lifted his hand and stepped forward. The skin on his arm went numb as he touched the darkness of the hole. Breathing out, he pushed every ounce of his healing abilities out and began to repair the rip in Sean's mind. When he felt his connection waver, Davin concentrated as hard as he could until one last healing blast poured out of him. All the hate, guilt and doubt that had filled Sean was pushed away, the deep internal wounds stitched up. With a gasp, Davin pulled back, breaking both the physical and mental connection.

When Davin opened his eyes, he was looking at the shocked face of Sean. He could see Sean searching for that darkness, looking for the old anger that had sustained him for so long. Davin reached up and squeezed Sean's shoulder. It was only then that Davin realized Taber had come up beside them, frowning deeply.

"What's wrong?" he asked, his deep voice full of concern.

"Someone was trying to take over Sean's mind." Davin swallowed hard, a wave of exhaustion hitting him. "I broke the connection and repaired some damage. It looks like it had been there a long time."

"What?" Taber looked between the two of them.

"It's the Ecada," Sean managed, his voice shaky.

"Impossible. We checked the entire planet, including the mine. There weren't any."

Sean straightened, his jaw muscles twitching. "There's at least one. And it's injured. The pull was very weak but definitely here. It must be using the miners somehow to boost its power. That's why I felt it now."

"It's the Ecada that's infecting the miners with the parasites. It was trying to take you over again. I managed to kill them off. It's easier now that I know what they are."

"If it is the Ecada, then we have a serious problem." Taber straightened. "Ryans, report back to the administrator. Tell him that we suspect we have an Ecada trapped in the mine and we need reinforcements. Now!"

Having touched that evil, Davin couldn't wait. He needed to find Sara and get her to safety. He pushed past the other men and jogged down the corridor toward one of the tunnels that led deep into the heart of the mine.

"Davin!" Sean caught up to him. "You can't take the Ecada on alone. It's probably controlling the miners."

He stopped dead in his tracks and spun to face Sean. "I'm not going to fucking sit around while that *thing* has Sara."

Taber joined them and the three men stared at each other. Davin slapped his open palm against his thigh. "The three of us can do this. We have the element of surprise and we now know what we're up against."

"It may not be much of a surprise," Taber said shaking his head. "It will know you prevented its ability to control Sean."

"I doubt it recognized who I was. It would have been too busy fighting off my attack to know who or what I am."

Sean nodded slowly at first but finally with confidence. "It probably got trapped here when they pulled out after the attack. The mine was empty at the time and it could have entered from one of the natural caverns that lead here. If it's weak, we can kill it and once it's dead the miners should return to normal."

They both looked at Taber who, after a few seconds of silent contemplation, simply shrugged. "We best hurry then."

Sean took the lead and brought them down a narrow path that led to a smelting area. Davin remembered this as being a heavily guarded area the last time he'd been here. He'd been told it was off limits when he'd asked around. Something to do with a problem with the stability of the tunnel. If it really was the Ecada, then it would be the most likely hiding spot for it to be.

They had to jump behind an outcropping of rocks to prevent from being seen when they finally entered the area. It looked like most of the sixty miners from this shift were busy blasting and digging their way through the rock.

"What are they looking for?" Davin whispered to Sean.

"Not sure. There's no silicate in these rocks. Nothing of value."

"Nothing unless you're an Ecada," Taber whispered. Both Sean and Davin turned to look at him. "The minerals in these rocks act as an amplifier for the Ecada's psychic control. The more of the mineral that's exposed, the further its reach."

"Explains why it reached me back at the medical area," Sean whispered, his fingers flexing on his blaster.

Davin reached out and touched Sean's arm. "You should be fine now. I broke its connection to you."

Sean nodded, but Davin could still see the tension in him. Their conversation died down as they watched the miners trudge back and forth between drilling the side of the wall and carrying large rocks to the metal grate that hauled them away for processing.

It took a few minutes, but Davin finally noticed three men emerge from a circular tunnel in the far corner of the cavern. One of them he recognized as Grit, the man who'd led him and Sean to Sara when they'd first arrived at the mine. He'd been very attentive to her the whole time she'd been helping the miners. *Too* attentive.

"I want to check that out," he said and pointed.

"How do you propose we get there?" Taber asked, looking over the tops of their heads to where Davin indicated.

"Like this."

Davin stood and grabbed a mining ax as he shuffled toward one of the walls. He paused long enough to blast part of the wall and grab a heavy boulder. He soon felt Sean and Taber come up beside him, doing the same.

"Keep your head down and eyes on the floor. Otherwise it might attract attention," Sean muttered under his breath.

It took a few minutes, but they made their way undetected to the far end of the cavern. They had to wait for Grit and the two other men who'd come out of the back to move away, leaving the entrance unprotected.

"Now," Davin hissed and moved before the others reacted.

He went through the entrance and broke into a run. He made his way down the twisting pathway until a buzzing in his mind grew so loud it sent his body staggering. He lurched to a stop as pain lanced through his body.

"Davin!" Sean yelled, coming to a skidding halt behind him.

When Davin was finally able to push past the numbing feeling and could look up, he saw something that made him shudder. A large beast with a giant jaw filled with teeth lay in a corner in front of them. Its silver scales seemed to glow in the faint light of the cavern, a deep rumbling growl came from its chest.

"By the goddess," Taber hissed behind them.

"An Ecada, I presume?"

"How very observant of you, Captain."

The trio turned to see Grit holding Sara, who was gagged and staring wide eyed at them. Davin took a step forward, but the Ecada behind them let out a low roar. Paralyzed, he didn't know what to do. Fuck, she looked so scared.

"Let her go," Davin managed to get out.

"No. We need her to keep the men going. We're almost done." Grit said in a voice that didn't sound quite normal. He seemed to be looking through Davin rather than at him.

"Done with what?" Taber asked, taking half a step closer to Davin. His shoulder was pressed against Davin's back.

"We're hungry and need to eat. We want to leave." Grit's eyes were wide, like he wasn't aware of what he was saying.

Davin mentally reached out and could feel the thread of control the creature had over the man. It was the same dark thread that had been buried deep in Sean's mind. But he couldn't do a fucking thing about it. He needed to be in contact with the man in order to break the mental control and there wasn't any way to do that without Sara getting hurt.

"What do you mean *we*?" Taber asked.

Davin was about to take a step forward away from Taber when he pressed something into his hand. Trying not to move, Davin turned it around in his hand until he realized what it was—a sonic grenade. He tightened his grip around the cool metal and tried to gauge which would be the best target.

"We were left behind," Grit said, his grip on Sara loosening slightly. "We're hungry, but the food isn't good. It's dirty and weak. We need to leave."

"You're Ecada?" Sean asked, looking from Grit to the beast behind them.

"Yes," he spoke as the beast growled.

"Why are you making these men work here?" Davin asked, needing to keep both the man and the beast distracted while he prepared to toss the grenade.

"We need them. They feed us."

Sean shuddered as he took a step away from the Ecada, his back pressed closer to the rock wall. Davin risked a glace at Taber, who nodded ever so slightly.

"I think there's been enough eating in here. Let Sara go and we can talk about getting you off this planet."

"No!" the man shouted a second before the Ecada growled and surged forward several steps. "We need her to heal them! We need them strong so we can leave."

"Well, you can't have her." Davin turned to face the Ecada.

He was about to move when Grit pulled out a small clear vial of a bright green substance. Davin instantly recognized it as stocolran gel. There wasn't enough of it to kill all life on the planet, but no one in the mines would survive.

"We will kill everything before we let her go," all three of the miners said in unison.

The sudden surge of anger welled up in Davin. He'd seen the aftereffects of what that gel could do to a living creature. Their bodies were distorted and split. The pain a death like that would create was devastating. He couldn't let that happen to Sara. With a scream, he drove himself forward, the loud buzzing in his head feeling like a thousand needles picking at him.

"Davin!" Sara's scream echoed in the cave.

Taber's shout blended with hers. "Stop!"

Every warrior instinct was pulled taut as he leapt in front of the Ecada, his blaster and the sonic grenade poised, ready to hit their marks. He fired shot after shot at the beast, who howled as several seared its flesh. Davin was about to let the grenade fly when a pain lanced through his head behind his eyes. It brought him to his knees, screaming, both weapons falling uselessly to the ground. He felt both Sean and Taber collapse close beside him.

Panting, he managed to look over at Sara. She'd been thrown clear of Grit and the other miners, who were also holding their heads. Despite the look of agony on her face, she'd managed to crawl clear of her captors, pausing only long enough to grab the gel vial that Grit dropped. It wasn't until she was close to Taber that he knew she'd be safe.

Concentrating as much as he could to push past the Ecada's attempts at controlling his mind, Davin knew he had only one shot at this. With shaking hands, he picked up the sonic grenade and stumbled to his feet. The Ecada was glaring at him with its bug eyes, its large jaws opening and snapping shut. Davin managed to take a half-step forward as he slid the arming mechanism into the armed position.

The Ecada must have realized how much of a threat Davin was because the moment he took a second step forward, he felt a dramatic increase in the beast's mental attack. But he was ready for it. Davin quickly erected a mental wall, trapping the Ecada's connection so it couldn't retreat. It was just the two of them now. It growled at Davin, which made him grin.

"You're picking on the wrong Raqulian, *janva*!"

Behind him he heard moans of the others, the shuffle of feet in the rocky dirt. He knew that with the Ecada's attentions solely focused on him, the others would be able to escape.

"What the fuck," one voice muttered.

"Davin?" the Briel's voice now. "Back up."

"Get Sara out of here, Taber." He had to concentrate to say each word. Any distraction would break their connection and they'd all be dead.

It was then he heard Sara's muffled cries. He almost lost his hold on the mental barrier, only refocusing at the last moment. Another shuffle and he heard Sara gasp.

"Davin." The fear in her voice was loud and clear.

"Get out of here, wild one. I can't hold him off much longer." He held out the grenade so everyone, including the Ecada could see it. "The second I'm about to lose my hold on it, I'm releasing the button. Now run."

"We're not—"

"Run!"

"Come on, Sara!"

Davin heard Taber pull Sara along, the voices of the other miners, now free of the Ecada's influence, going with them. It was the other sound that caught his attention.

"Sean?"

"Taber's getting everyone else out of here. Grit and the boys are confused, but they seem free from this fucker now, thanks to whatever you just did." Sean paused, giving Davin a solemn nod. "I'm not leaving you to face this shithead alone."

"We're not walking out of here." Davin's voice was surprisingly calm as he spoke. He took another step forward so he was only a few feet away from the Ecada now.

"You release the grenade, I'll fire the blaster, but you'll have to stab it. Its throat is the most vulnerable. I doubt I'll be much good to you after the sonic blast."

Davin braved a quick look over at his new friend. Sean looked as calm as he sounded, like he'd reached an impasse in his life and finally made a choice. He nodded at Davin and turned his attention back to the killer in front of them.

The next few seconds seemed to drift into an eternity. Davin focused every bit of his healing powers on his ears and keeping the mental barrier in place. When he pressed the activation button and tossed the grenade at the Ecada, there was a brief pause in the insanity, a beat of silence as all three of them watched the small silver ball gracefully fly through the air in a long arc toward the Ecada. Sean opened fire at the beast, landing several shots on the top of its head, distracting it from the grenade and preventing it from catching and crushing it.

A silent blinding light was quickly followed by an earthshaking sonic boom. The pressure of the sonic wave threw them back hard, sending them in a heap against the side of the cavern. As soon as Davin hit the ground, he felt the mental cage he'd erected slip. He knew he didn't have time to worry about it. Sending a healing blast of what little energy he had left to repair the damage to his ears so he could stand and fight, Davin picked up his knife from the ground.

He struggled to his feet, knife in hand and stumbled over Sean's unconscious body. Launching himself at the Ecada, he struggled with the beast's mental attack as it snapped its powerful jaws at Davin's head. He managed to tuck his body into a roll and slide out of the way. He then had to twist sideways to avoid being stomped by a large, clawed foot.

The Ecada let out a frustrated growl loud enough to shake the cavern walls. It gave Davin the advantage he needed. He pushed his body forward, diving directly for its neck. But the Ecada saw him at the last moment, whipped its head to the side and dug its long teeth into Davin's neck and shoulder.

The pain was greater than anything he'd ever imagined. Fire seemed to take the place of his blood, scorching him from the inside out. His fingers were suddenly wet, making it difficult to hold the knife in his left hand. Davin thought it was drool from the Ecada, but looking down, realized it was his own blood.

Everything in the room began to fade away until all he could see was a tiny spot in front of him. It was the Ecada's throat, exposed and at an awkward angle because of how it bit down on him. With the last bit of strength he had left, Davin thrust the knife deep into the beast's neck. The pressure on his shoulder lessened, giving him enough leeway to lean in and twist the knife.

The Ecada dropped Davin to the ground and staggered backward. It tried to claw at the protruding knife, but it couldn't reach it with its short front legs. Finally it fell to the ground and let out one last growl before it stopped breathing.

Davin smiled. He'd done it. Sara and the others would be safe and could continue to grow and build their wonderful home. And for the first time in his life, Davin felt at peace with himself. He'd been a warrior for years, running from the part of his nature that could heal. He'd needed all his skills to survive, to save the others. To save Sara.

He'd actually forgotten he was injured for a moment and tried to stand. When he landed on his wounded shoulder, the pain jolted him back to reality.

"*Friken*," he muttered.

"Davin!"

Sara's shriek announced her return and she was at his side before he had time to process what was going on.

"Sara?" His voice barely wanted to work.

"Don't move. *Med kit!* Just don't move, baby. I'll get you fixed up. Taber, get me that *fucking* med kit!"

He felt the pressure of her hands on his shoulder and knew she was trying to stop the bleeding. Davin looked up and was finally able to see her face. She was saying something, but his ears didn't want to work to pick up the words. Wanting to hold on, he reached out and tried to use his healing ability to seal the wound. The familiar tingle of repairing skin lasted only for a second before fading away. He was too tired. Instead, he tried to smile and reached up with his good hand to brush a lock of her hair from cheek.

"I love you," he whispered, his throat constricted with unshed tears.

Sara stopped moving, cupped his face with her hands and looked him straight in the eye. *I love you too*, she mouthed. It was the last thing he saw before he blacked out.

* * * * *

"No, no, no! Don't you give up on me, Davin. Davin!"

Sara wanted to shake him awake but knew it would do any good. She turned to look for Taber when the med kit was thrown open beside her.

"I'll assist." Taber's steady voice was at her ear.

It took everything she had to keep her emotions pushed back enough so she could concentrate on the wound. Davin didn't have time for her to lose her professional perspective right now.

"Cauterizer." The cool metal laser was slapped into her hand.

She set about doing her best to seal the ripped veins, repairing the damage enough so she could move him back to med bay. If she couldn't, he wouldn't survive an hour.

"There's too much fucking blood. I can't see." She wiped a tear from her face.

"His breathing is getting shallow," Taber said softly.

"We're not giving up on him yet. Get me some gauze."

A soft roll was pressed into her waiting hand. She pressed it deep into the wound and hoped it would somehow stop the bleeding. "More. Taber, give me everything."

After a minute she had the rest of the gauze packed into the wound. Looking at his face, she was shocked to see how pale he'd grown. Of course there was a lot of blood loss, but this looked different.

"The parasite," she whispered.

"You think they came from the Ecada?" Taber looked at her, frowning.

"How it controlled everyone. God, they'll kill him faster than the blood loss."

"No, it was that thing that killed the people."

Sara turned to look at the miner who'd kidnapped her, who was standing beside Grit. He was staring at Davin, looking like he was ready to turn and run screaming. Or like he'd just woken up from a nightmare.

"Whenever the parasites were attacked, the Ecada killed the person rather than let what they knew come out," Grit said, his voice shaky.

"That means the antibodies the computer generated back at the station were working," she gasped and turned to look at Taber. "We need to get him back."

"He'll never make it." Taber's gaze was direct, but there was sadness in his eyes.

Sara found it hard to breathe, to focus on anything except the fact she was about to lose the man she loved. If she could get the parasites out of his system, she might be able to keep him alive long enough that his natural ability to heal could kick in. Maybe.

She was about to signal the station when it hit her. Her head snapped up and she grinned at Taber.

"We might have a chance. Can you carry him?"

"It won't be comfortable for him, but yes. Where to?"

"Follow me. Quickly!"

Taber stood and with the help of the other men, he slung Davin over his shoulder. They raced past the crowd of disoriented miners who were out in the smelting area, back toward the tunnel that led to the underground pool.

When they got there, Sara jumped in, not waiting for Taber to round the corner. When he stepped up to the edge, she beckoned with her hands.

"Drop him in. There's something in the water that killed off the parasites. That's why the Ecada tried to kill me when I was wounded."

Taber didn't hesitate and jumped into the pool with Davin. After some adjustment, they had him floating on his back, his wounded shoulder down in the water. They stayed that way for a long time. Sara kept stroking Davin's hair, keeping it from his eyes and cooing in his ear. She kept talking to him, encouraging him to keep fighting, telling him that she loved him. Mostly that she loved him.

An hour went by without his condition changing. No improvements, but he wasn't getting any worse. At some point, Sean came into the cavern and looked down at them.

"Davin, Sean's here. He's fine. He's really worried about you, so you have to get better, okay?"

Davin's body twitched. It was a subtle change, but she felt it nonetheless.

"That's right, Sean. And Taber's been here too. He's never left your side. Even carried your sorry ass all the way to this pool. So you can't go and die on us now. You hear me?"

She didn't know when she'd started to cry, but the tears rolled down her face to drip into the water below. God, she couldn't lose him. She'd been alone for so long. Hadn't even realized there'd been a large hole in her life, one she was waiting to fill with her love for someone else. That hole had gotten larger every day she'd watched how happy Haylie and Kamran were. Jealousy eating at her.

"You crashed into my life. I'm not letting you get away that easily," she whispered and rested her cheek on his forehead.

Sara relaxed the same way she had when they'd made love. Hoping she could feel a tiny strand of him still there. She reached out with her senses, straining against the blackness and her own human limitations.

When she brushed against a small spark, she almost missed it. Taking a deep breath, she relaxed even more and floated back to where she'd felt the spark. It took her a second, but she found it again and grabbed on tight.

Davin, hon, come back to me.

Silence answered her. She tried to feed her energy into that spark, hoping it would take flame. Over and over she let it fan out as she silently whispered to him.

Davin, come back.

Sara.

It sounded more like the wind blowing through the trees than her name, but she knew it was him. Again, she tried to feed him her energy, her strength and prayed he wasn't too weak to take it.

The second he grabbed on, Sara felt suddenly pulled into a dark pit. She had to struggle to hold on, knowing if she lost control he was likely to drain her dry. Holding on, she felt him grow stronger and stronger until the spark roared into a fire.

Davin?

Sara!

She didn't know when or how, but he was kissing her. His mouth gentle against her lips, licking and nipping at her. She felt him shiver and she pulled him close to her body, needing to feel his body.

"I think he's going to live."

The sound of Taber's voice brought reality back and Sara pulled away. When she opened her eyes and looked down into Davin's half-open ones.

"Hi," she whispered.

"Pain," he muttered.

"I'm going to get you back to the station. You're going to be okay."

"Thank…"

"No, not yet. Not until I know you're stable."

"Love…"

Sara felt her heart soar. "I love you too. Now shut up so we can get you back to the station."

Chapter Fifteen

"If you won't let me get out of this bed soon, I'm going to scream."

Davin really had tried to relax and rest like Sara had told him to. But after a week of being forced to sit around while his body got back up to full strength, he'd had enough of being coddled. He'd gotten rid of the sling that had held his wounded arm and shoulder steady yesterday and was eager to try it out.

"Sara?"

"Not until I have a chance to give you a final physical," she called to him from the bathroom.

At least she'd let him recover back in the guest quarters and not in the med bay like she'd originally wanted. The soft blankets that covered his half-naked body seemed to make his skin more sensitive, especially since Sara had arrived a few minutes earlier. She'd spent every minute she wasn't on duty with him. And when she wasn't here, she'd called to check in with him. Not that he minded the constant connection. Every day he felt this bond with her grow closer, tighter until he didn't think he could live without her.

For the first time in his life, he could honestly say he was completely and hopelessly in love.

Davin lay back in the bed and laced his hands behind his head and hoped Sara would enjoy the view of his naked upper body. He *really* enjoyed the close scrutiny she put him under with these exams. Even now his cock was pushing hard against his pants, wishing he could thrust into her sweet cunt right now. It had been too long since they'd made love. Way too long since he'd had her under him, on top of him, anywhere and everywhere he could get her.

"Are you just about done? I'd like to get the go ahead from my doctor so I can get up and rejoin the living."

"Holy shit, you're impatient. Just give me a minute."

He chuckled and closed his eyes. "Sean stopped by earlier to say hi."

"Has his hearing improved?" Her voice drifted out to him.

"I helped move things along for him. The damage to his inner ear was tricky, but I think I was able to heal most of it. He said they were able to dispose of the stocolran gel."

He opened his eyes when something soft hit him in the face. Looking down, he saw the white lab coat she'd had on when she first came in lying in a rumpled ball on his chest. Sara was nowhere to be seen. "Abusing your patients now?"

"You weren't supposed to even think about healing someone for at least a month. You know what your father said."

Davin was still in shock that Sara had contacted his father after she'd managed to get him back to the station. He'd blacked out for most of the first day and a half until his body had been able to repair the bulk of the internal damage. Sara wasn't sure what had happened and hoped his father would shed some light on things. She didn't know that without her help, he wouldn't have had the strength to repair his wounds. His father reassured her she'd given Davin the edge he'd needed to live.

What Davin hadn't expected was the four-hour conversation he had with his father after he'd regained consciousness.

"He's been wrong about a lot of things. He even admitted it to me."

"I'm just glad the two of you are talking again."

The pain was still there, but the two of them were finally beginning to see each other's perspective. Davin didn't blame him for his mother's death. After seeing the good he could do, he understood what drove his mother to help. His father would have been powerless to stop her even if he wanted. His father had also told him things about his mother Davin hadn't been aware of. She was the one who wanted to heal the mental wounds of the soldiers. His father had wanted her to back away and deal only with injuries of the body, not mind. She'd been consumed with her need to help others.

But his father was the last thing he had on his mind at the moment.

"What are you doing in there, Doctor? Your patient is tired of…"

The rest of his words died in his mouth when Sara stepped out of the bathroom wearing a black nightgown that hugged her curves and stopped mid thigh. Her blonde hair was lying in loose curls down over her shoulder and along her back. Davin could see her erect nipples poking out from behind the shimmering cloth and had to swallow hard.

"Are you ready for your checkup?" she asked with a perfectly serious expression on her face.

Davin swallowed again before he managed to say, "Absolutely, Doc."

"Good. I hate it when I have to restrain my patients."

Images of Sara tying him down and having her way with him were almost more than he could handle right then. He had to take a deep breath and pray he would be able to control himself once she got near him.

Sara took a step into the room, and keeping her gaze fixed on his, pulled out an odd-looking device.

"What's that?"

"A stethoscope. It's an old Earth instrument that doctors used to use to listen to their patients' heart and lungs."

He found himself frowning as he eyed the odd-looking contraption. "How does it work?"

"It's simple, really. I put these in my ears," and she placed the earpieces where they needed to be. "And this part goes on your chest."

As she spoke, she moved closer and closer to him. The sway of her hips as she walked was hypnotic. Davin felt his cock twitch and grow and his hands itched to reach out and touch her. She was perfect.

"Does it hurt?" He really didn't care if it did or not at this point but felt he'd best be ready for anything.

Sara smiled as she knelt on the side of the bed. The sweet, light scent that was distinctly her drifted to him. The material of her nightgown was soft and brushed his side, sending a powerful jolt of lust through his body.

She brought her hand up holding the small round part of the stethoscope and hovered an inch above his chest where his heart was. "Won't feel a thing. Ready?"

"I'm always ready...hey! That thing is cold."

Sara giggled. "Shh, I'm trying to listen."

It took a minute, but the cold metal of the stethoscope eventually warmed up against his skin. Not that he was really paying attention to it any longer. Sara's hair had slipped forward, sending soft waves of her silken strands over her shoulder to collect on his chest. Davin wanted to lose himself in it. Wanted to rub her softness over the hard planes of his body until they were both ready to burst from need.

He wanted to fuck her senseless.

"Prognosis, Doctor?"

Sara pulled the stethoscope from her ears and tossed it aside. She then leaned in and placed a kiss on the spot where the metal had been moments before.

"Your heart is in perfect condition." Her breath was hot as she spoke the words against his skin.

"It is now," he whispered.

"But I'm not so sure about the rest of your body," she said with a smirk. "I might have to give you a closer examination."

Her fingers pressed gently over the muscles of his chest, circling every faint bruise that remained. She stopped to kiss each one lightly, marking him with her wet tongue. Davin had to fight to keep his body still so she could play her game.

She continued to kiss his chest and then moved down to kiss the muscles that covered his stomach. Her hands didn't stop moving either. She reached down and slid her hand inside his shorts that barely held his swollen cock. Her cool fingers wrapped around his shaft and squeezed him hard, causing him to suck in a deep breath. Davin's eyes threatened to close, but he needed to keep them open, to watch what she was doing to him. When he felt the gentle scrape of her nails against his balls, he almost exploded with pleasure.

When she looked up at him, he knew she could see how much he loved her. But that wasn't going to stop him from telling her.

"I love you, Sara."

He watched the tears swell up in her eyes as she reached forward and ran her fingers down along his cheek. "I love you too. So very much."

Not willing to wait any longer, Davin pulled her hard against him. The soft swell of her breasts was crushed against the muscular wall of his chest. He could feel her beaded nipples as he dragged her along his body so he could claim her mouth for a kiss.

Her lips opened for his mouth and he slid his tongue in, probing and teasing her as he went. Sara sighed as she snaked her hands into his hair and along the back of his neck. Her nails dug into his skin, making his hips buck up, pressing his cock hard against her stomach.

Davin rolled Sara over onto her back, kissing her harder than before. When she started cooing and moaning against his lips, he knew she was more than ready. She needed him just as badly as he needed her. He led a trail of kisses down her jaw and along her neck. The thin straps of the nightgown were already pulled halfway down her arm because of their actions. Davin continued to kiss and lick her neck and down to her shoulder where he'd bitten her before.

His tongue circled the faint mark that was still there, sending a shudder through Sara. She clutched at his shoulders and pressed her hips hard against his.

"Mine," he whispered.

"Always," she said against his temple, sealing it with a kiss.

"I want to mark you again." And to let her know he was serious, he growled and nipped at her neck.

Instead of the giggle he'd half expected, Sara moaned and wrapped her legs around his waist. "Yes," she sighed.

The warrior in him reared up and he barely caught himself in time. She wasn't ready for that. Not yet. But soon.

With steady fingers, he pulled the front of her nightgown down, exposing the white skin of her breast and the pink flesh of her nipple. The pebbled tip rose and fell with the harsh rhythm of her breathing, teasing him.

"Oh my, Doctor. What do I see here?" Davin leaned forward and touched the tip of his tongue to her nipple, wetting it. "It seems your body is in distress."

"I think I need a healer to help ease my pain. Do you happen to know any?"

Davin smiled and flicked his tongue over the tip again. "I think I can find one."

Sara closed her eyes and pushed her breast forward closer to his mouth. Not wanting to disappoint, Davin latched on, sucking the sensitive tip into his mouth, flicking it over and over with the tip of his tongue. Her moans of pleasure and aroused scent consumed him and he needed to plunge his cock into her now.

Reaching down, he pushed the hemline of the nightgown up, exposing her thighs. The feel of her skin intoxicating, making Davin nip at her neck again as his head buzzed from pleasure. But there was someplace else he wanted to taste.

Pushing his body from hers, he kissed his way down her body as he pulled the nightgown higher and higher. Her flat stomach earned his attention and he circled her bellybutton with his tongue. She did giggle that time, so he did it again as his fingers continued to explore her sides.

"You're so soft," he said and kissed her belly as he moved lower.

"Davin," she said as she ran her fingers through his hair.

He loved it when she did that. Fuck, he loved everything about her.

When he reached the top of the tiny pair of black panties she'd put on, he felt a growl come out of him again. The scrap of fabric was a thin but present barrier he'd have to get through. Instead of pulling them off, he ran his finger along the edge of the band that hugged her thigh. He could smell her musky arousal and it made his mouth water, wanting a taste.

Leaning in, he placed a kiss on the sensitive spot where her leg met her body. She twitched and then bucked when he ran his tongue down along the skin where it met her panties. He could see how wet she was, her cream soaking the thin material. Davin pressed his nose to her pussy and inhaled deeply.

He felt the sudden buzzing as his abilities reached out and connected to her inherent energy. It added to his pleasure and he knew Sara felt it too. He needed more from her, needed to feel her come. Hooking his finger around the edge of her panties, he pulled it aside, revealing the swollen pink tip of her clit.

"Let's see how well I'm feeling, Doctor."

He flattened his tongue and licked up the length of her pussy, lapping up her cream and teasing her clit. Sara bucked off the bed, her hands flying to the mattress beside her body, squeezing the sheet.

Again he licked, this time careful not to apply too much pressure to her sensitive clit, knowing it wouldn't take much to push her over the edge. He licked around the nub, wanting to delay her release as long as possible.

"Davin, please," she begged, her head thrashing on the bed.

"Please what? Please this?"

He pushed two fingers deep into her pussy, rubbing against the secret spot inside her that was sure to drive her wild. Her hips thrust up to meet his hand as he continued to lick around her clit. She was so wet, her juices were running down his hand and covered her thighs. He wanted to push her over, feel the rush of energy through her body as she came.

Latching on to her clit with his mouth, Davin sucked hard, thrusting his finger in at a relentless speed until Sara's body spasmed around him, her screams of pleasure filling the room.

Spent, her body fell back down on the mattress, her breathing coming out in gasps. Davin ran his tongue one final time up the length of her pussy, savoring the taste of her cream. He'd never have enough. He rolled to the side and settled in behind her, tucking her ass firmly against his groin.

"Wow," she muttered after a few minutes.

"It seems my strength has returned. As well as the use of my arm. I think I may be cured, Doctor."

She chuckled, her voice low and husky. "I'm the only one who gets to make that diagnosis."

"Really? And when can I expect my physical?"

Sara looked back at him and grinned. "If you take your pants off, I can begin."

Davin was on his feet and pulling at the material, determined to get to her before he came in his pants. She smiled, her gaze fixed on his body as he removed the last shred of clothing he had on. Finally, blissfully naked, he stood there, letting her enjoy the sight of him. When she licked her lips, Davin's cock twitched.

"Come here," she whispered, running her hand along her exposed hip and thigh.

When she tried to move, Davin held her in place. "Like before. I want to feel you in front of me."

He pressed his body behind her once more, this time lifting her leg to give him access to her wet pussy. Positioning his shaft so it was at the entrance of her pussy, he pressed forward slowly, enjoying the sensation of stretching her inner sheath wide. Davin groaned when he reached as far as his shaft would allow and wrapped his arms around her.

With each thrust, he felt their connection growing closer and closer. Their energy mingling and strengthening as they collided. He slid his hands down to cup her breasts, stopping to pull and tug on her nipples. Sara bucked back against him, her own hands reaching back to press the side of his hip closer.

Davin's heart pounded, his breath coming in short gasps as he sucked in Sara's scent that drove him wild. Her neck was before him, beautifully exposed and open to him. Placing a kiss on her shoulder drew a moan and a gasp as he thrust even harder into her.

"Mine," he growled again by her ear.

"Forever," she gasped as she reached up and pulled his face down to her shoulder.

His orgasm was there, close, and he could feel Sara was right there with him. He slipped one hand from her breast to rest between her legs, pressing her clit. As soon as he felt her cunt tighten around him, he began to pound into her as hard as he could.

She screamed her release again, only this time he came with her. As his seed filled her body, Davin dipped his head and bit her neck. Sara pulled his head down, holding him there as she continued to ride him hard.

He wasn't sure when they stopped, if they even had. The next thing Davin realized was the feeling of absolute bliss that cocooned them in the room. His still-hard cock was nestled deep inside her as his leg lay draped over hers.

"So, how am I, Doc?" he murmured next to her ear, licking the lobe.

"Clean bill of health."

"Clean enough that I'd be given clearance to become a resident of the station?"

Sara pulled away from him, turning so she could look at him directly. "What?"

"When I said that I loved you and you were mine, what did you think that meant? I'm not about to leave you now. Though Silas won't be happy. He'll have to find another ship to maintain."

"I thought you wanted to leave. I don't want you to stay just because of me. You'll end up hating me for keeping you trapped in one spot."

Davin kissed her arm, rubbing his nose against her warm skin. "I could never hate you. You've helped me in more ways than you'll ever realize. And one of those things was helping me accept who I am. Now lean back."

He felt her sigh as she snuggled deep in his arms. "I'm going to hold you to that. So what do you think you'll do here?"

"Kamran mentioned to me he was looking for someone to help establish trade relations with other planets in the sector. I think I might take him up on the offer."

Sara placed a single kiss on his arm that cradled her head. "You're really going to stay."

"Happy?"

"More than you'll ever know."

Davin pushed his hips forward, rocking his cock back inside her. "I love you."

Sara pushed back against him, driving him in deeper, and growled a very feminine, "Mine."

He laughed, wrapped her tight in his arms and promised her he'd never let go.

Christine d'Abo

Also by Christine d'Abo

eBooks:
Chasing Phoenix
Mistress Rules
No Quarter
Primal Elements
Sweet and Spicy Spells
The Bond That Consumes Us
The Bond That Heals Us
The Bond That Saves Us
The Bond That Ties Us
Wizard's Thief

Print Books:
Amethyst Attraction (*anthology*)
The Bond That Ties Us

About the Author

It took Christine a lot longer than the average bear to figure out what she wanted to be when she grew up. When she was home on maternity leave, she decided to take a stab at saving her sanity and sat down to write a romance novel. After dabbling with various sub genres she realized she really enjoyed creating strange new worlds and writing about sex. Whether due to the pregnancy hormones or sleep deprivation, she thought this was a great combination.

Many years later her kids are in school and she's back at her day job, but the writing bug is here to stay. When not torturing her characters, she's busy playing with her children or conducting "research" with her husband.

Christine welcomes comments from readers. You can find her website and email address on her author bio page at www.ellorascave.com.

Tell Us What You Think

We appreciate hearing reader opinions about our books. You can email us at Comments@EllorasCave.com.

Why an electronic book?

We live in the Information Age—an exciting time in the history of human civilization, in which technology rules supreme and continues to progress in leaps and bounds every minute of every day. For a multitude of reasons, more and more avid literary fans are opting to purchase e-books instead of paper books. The question from those not yet initiated into the world of electronic reading is simply: *Why?*

1. ***Price.*** An electronic title at Ellora's Cave Publishing and Cerridwen Press runs anywhere from 40% to 75% less than the cover price of the exact same title in paperback format. Why? Basic mathematics and cost. It is less expensive to publish an e-book (no paper and printing, no warehousing and shipping) than it is to publish a paperback, so the savings are passed along to the consumer.
2. ***Space.*** Running out of room in your house for your books? That is one worry you will never have with electronic books. For a low one-time cost, you can purchase a handheld device specifically designed for e-reading. Many e-readers have large, convenient screens for viewing. Better yet, hundreds of titles can be stored within your new library—on a single microchip. There are a variety of e-readers from different manufacturers. You can also read e-books on your PC or laptop computer. (Please note that Ellora's Cave does not endorse any specific brands.

You can check our websites at www.ellorascave.com or www.cerridwenpress.com for information we make available to new consumers.)

3. **Mobility**. Because your new e-library consists of only a microchip within a small, easily transportable e-reader, your entire cache of books can be taken with you wherever you go.

4. **Personal Viewing Preferences.** Are the words you are currently reading too small? Too large? Too… ANNOYING? Paperback books cannot be modified according to personal preferences, but e-books can.

5. **Instant Gratification.** Is it the middle of the night and all the bookstores near you are closed? Are you tired of waiting days, sometimes weeks, for bookstores to ship the novels you bought? Ellora's Cave Publishing sells instantaneous downloads twenty-four hours a day, seven days a week, every day of the year. Our webstore is never closed. Our e-book delivery system is 100% automated, meaning your order is filled as soon as you pay for it.

Those are a few of the top reasons why electronic books are replacing paperbacks for many avid readers.

As always, Ellora's Cave and Cerridwen Press welcome your questions and comments. We invite you to email us at Comments@ellorascave.com or write to us directly at Ellora's Cave Publishing Inc., 1056 Home Avenue, Akron, OH 44310-3502.

Discover for yourself why readers can't get enough of the multiple award-winning publisher

Ellora's Cave.

Whether you prefer e-books or paperbacks, be sure to visit EC on the web at www.ellorascave.com

for an erotic reading experience that will leave you breathless.